AVENGED

Daniel Judson

THOMAS & MERCER

Published by Thomas & Mercer, Seattle

Originally published as a Kindle Serial, November 2013

www.apub.com

ISBN-13: 9781477819838
ISBN-10: 1477819835

Cover design by Bob Newman

Library of Congress Control Number: 2013920601

Printed in the United States of America

for Alison Gaylin

Prologue
Tuesday

Muted light greets her when she is at last able to open her eyes.

Seated directly across from her is Miles, his hands, like hers, bound behind him. It takes a moment before she realizes that he is speaking, and another for his words to actually reach her ears.

Her mind, newly conscious, is reeling.

"You okay? Elena? Are you okay?"

Still groggy, she nods, then looks down at her right shoulder. She is dressed only in her camisole and black jeans, her bloodied sweater gone. She can only conclude that it had been removed and disposed of while she was unconscious.

The sterile tape her brother had wound tight around her wounded shoulder has been replaced by a single large bandage. Crisp and white, the gauze shows no hint of seeping blood.

"Someone stitched you up," Miles explains.

Elena looks at him. She finds it difficult to keep her head up. She remembers getting captured as they tried to flee, then the two of them being injected as they sat shoulder to shoulder in the narrow backseat of the Audi.

Waking bound to a chair that faced her half brother, he bound to his own chair, was the next thing she knew.

The powerful tranquilizer has left a bitter, metallic taste in her mouth, and there is a steady, sickening throbbing in the dead center of her skull. The wire holding her wrists together is sharp and wound tight.

"Who stitched me?" she says.

"I don't know. He had one of those black leather bags. Like doctors used to carry. So a doctor, I guess."

"When was this?"

"I'm not sure," Miles says. "Jesus, my head is killing me."

"Any idea where we are?"

"No."

Elena looks around. This room is a basement, that much is obvious. The floor is concrete, uneven and cracked, an indication of many years of frost heave. The walls are fieldstone and crumbling mortar. A far corner is occupied by a furnace the size of a ship's smokestack, and not far from it stands a large, oval-shaped tank, most likely containing heating oil.

So, the basement of an old house.

But where?

She finds only one window. Located directly above the tank, where the top edge of the stone wall meets the wood beam ceiling, it is boarded over.

The source of the muted light, she realizes, is a small quartz heater standing several feet away.

Its warmth barely reaches them.

——— ⌣ ———

Miles is saying, "They're going to kill us, aren't they? When they get what they want, we're both dead, right? Elena?"

She emerges from what must have been a brief blackout.

"Yes," she says.

"And they'll make it look like a murder-suicide. I killed you, then myself. Two heirs fighting over their dead father's money."

"That sounds about right, yeah."

Miles cringes. She knows he does so not at the idea of dying but at the thought of his son going through life thinking his father had killed himself.

The father who promised to come back no matter what.

The thought is, for him, simply too much to bear.

"I'm thinking there might be a way for you to get out of this," Miles says.

"What do you mean?"

"Offer to take them to where you hid the real flash drive. If that's what they want, give it to them. Maybe you'll get lucky on the way and see a chance to make a break for it. They need you alive, so that gives you the advantage, right? They can't just start shooting at you if you run. And like you said, you're better at this than I am." He pauses, then: "And who knows, maybe you'll even see a chance to kill them and put an end to all this once and for all."

"And if they decide to kill you first? Or if one of them stays behind with orders to kill you if the others don't come back? What then?"

It takes Miles only a second.

"Then take care of my son, Elena. Provide for him and protect him. Tell him I didn't abandon him. When he's old enough to understand, tell him what really happened. Will you do that for me, Elena?"

She shakes her head. "I'm not leaving without you."

"It's me or it's the both of us. You know I'm right. This is the way it has to be."

Before Elena can respond, Miles raises his head and calls toward the ceiling, "Hello! Anybody up there? Hello!"

"Don't." It is all she can say.

He ignores her and continues calling till the door at the top of the plank stairs finally opens.

A corridor of harsh light is cast downward. Though it doesn't reach them in their far corner of the basement, it is still bright enough to cause Miles and Elena to turn their heads away.

Someone starts down the stairs. It is easy enough for Elena to tell who by the sound of the footsteps.

The woman stops a few steps from the bottom. "What?" she demands.

Despite the fact that the woman is backlit, Elena can still make out her split and swollen bottom lip.

"Tell your boss I have a deal to make," Miles says. "Tell him I want to talk to him. Now."

The woman hesitates, glances at Elena, and then looks back at Miles. Dark curly hair frames her exquisite face. Finally, she turns and starts up the stairs. She moves quickly, with purpose. When she reaches the top, the door closes.

Near darkness again, and a long silence that Elena eventually breaks with a simple plea.

"Don't do this."

Miles shakes his head. "This is the way it has to be, Elena. It doesn't matter what happens to me. Kill them, then save my son. Do what you have to do. Promise me that, okay? Promise me you'll do whatever you have to do to keep my son safe."

Elena is silent. She is beyond exhausted, beyond broken.

"Promise me," Miles presses.

She finally nods. "Yes. Okay. I promise."

Miles sighs, and Elena knows by this that her half brother is unaware that what must follow won't be as easy as that.

The flash drive is useless without the ten-digit code that unlocks it, and only she knows that code.

Only she knows where the drive is hidden.

And their captors will stop at nothing to possess it.

It isn't long after this that the door at the top of the stairs opens.

More than a single set of footsteps are moving down them now.

Two belong to large men.

And one of those belongs to the man who murdered their father.

Crossing the dimly lit basement and standing together, the woman and the two men who employ her face their captives like a wall.

"You have something you want to tell us, Miles," one of the men says.

He smiles as if he and Miles are old friends. He is the younger—and smaller—of the two. The other man has a torso like a keg and short arms and large hands.

Butcher's hands.

Elena can tell by the look in his eyes that he is eager to get to work. Eager to do what he does best.

Make one of them talk.

"Don't do this," Elena says one last time.

Despite her fading strength, she tries to work free of her bonds, but the cold wire cuts deep into her wrists, and she is forced to surrender.

Her eyes lock with those of the larger man.

Miles ignores his sister's plea and tells the younger man to take a seat.

The butcher's eyes linger on Elena for a moment, then shift to the young man in the chair across from her.

All eyes, in fact, are now on him.

Six Days Earlier

Wednesday

One

Elena Aureli wakes too frightened to move.

Unable at first to even breathe, she counts those of the man beside her.

One, two, three.

The steady inhalations of someone in deep slumber.

Releasing the contents of her aching lungs, she draws in through her nose the chilly air that surrounds them. Lying still, breathing deeply, she waits for the powerful grip her nightmare still has on her to ease.

When it does and she is at last able to move again, she rises and, wiping the tears from her eyes with the backs of her hands, sits on the edge of the mattress.

There is only one window in their small bedroom, and she searches the near-total darkness for it.

The drawn curtains—ten feet of heavy cloth a color slightly darker than blood and embroidered with thick golden threads— stand just feet from the bed. She can tell by the complete absence of light along their straight edges that beyond it is now night.

Glancing at the clock on the bedside table, she focuses through her lingering tears and sees that it is just past five p.m.

Seven hours till midnight, and so much still to be done.

Behind her, Pavol's breathing is unchanged.

He always did sleep well, is lucky in that regard, and this difference between them is, or so she likes to believe, one of the few ways
in which they are not equals.

Eventually, though, he stirs; the absence of her body beside his
always disrupts his deep sleep soon enough.

Rolling onto his side, he reaches across her vacant half of the mattress. He finds her in the darkness and places his hand on her back.

His touch presses a T-shirt soaked with cold sweat against her
skin. As discreetly and quickly as she can, she wipes the last of the
distorting tears from her eyes.

"*Mi milenec*," he says. *My beloved*, in his native Czech. He speaks
softly, almost cautiously. "You okay?"

"I'm fine," she lies.

A powerful man, Pavol isn't much taller than she but easily more
than twice as wide. Built like an anchor, her father had said after first
meeting him. His hands are broad and strong—butcher's hands—
but his touch can be remarkably gentle, as it is now.

Sitting up, he closes the distance between them, placing himself
directly behind her. His right hand still on her back, he rests his left
on her shoulder.

"Your heart is pounding," he says.

She nods, the movement of her head both slight and abrupt.

Her waking in this manner has been a nearly nightly event for
the past ten months.

Or has it been eleven? She has lost track.

So there is no need to tell him the nightmare replayed itself yet
again. Nor is there any need for her to describe it to him.

He knows that in her dream she is chasing her father through a
maze of old streets, following the man but unable to catch him or,
even as she calls his name, get his attention.

Pavol knows, too, that the dream always ends in the same way,
with her father stopping finally and turning to face her, only to show
her the wounds in his temples from which pours precious blood.

Self-inflicted wounds, it was determined by a Geneva coroner, one hole where the single bullet entered and a larger, jagged hole where its fragments had exited.

Placing his hand under her T-shirt, Pavol says, "We should get you out of this. It's cold, and the last thing you need right now is to get sick."

"In a minute. Okay?"

He nods. Her solid back—an athlete's back—rises and sinks beneath his broad hand.

Nightmares can paralyze, Pavol knows this, both from these past months of waking beside Elena but also from his own experience recovering from violence witnessed and violence committed.

He knows, too, that remaining silent about nightmares can give them even more power.

He asks if the dream was especially bad tonight.

She nods, her eyes fixed on the curtain; its vague shape is still all that she can make out in this darkness. "Yeah," she says.

"What made it so bad exactly?"

She shakes her head in refusal.

"A nightmare is like poison, Elena. It needs to come out. And the faster, the better."

She takes a breath, holds it, exhales, then: "He looked right at me and actually said something."

"What did he say?"

She shakes her head again.

"What did he say, Elena?"

"He said, 'What will you do?'"

Pavol understands the significance. He begins tracing small circles on her back with his palm to help calm her. After a moment, he says, "Dreams are our subconscious trying to communicate with us. Things we can't face consciously, when we're awake, they often come to us in our sleep."

"It was like looking at his body again," she says. "It was that real.

But he wasn't dead and in a casket, he was alive and looking back at me." She pauses, then: "I could have reached out and touched him."

"It wasn't real, though. You need to remember that."

"It felt real."

"I know."

"So if it is just my subconscious trying to tell me something, what is it trying to say?"

"Maybe it's asking you a question your conscious mind isn't willing to ask. Maybe it wants to know what you're going to do if everything works out tonight."

"If it works out?"

"When it works out."

"What else can I do?"

"But can you actually do it?"

Again she nods. The movement of her head is as jagged as it was a moment before.

"First of all, Elena, it's not as easy as that. Killing someone. It's not easy at all. Trust me." He pauses. "Second, it's not too late to call the whole thing off."

"That's not an option."

"Yeah, well, maybe that's the problem right there. You think you can't walk away when the truth is you can. You can say the hell with this, and we can just go back home and live our lives. You can warn your brother, send him his share. He'd have the means to hide then."

"I can't do that."

"Because of the letter."

She nods.

He waits a moment, then says, "I'd tell you that vengeance is best left up to God, but I know you don't believe that, so I won't waste our time. But if a task is impossible, for whatever reason, then it's impossible. And there's no shame in being wise enough to know it's impossible. There's no shame in knowing the value of your own life."

Turning her head, she looks at him. She can barely see him through the darkness but doesn't really need to.

At thirty-eight, Pavol is older than her by ten years—hard years, by the scars on his body and face. His mother was Israeli but his father was Czech, and it is his old man that he resembles most: hair like black thatch, a square chin and sharp cheeks, deep-set eyes darker than any Elena has ever seen.

Elena's mother, too, was Israeli; her father, though, was an American of Greek ancestry. She is her mother's daughter only outwardly—short black hair, slender but surprisingly strong, a cutting stare. Inwardly, she is her old man's daughter—tireless, cunning, driven to the point of obsessive.

Being seen as outsiders in the land of their mothers was what initially brought Elena and Pavol together. They met three years ago, not long after he left the Sayeret Matkal, the elite unit of the Israeli Defense Forces in which he'd served for eight years.

Perhaps it was the very fact that she is her father's daughter that caused her to be drawn to a man of such particular skills.

Reaching out now, she finds Pavol's face. Though he shaved last night—as she sat on the edge of the tub, watching—she can feel thick stubble beneath her fingers.

"I can't do it without you," she says.

"You won't have to."

"That a promise?"

"It is."

She offers him the best smile she can find. It doesn't last for long, though.

"I need to find them, Pavol. I have to. No one knows what they did. No one knows the truth. Anyway, *he* wants me to find them. Dreams may mean one thing to you, but they mean something else to me."

"You think it's him coming to you."

"I do. Yes." She pauses. "He was murdered, Pavol. I know it, and you know it. I can't let them get away with that."

"Vengeance is a dangerous pursuit."

She nods. "They won't stop till they get what they want. They'll kill us, just like they killed him. They'll kill anyone who even remotely stands in their way."

Pavol thinks about that, then says, "So we'll do this. We'll do this and then go somewhere and start our life. A new life for the both of us. And when the time comes, when we find them, I'll be right there beside you. If you need me to kill them, I will. I'll do whatever it takes to get you back. And anyway, I've killed before, so it doesn't matter. I'm already damned. You, on the other hand . . ." He doesn't finish his thought. "Understand?"

Elena nods.

He tilts his head forward and kisses the back of her neck. He means it as a comforting gesture, but his breath on her cold skin sends a sudden current of warmth spilling through her. It cascades quickly from her heart down to her groin, and from there into her legs.

She closes her eyes and smiles. There is nothing forced about it this time. "Help me take this off," she whispers.

Heavy with sweat, the T-shirt stubbornly clings to her skin. It takes the two of them to remove it, Pavol pulling up, she twisting and wriggling, her arms raised. Dropping the sodden shirt to the floor, Pavol places his arms around her waist and kisses the back of her head. She lowers her arms, holding his close to her.

Her dark hair, also soaked, smells of lavender. Naked and damp, she trembles in the chill.

"I think you need to warm me up a little," she says.

"Do we have time?"

"Jean-Claude won't be here till seven."

"I should probably shave first."

"No, it's okay." Her voice is again a whisper. "A little roughness might be good for me right now."

Afterward, she showers, then dresses.

Black canvas pants, black turtleneck sweater, black boots—rugged military-type boots, not unlike those she wore during her requisite service in the Israeli army.

Pavol is already similarly dressed and waiting in the living room. In the center of that room stands a long oak table that has served since their arrival a month ago as their workstation.

On this table sits a desktop computer with dual flat-screen monitors, a portable satellite dish, and several impact-resistant carrying cases containing various pieces of equipment, among them a long-distance listening device, lock-picking kits, and a half dozen prepaid cell phones still in their packaging.

Under the table is a metal case kept locked and chained to one of the sturdy legs. In it are two Czech-made CZ-75 semiautomatic handguns, ammo, and extra clips.

Everything they could possibly need.

Standing by one of the two front windows overlooking rue Saint-Denis, Pavol is watching for Jean-Claude, as well as any hint of something unusual.

It was Jean-Claude who found them the apartment, in the Latin Quarter, just a few blocks west of the university. *A good place to go unnoticed,* he had assured them.

He also instructed them of the city's layout and obtained most of the items, both legal and illegal, currently on the oak table. A "clean" vehicle, should she and Pavol need it, for any reason, is parked in a lot a few blocks way. Elena paid Jean-Claude ten grand for it, and how exactly he obtained it she does not know or care.

"It's quiet out there," Pavol observes.

Being a Wednesday night, quiet, even for this university neighborhood, is normal.

Elena steps to the other window to have a look for herself. She instantly feels the cold coming off the glass. Though it is only just past mid-November, the temperature at night already dips down to freezing.

Montreal is a long way from Haifa.

The few people on the sidewalks below are bundled up and moving quickly, and the long row of clothing shops on both sides of the street are closed. Only the eateries, of which there are many, remain open after dark.

After a few minutes of looking at nothing, Elena heads into the adjoining kitchen to make tea.

As she sets the half-filled kettle on the gas burner and waits for the water to boil, she thinks of the dream. The raw sorrow it had stirred has passed. What better way to get rid of such feelings than prolonged sex with the man she loves? What better way to relax than to touch upon, if only briefly, the rage that fills her day and night?

It is perhaps strange that while Pavol believes in God and she does not, dreams are for him merely subconscious thoughts rising toward consciousness, while for her they are nothing less than visitations from the beyond.

Visitations from a murdered man pleading for justice.

From a father determined to protect his two children.

Closing her eyes, she sees her beloved father again, walking but dead, asking what she will do.

Will she ever be free of this vision? Will she ever be able to remember him as he was when he was alive?

She tries for a peaceful memory—the first time he met her Pavol, the two men she loved shaking hands and nodding hello.

But it doesn't last. Like a stronger signal overtaking a weaker one, her memory is overtaken by her nightmare.

What will you do?

The next thing Elena knows the kettle water is on the verge of boiling. And not long after that she hears Pavol announce, "Jean-Claude's on his way up."

She opens her eyes and reaches for the screeching kettle.

Two

A corner of the table is cleared, and Jean-Claude places a small Fed-Ex box down upon it.

Pavol stands on one side of him, Elena on the other.

"Talk about cutting it close," Pavol says. "These just arrived?"

Jean-Claude nods and pulls a pair of latex gloves from his back pocket. "Yes. This item was not easy to obtain. We are lucky to have it at all, never mind on time."

He wears his black hair long, has a thick brush for a mustache and a week's worth of patchy stubble on his jaw and chin. Tall, lanky, he is somewhere between Elena's twenty-eight and Pavol's thirty-eight, though neither Elena nor Pavol could pinpoint which.

A drinker—Elena's guess, by the dullness of his eyes and skin—but neither has ever once seen him drunk.

There's never a time, however, when Jean-Claude doesn't have a handful of mints in his mouth, which, coupled with his thick French accent, often makes understanding him something of a challenge.

Once the latex gloves are on, Jean-Claude slices the box open with a long folding straight razor he always has with him, then expertly closes and pockets the razor with one hand. Pulling back the four flaps, he exposes, within a tightly packed nest of Styrofoam peanuts, a rectangular Mylar bag.

Removing the bag, he opens it and extracts its contents.

Ten fifty-dollar bills, American, each one in its own sleeve of transparent plastic.

Jean-Claude removes one of the fifties from its sleeve and holds it for Elena and Pavol to see.

"It looks real," Pavol says. "How does it feel?"

"It's a little thicker than an actual bill. And the feel is different, more like paper than cloth. But it isn't meant to pass as a counterfeit."

Raising it up and holding it between them and the crystal chandelier suspended from the high ceiling, Jean-Claude points to the left half of the bill and says, "That's it, right there."

Elena can see the outline of something square, about twice the size of a large postage stamp, inside the fake fifty.

Next to it is what looks like a metallic ribbon running from the top of the bill to the bottom.

Placing the bill on the table, Jean-Claude begins removing the others from their sleeves.

"I've never even heard of anything like this," Pavol admits.

"State of the art, my friend. It's called a tracer bill."

"How does it work, exactly?"

"That square thing inside is a circuit card, and the strip next to it is a chemical battery. The card transmits a continuous signal on a preset frequency and has a range of about a mile."

"That's not much."

"It is, actually, considering the size of the transmitter. The battery only lasts five days. Again, that's impressive when you take into account that it's basically the size of thread. As the battery begins to weaken, so will the signal. During the fifth day the range steadily diminishes down to zero."

Pavol leans in for a closer look at the unsheathed bill. "The battery must be inactive, right? Otherwise it would start draining the moment the bill is manufactured."

"Correct."

"So how do we activate it?"

Jean-Claude takes another Mylar bag from the box, opens it, and removes a small box made of hard plastic. It is the size of Zippo lighter.

"This is a sensor. When we're ready, we simply pass it a few inches over each bill, and the chemical reaction inside the battery is triggered. Like I said, we are lucky to have these at all. This is prototype stuff, cutting-edge. They were originally developed to track drug money. Stick the bill inside a stack of fifties, and as long as you're within a mile, you can pinpoint the location of your money with a tracking device that's tuned in on the correct frequency. Give it a year or two, and I'll bet you the signal gets increased to ten or twenty miles, and they'll come up with even smaller batteries that'll last up to a month. But for your needs tonight, they'll do the job fine as they are now."

"I'm impressed," Pavol says. "Is there anything you can't get?"

"Only your attempts at French," Jean-Claude deadpans.

"We should get started," Elena says.

Pavol hurries into the bedroom, where a combination safe is hidden in the bottom of a cabinet. He opens it quickly. It contains a canvas duffel bag, a clear plastic Baggie containing their several passports, a black Moleskine notebook, and a thumb-sized flash drive encased in titanium and fitted with a thick silver neck chain.

Removing the canvas duffel, he closes and locks the safe, then returns to the living room and places the duffel onto the cluttered table.

He zips it open. Inside is fifty thousand in cash.

Ten stacks of American fifties, five grand per stack, paper bank bands still wrapped around their centers.

Without another word, they go to work. First Pavol opens one of the nearby carrying cases and switches on the tracking device. It is a portable unit, no bigger than a paperback book. On its face are several buttons and a row of ten LED indicator lights.

Pressing the button marked "Test," Pavol watches as the row of lights illuminate, one right after the other. When all ten lights are lit, he takes his finger off the button and announces, "Good to go."

Elena has put on her pair of latex gloves and laid out the tracer bills. Jean-Claude is holding the activating sensor.

"We should test them all individually," Pavol says.

Jean-Claude nods, pauses, and then says, "You know, using them all like this is overkill. We only really need one, right? So there's no strength in numbers here. I could resell the rest, make you a tidy profit."

Elena shakes her head decisively. Profit is not her concern. "No, I want backups, in case one fails."

"So let's put in two or three."

"No, I want them all."

Jean-Claude shrugs again. "You're the boss."

He passes the sensor over the first bill, and immediately all ten indicator lights on the tracking device are illuminated. This is accompanied by a series of rapid beeping sounds emanating from a small speaker just below the lights.

"This one works," Jean-Claude says. "That's two grand well spent. Let's try the next one."

Pavol slips the activated bill into the Mylar pouch to block its signal, and Jean-Claude passes the sensor over the second bill. The ten lights on the tracking device light up again. They repeat this process for the remaining eight bills, after which they each take a stack of fifties and pull from each one a single bill, then wedge a tracer bill in its stead, placing the bill as close to the bottom of the stack as possible.

As they work, Elena asks Jean-Claude to go over again his part in tonight's plan.

"After your contact gives us the files, we give him the money. When he leaves, I track him, go wherever he goes, no matter how far away."

"It'll take Pavol and me a few hours to go through the files. Once we find what we're looking for, we'll call your cell, and you can turn around and go back home. But until you hear from us, you stay on his tail."

"Simple enough," Jean-Claude says.

When the tracer bills are all in place, Pavol tosses the stacks one by one back into the duffel, then zips it closed. Turning off the tracking device, he closes its protective carrying case.

Jean-Claude unwraps another mint and pops it into his mouth.

"You'll meet us at the location at eleven thirty?" Elena asks.

Jean-Claude nods.

"And the gear is there?" Pavol asks.

"It's all set. Everything that you asked for." He pauses, then says to Elena, "You'll wire the remainder of my money to my account?"

"The minute we confirm the files are authentic."

Jean-Claude nods. "All right then. I'll see you at the place at eleven thirty."

———

At 11:10 Elena and Pavol exit the apartment and walk several blocks to boulevard Saint-Laurent, where they catch a cab.

Sitting close together in the backseat, they ride in silence, leaving the Latin Quarter and passing into Vieux-Montreal—Old Montreal. Crossing rue Notre-Dame, they enter Vieux-Port, a place even older looking than Old Montreal. Narrow cobblestone streets, many of them one-way and curving, wind past boutiques and art galleries and bistros.

Here, a few blocks from their destination, they exit the cab.

The sky is overcast, the cloud cover low, but Montreal, particularly the Old Port, is well lit. Elena, in all her travels with her father, has never seen a brighter city.

At eleven thirty sharp they meet Jean-Claude on the corner of rue de la Commune and place Jacques-Cartier.

Where the Latin Quarter was quiet, Vieux-Port is almost desolate.

Their destination is a five-story building—gray stone, three full-length windows to each floor, their wooden frames painted glossy black, but not recently. Though the face of the building is on Commune, a wide boulevard that follows the edge of the Saint Lawrence

River, the entrance is on Jacques-Cartier, an even wider street that slopes steeply down from Notre-Dame to Commune. The door itself is strangely short, more like the hatch on a ship, requiring that they each duck as they pass through.

The space that Jean-Claude secured for them is an office on the third floor. Or at least had been one once. Dark and cold, it is empty save for all the equipment he spent the day transporting here. Many of the pieces are duplicates of what Elena has already amassed back in the cluttered apartment.

She takes a quick inventory—two notebook computers with Internet access, both up and running; four two-way radios on a bank of chargers; a pair of powerful binoculars; and several hard plastic carrying cases of varying sizes.

Along the dirty tile floor are a dozen car batteries daisy-chained together and connected to a power converter. Everything in this room is powered by this. Elena has no doubt that the batteries are stolen. No doubt, and no care, one way or the other.

The building, from the boarded-up storefront on the ground floor to the offices above, is vacant. Like the buildings surrounding it, this one is easily several hundred years old. And by the look of its interior, it hasn't been updated for at least the last fifty of those years.

Every neighborhood in every city has a place like this, Elena thinks. Somehow, at the same time, worth a fortune and worthless.

Immediately upon entering, Elena steps to a row of tall windows, where a long plank of wood and two stacks of milk crates form a makeshift workstation.

These windows offer a clear view of the four piers—quai Alexandra and quai King-Edward to her right, quai Jacques-Cartier straight ahead, and quai de l'Horloge to her left. Beyond them is the Saint Lawrence River, its moving surface both dark and sparkling.

Her eyes go directly to the pier to her left—quai de l'Horloge. The place where the exchange is to be made. It is several hundred yards away, but even with her naked eyes she can see it clearly.

The only structure standing on it is an old two-story hangar. Painted gray, it has seven large doorways along its side, each one open but blocked off with foot-high concrete dividers. Over its front entrance hangs an orange awning on which, in large white letters, is printed a single word: "Labyrinthe."

The front third of the hangar, where the main office was once located, is an open space available for rent—children's birthday parties, holiday theme-parties, corporate team-building, and so on. The remainder of the building—a hulk of corrugated iron over steel I-beams on concrete footings—is a city-run parking garage used mainly by the day-tourists come to shop the overpriced boutiques at the palatial Marché Bonsecours across the street.

Open twenty-four hours, the garage is equipped with an automated gate, so it is fairly certain that there would be, at midnight on a Wednesday, not a soul present.

The location was her contact's choice, one he'd kept secret till two days ago. Jean-Claude scrambled to secure the right place from which Elena could observe the transaction.

But that—scrambling, providing, pulling off fast last-minute miracles—is what she pays him for.

Picking up the binoculars, Elena scans the port area. Her perch is high enough that she can see over the tops of the double row of trees lining the long promenade that separates rue de la Commune from the river's edge.

Her initial scan takes close to a minute, and she sees not a single person anywhere.

Returning the binoculars to the plank workbench, she turns to Jean-Claude and says, "Good job."

A candy clicking in his mouth, he replies, "*Merci.*"

Pavol steps to Elena's side. They look at each other for a moment. She nods a single, determined nod. Her answer to his unspoken question.

You sure?

Pavol turns to Jean-Claude and says, "All right, let's gear up."

Buttonhole surveillance cameras hidden in their heavy jackets, Ear-bone radio receivers placed in their right ears, and wireless transmitters attached to their belts, Jean-Claude and Pavol stand ready.

A split screen on the display of one of the notebook computers shows Elena the real-time view from both cameras. The images are black-and-white but crystal clear. Every moment captured by these cameras will be automatically recorded to the hard drive as an MPEG file.

Seated on a milk crate at her makeshift command station, Elena pulls one of the two-way radios from its charger. Facing both men, she speaks into the radio. They nod to indicate they can hear her. Pavol speaks, then Jean-Claude, and their voices, captured by the tiny microphone attached to the Ear-bone, come over the radio in Elena's hand loud and clear.

Pavol opens his jacket and removes the CZ-75 from its shoulder holster, makes a quick check of the weapon, and then holsters it again. Jean-Claude grabs the duplicate tracking device from one of the carrying cases and turns it on. Its ten LED lights spike immediately, its alarm clicking at full speed. Switching it off, he places the device in the inside pocket of his winter coat.

Finally, Pavol picks up the canvas duffel containing the fifty grand and slings it over his shoulder.

Elena feels her stomach tighten and her heart race.

Nearly a year of searching, and just moments away now.

They leave the office together but exit the building separately—Pavol first, followed a half minute later by Jean-Claude.

Elena watches through the binoculars as they make their way toward their positions. It is a five-minute walk to the end of the pier—she and Pavol made a reconnaissance trip here at dawn this morning to time it out.

It feels to Elena now, however, as though it is taking much longer. Five minutes is a long time to do nothing but watch and wait.

Finally, Pavol reaches the entrance to the pier. When he is halfway across it, passing the fourth of the seven hangar doors, he says, "So far, so good."

Panning to her left, Elena finds Jean-Claude. He is maybe a hundred feet from his position—but suddenly he isn't alone.

A man is approaching him on an intercept course.

Elena grabs the radio and informs Jean-Claude of this.

"I see him," he says.

Elena looks down at the computer display. Since both men are walking, the images caught by their cameras are jittery. She focuses on the left-hand side of the screen—the view from Jean-Claude's camera—and sees nothing but chaotic motion.

"It's okay," Jean-Claude says, "it's just a panhandler."

Looking through the binoculars again, Elena tries to get a good look at the man. All she can see, though, is that he is tall and staggering a bit, has long hair and a long beard, and is wrapped up in a full-length and weather-beaten wool overcoat.

Reaching Jean-Claude, the man is close enough to him for the Ear-bone microphone to catch him asking in French for spare change.

Panhandlers are common in Montreal; during their first night out after arriving a month ago, Elena and Pavol were approached by three. Most are modest and polite, but some can be colorful characters who don't take no for an answer and seem to derive pleasure from making it perfectly clear that the money they seek is to buy another drink.

Despite the fact that the appearance of a panhandler isn't an extraordinary thing, Elena watches carefully as Jean-Claude, without breaking his stride, tells the man to go away.

Stopping short, the scraggly man calls after Jean-Claude, saying all he needs is a few dollars.

Because Jean-Claude's back is to him, Elena keeps the binoculars fixed on the panhandler for a moment more, making sure he doesn't pursue her scout—or worse.

When the panhandler finally turns and starts to walk away, heading back toward Commune, Elena quickly pans past Jean-Claude to the pier.

Pavol, hearing the exchange via his Ear-bone, had stopped by the fifth doorway.

She radios that it's okay, he can keep moving.

It is a few minutes to midnight when both men have reached their positions—Pavol at the pier's end, Jean-Claude at its entrance, the large hangar between them.

And it is just seconds after midnight when the man they have come to meet suddenly appears, crossing Commune from the far side of Marché Bonsecours and heading straight for Jean-Claude.

Three

Elena watches through the binoculars as the man crosses the few hundred feet between Marché Bonsecours and the pier.

When he finally reaches Jean-Claude, she once again turns to the computer screen.

As instructed, her scout faces the man squarely, allowing Elena her first look at him via the buttonhole camera.

He is dressed in jeans, mud boots, and a B-15 flight jacket made of shiny black nylon, its faux-fur collar turned up. The man's appearance surprises Elena somewhat; being an associate of her father's, she expected he would be as well dressed as her father had always been.

She expected, too, that he would have something in his possession— a briefcase or messenger bag, something large enough to contain the hundreds of pages of documents he promised to deliver to her in exchange for fifty thousand in American fifties.

Elena says into the radio, "Why isn't he carrying anything?"

Almost immediately, she hears Jean-Claude say, "You've come empty-handed."

The man's reply is calm yet vague. "A last-minute change of plan was necessary."

Elena, concerned by this deviation, as well as the vagueness of the answer, hesitates.

The deal was that the man gives Pavol the files, and Pavol gives him the cash. Everything to follow counted on this—on Elena and Pavol poring through the pages in the third-floor office while

Jean-Claude tails the contact in case the documents turn out not to be what he promised.

But to come this far and get this close only to turn back—Elena can't even imagine doing that.

She depresses the "Talk" button and says into the radio, "Go ahead. Bring him."

Jean-Claude turns and escorts the man toward the hangar. Elena gets glimpses of its interior via Jean-Claude's button camera as he passes.

The place is devoid of any vehicles, which is as it should be, and yet crowded with the shadows of many thick support beams.

Plenty of places for an ambusher to hide.

It takes a minute for the two men to reach the pier's end. Pavol and the contact stand face to face. Elena, carefully watching both sides of the split-screen display, can see the man now from two angles.

"Why exactly was the last-minute change necessary?" Pavol asks.

"You heard that?"

Pavol nods.

The man glances over his shoulder at Jean-Claude, then looks at Pavol again. "I had reason to believe I was being tailed. Since my copies are the only ones in existence, I thought it would be best if I adapted and took certain precautions."

"What kind of precautions?"

"I scanned the files and uploaded them to an online storage facility, then destroyed the hard copies. You give me the money, and I give you the means of accessing the storage facility."

Pavol says nothing.

"I'm assuming you are in contact with her at this moment," the man says. "The three of us can all wait right here while she goes online and downloads the documents. Once she is satisfied that they are what I claim, you give me the money."

Again, Elena hesitates. By extension, Pavol is silent as well.

The man smiles. "I assure you, I didn't come all this way to rip you off. And if that were my intention, I would have asked for more than fifty grand. If all I cared about was money, I could have easily sold these to others for much more."

"What others?"

He says flatly, "The men who killed her father."

Elena's heart stops. This is the first confirmation of what she believes—what she knows—to be true.

But he said *men*, not *man*.

"So why didn't you just sell the documents to them?" Pavol asks.

The man shrugs. "Let's call it justice."

Elena doesn't need to hear any more. "Tell him to proceed."

Pavol hesitates. Elena knows why—things that appear too good to be true generally are, or so her lover would tell her. If she were a ship, Pavol would be her anchor.

But she wants none of that now.

"Pavol," she prompts.

"Proceed," he says.

The man reaches for his jacket's zipper, but before he even is able to touch it, Jean-Claude moves and is standing right behind him, straight razor out and open.

"It's all right," Pavol says.

Jean-Claude takes a step back, closing the razor. The man unzips his jacket and reaches inside. Removing his hand slowly, he holds up an index card. It is folded over, and clipped to it is a pen.

Opening the card, he writes three things on it, then hands the card to Pavol.

Instead of reading aloud what the man has written, Pavol holds the card a few inches from the camera mounted in the buttonhole of his jacket.

"Can you read it?" he says.

Elena tells him that she can. Putting down the radio, she quickly turns to the second computer, which is online via a personal Wi-Fi hotspot. She types in the first thing written on the card—a web address—and the fast connection delivers her instantly to the homepage of an online storage site.

She enters the username and password—the second and third things on the card—and is brought to a page that displays the icon of a filing cabinet. Clicking on that, another page opens, this one displaying the icon of a paper folder. When she selects that, the folder opens and long list of PDF documents begins to spill down the page.

She starts by opening the first document, which appears to be the copy of an invoice for several pieces of surveillance equipment, dated three years prior to her father's death.

Clicking on the next one down, she is looking at a field report from someone named "Don Quixote." On it are several dates and times, and next to each of these are either the words "pick-up" or "drop-off."

Scrolling down the list—it has quickly become obvious to her that there are, in fact, hundreds of documents here, if not close to a thousand, many of them several pages long—she moves the cursor to a random third file and clicks on it.

What opens is an organizational diagram—a single square at the top of the page with two squares below it and four squares below those, and so on, a different word—code names, no doubt—within each square.

In bold letters above the first square is the word "Pipeline."

So here they are. Her father's business records, missing from his apartment in Geneva.

And exactly what she was promised.

She begins closing the documents, saying into the radio as she does, "Got them. Pay him and get out of there."

Once the documents are closed, she backs up to the page displaying the icon of a single folder, right-clicks on that, and selects "Download to Computer" from the drop-down menu.

A box opens up, showing a segmented progress bar beneath which reads: "Est. Time: 60 Seconds."

Fixated on the progress bar, she is paying no attention at all to the split-screen display on the other computer, so she only hears Pavol hand the duffel bag over to the man.

A few seconds later the sound of the bag being zipped open comes over the radio, and a few second after that, the man speaks.

"There are people who aren't going to be happy that she has these."

Elena sees the progress bar reach the halfway point.

Thirty seconds remaining.

"That would be the idea," Pavol replies.

Twenty seconds.

Fifteen.

"It was a pleasure doing business with you," the man says. "And good luck to you both."

Ten.

Five seconds.

It is the very instant the download is completed that Elena hears the first gunshot.

Little more than a crack coming from the radio's speaker, it is to her ears the unmistakable whispered spit of a bullet emerging from a handgun affixed with a suppressor.

Her first reaction is to look at the other computer in hopes that she is mistaken, that the sound she has just heard is something other than what she at first believed. But all either camera shows her is jittery, frantic chaos.

The only sounds coming over the radio are raised voices and scuffling feet.

Panic, surprise, movement.

Then, before she can do anything else, the sound of a second suppressed gunshot erupts from the tiny speaker.

Rising to her feet, she grabs the binoculars, aiming them through the window and toward the pier. All she sees at first is just more confusion. A surge of adrenaline has hit her blood, causing her heart to pound and her hands to shake. When she is finally able control herself, she focuses on the pier's end and sees that Pavol is standing and that the man with the duffel is lying in a heap just a few feet away.

A third shot breaks over the radio, and suddenly Jean-Claude comes into view. He is running—away from something, by the way he is looking over his shoulder—and his straight razor is in his hand, its long blade glinting under the floodlights.

Suddenly dropping to one knee—he has been shot, this much is clear—he tries immediately to stand again, but a fourth shot is fired, and he falls instantly.

It is then that the shooter emerges from behind the far side of the hangar. His left arm is outstretched, the weapon in it, a Sig Sauer fitted with a suppressor, aimed directly at Pavol.

She recognizes the man immediately.

The long-haired and bearded panhandler, walking now not at all like a man who has had too much to drink but one with a definite and singular purpose.

It is obvious what is about to happen.

Elena feels a dose of dread rush through her.

Dread and anger and sorrow.

Pavol has managed to reach into his jacket, but that is as close to drawing his weapon as he gets. The panhandler approaches him quickly, and as he does, Elena hears Pavol's voice over the radio.

Calm, quick, insistent, soft.

"Get out of there, Elena," he says. "Get out of there now."

Elena whispers, "Pavol," but as she says it the panhandler fires a single shot.

A small cloud of fine mist bursts from the back of Pavol's head.

And he, too, simply folds and falls.

Standing over him, the panhandler fires two more times into Pavol's head. Elena flinches hard with each shot.

For the second time tonight, she is unable to breathe or even think.

All she can do, in fact, is watch in horror as the man disguised as a panhandler, the only person left standing at the pier's end, opens his tattered overcoat and holsters his weapon.

Quickly stepping to where the contact lay dead, the panhandler grabs the duffel bag containing the money. Slinging it over his shoulder, he moves swiftly to Pavol's body, kneels down, and pulls something from Pavol's hand.

The index card.

Then, as though he not only knows he is on camera but where exactly that camera is hidden, he looks straight into the lens.

Elena glances down at the computer screen and sees his face, bearded and smudged with dirt.

"Run, little girl," he says. "Run."

His voice is an unfriendly whisper, a snake's hiss. His accent, as before, is French, but she knows this could be as much of an act as his drunken stumbling had been.

As much of a disguise as the long beard and filth.

He exits the camera's frame, and Elena lifts her head to look out the window in time to see the man disappear once more behind the large hangar.

When he reemerges at the other end he is moving in an all-out sprint. Exiting the pier, he crosses the tree-lined promenade and, turning right, runs north on rue de la Commune.

His hard pace never lets up, and within seconds he has disappeared into a side street.

Elena looks back at the pier's end. She is numbed by shock. All she knows, in fact, as she stares at her motionless lover—all she can let herself know right now—is that there is no time to waste.

No time for the anguish clawing at her gut from the inside.

No time now to *feel*.

Except maybe fear.

In the dreadful silence surrounding, she hears her lover's final words to her.

Get out of there, Elena. Get out of there now.

Like the soldier she once was, she obeys.

——— ———

Leaning down to the second computer, her hand trembling wildly, she right-clicks on the folder icon again, this time choosing "Delete" from the drop-down menu.

A pop-up window appears, asking her to confirm this action.

She does, and within a few seconds—long seconds for her—the folder is permanently erased from the online storage site, making the copy on this computer the only one in existence and the information on the index card in the panhandler's hand useless.

Closing the two notebooks, she disconnects the power cords from the converter, then stacks both computers together, wrapping their cords around them. Placing the computers under her arm, she leaves the office, abandoning everything else it contains.

By the time she reaches the bottom of the dark stairs, she is already breathing hard. But this is more from shock than exertion. She pauses at the street door, a part of her unwilling to step out into the open. Finally, though, she forces herself through and climbs the steep incline that is Jacques-Cartier.

Turning left onto rue Saint-Paul, then right onto rue Saint-Vincent, she can barely hear the sound of her own steps over her breathing. Her mind is racing, and it takes concentration for her to discern that her steps are the only ones to be heard.

Emerging onto rue Norte-Dame, she spots several cabs in a rank in front of the Palais de Justice across the street.

She spots, too, a city police car on the next block, two uniformed cops seated inside.

Unlike before, she has to force herself not to move. She needs this moment to get complete control herself, or at least try to.

All hint of panic—in the way she moves, in the look on her face, in her body language—needs to be gone.

This takes everything she has.

Her heart is pounding, and all she can see is Pavol dead.

The cloud of shock is lifting, revealing a glimpse of the fear and sorrow and anger waiting beneath.

Calling upon all her training, however, she ignores all that and steps once more out into the open, crossing Notre-Dame as casually as she can.

She knows that every step she takes could be her last.

She knows, too, that she wouldn't even hear the gunshot, suppressed or not, that killed her.

To her surprise, though, she actually makes it across the street. Reaching the first cab in line, she knocks on the driver's window, her taps just a little too frantic, but there is nothing she can do about that.

The driver, a black man with a bald head and full beard, is slouched behind the wheel.

Sitting up, he waves for her to get in.

———

Back in the apartment, she takes an empty backpack from the closet just inside the door and stuffs the two notebook computers inside, then hurries to the table and gathers the two lock-picking kits, two of the several prepaid cell phones still in their packaging, a pair of binoculars, and, finally, the tracking device, which she switches on.

Standing at the desktop computer, she makes her way to an icon hidden deep within the C drive and clicks on it, opening a "scrubber" program. Following the prompts, she selects "Scrub All Drives," is asked to confirm this action, and does.

As the computer begins permanently deleting every scrap of information it holds, she kneels down and unlocks the chain securing the metal box to the leg of the oak table and places it beside the knapsack.

Moving into the bedroom, she opens the combination safe and grabs the Ziploc bag containing their passports—Pavol's two, her four—as well as the Moleskine notebook.

The final item she removes is the only thing remaining.

The thumb-sized, titanium-cased flash drive on a long silver chain. This she hangs around her neck and tucks inside her turtleneck sweater, its metal cold against her skin.

Back in the living room, she puts these items into the backpack, as well as the lock-picking kits and the cell phones.

As she picks up the tracking device, its audio alarm suddenly beeps once, then, a few seconds later, beeps again.

Looking at it, she sees that the first light in its row of ten is illuminated, indicating that the tracer bills are within a mile radius.

So, too, is Pavol's killer.

But the beeping doesn't continue, and the single LED light quickly goes dark.

Checking her watch, Elena sees that it is now close to one a.m. The tracer bills were activated a few minutes past seven. She remembers what Jean-Claude said. *The batteries only last five days.* She quickly does the math.

Five days is one hundred and twenty hours.

Minus the seven hours since activation means one hundred and thirteen hours remain before the signal terminates. But there is even less than that because, according to Jean-Claude, the signal begins to fade during the last twenty-four hours.

So, eighty-nine hours before any hope of finding Pavol's killer is lost.

Finding him before he can find her.

Killing him before he can kill her.

Holding the device, she watches it, unable to take her eyes from the row of lights. Eventually a single LED illuminates once more, but it flickers feebly and quickly goes dark.

Pavol's killer has moved out of range.

Still, he's out there, somewhere.

When she can no longer bear to stare at the unit—no longer bear its silence and inactivity—she switches it to standby and stuffs it into the crowded backpack.

Slinging the pack over her shoulder, she checks the progress of the scrubbing program. Seeing that it is nearly complete, she grabs the metal carrying case and heads for the door, pausing there for one last look around the cluttered room.

She will need to travel light from now on—well, light for her. For a month now she allowed herself to get caught up in the accumulation of tools. Everything and anything they might possibly need, she had to have it. A symptom of her obsession, yes, but she didn't care about that.

There is no way of knowing if any of the many things she is leaving behind are things she might need at some point. The cost of replacing them isn't the problem, but how to do so without Jean-Claude is.

Still, she will have to deal with that when the time comes. There is no other choice—this place is no longer safe, and she can only carry so much.

Crowded as it is with equipment, this room seems nonetheless suddenly both empty and large. She realizes that she has never before stood here without Pavol nearby.

The smell of him, the sound of his voice, the comforting balance of his steadiness and calm and reason—all absent now.

Her protector—from herself as much as from others.

What now without that?

What now?

Get out of there, Elena. Get out of there now.

Heeding these words, Elena hurries through the door. Closing it, she takes a box of waterproof matches from her pocket, removes from it a single match, crouches down, and then wedges the match between the door and the edge of the frame.

Should she need to return here for any reason, finding the match in the same location will tell her that the door has not been opened during her absence.

Finding the match missing or on the floor will tell her otherwise.

Pocketing the box of matches, she makes her way down the stairs to the street door, where she pauses to look around once more before stepping back out in the cold Montreal night.

A solitary woman moving casually but steadily, she heads toward the darkened eastern boundary of the Latin Quarter.

Friday

Four

In a barely furnished apartment in the city of South Norwalk, Connecticut, Miles Aureli is awakened from a shallow sleep by the sound of a ringing phone.

Sitting up, he grabs his cell from the nearby coffee table and, recognizing the number displayed on the caller ID, answers immediately.

As anyone with massive debt would, Miles never takes a call without first checking the incoming number.

"Jimmy, what's up?" he says. His own voice, which echoes sharply in the open space around him, is a mix of urgency and annoyance. It has been three days since he heard from his business partner—a long time to be out of the loop, considering what is going on and all that is at stake.

From the earpiece comes only hissing and static. When it ceases abruptly, Miles assumes the call he has been waiting for has been dropped.

Still, he says to the silence, "You there? Jimmy? You there?"

The hissing and static resume as suddenly as it ended, and through it Miles hears a faint voice.

"Yeah, I'm here. I'm driving, so I might lose you again."

All sounds cease once more, then return a few seconds later, this time with improved clarity.

"Jesus, man," the caller says, "where the hell are you?"

"I told you I was going to be out of the city for a while. Remember?"

"Oh yeah. Exile in South Norwalk. How's that going?"

"It's blast. I'm in the dark up here, man. What's going on? How did the auction go?"

"Not great."

"Shit."

"Pretty much, yeah."

Miles glances down at his wristwatch, sees that it is four thirty. But he doesn't care about the time. Looking at that watch reminds him of the five grand he could get for it in any pawnshop in the city.

A mint-condition platinum Rolex Submariner, thirty years old—just a few years younger than he is.

If he took it to the right place, he could maybe even get six grand for it.

Miles had found the thing—it had apparently belonged to his father—among his mother's possessions after her death twenty years ago.

It would, then, or at least should, take more than his current financial woes for him to part with it.

Miles stands and crosses the room to the tall front window that looks out at the Metro-North train platform standing across the narrow backstreet.

He watches the people waiting for the 4:38 to the city.

"How much did the sound system go for?"

"You don't want to know."

"How much, Jimmy?"

"Three grand."

"Jesus. It cost us, what, twenty grand just a few years ago."

"What can I tell you? The bidding opened at three, and there was only one bidder."

"So where does that leave us? How much do we owe?"

"I haven't figured it all out yet. Frankly, I'm not sure I want to. But if I had to guess, I'd say over fifty grand."

"Between us?"

"Each. Our distributors aren't the problem. It's the money we owe the bank that worries me."

"And how much is that?"

"Our credit line was seventy grand. We maxed that out. But then there's the interest and late fees."

Miles shakes his head. "We should have closed at the first sign of trouble."

When they first opened their jazz club on Delancey Street ten years ago, it was nothing less than a gold mine. Even in the months following 9/11, when a lot of businesses were hit hard and began to fold, they were making more money than they knew what to do with.

And with that kind of money, for two guys who were at that time still in their twenties, what else was there to do but spend it?

But when the downturn came, business all but disappeared overnight. Hoping it would return—needing it to return—they cut all the corners they could, were determined to do whatever it took to ride out the bad time.

After over a year, though, with their credit maxed and their savings depleted, there was nothing left to do but close the doors and attempt to settle as much of their debts as they could by selling everything that wasn't nailed down.

"Anyway, that's not why I'm calling," Jimmy says. "I need you to swing by the place."

"What for?"

"We should get what's left of that copper wiring out of the basement tonight. The leftover pipe, too."

"Why tonight?"

"Our dick of a landlord is putting padlocks on the doors tomorrow."

"We have two weeks left on the lease. More than two weeks, actually."

"I reminded him of that fact, and he said, and I quote, 'Sue me.'"

When he and Jimmy first found the bar for rent, it was a dive—rotting floor planks, substandard plumbing and wiring. Because of this, they got a cheap lease. Between the two of them they brought the place up to code, Jimmy handling the plumbing and Miles the electrical. The coils of copper wire and sections of copper pipe that were left over sat in a storeroom in the basement.

Jimmy says, "I was going to get it out of there next week, but you should go tonight and grab it."

"I'm supposed to pick up Jack in an hour. Can't you do it?"

"I just got on the turnpike."

"Let me guess. Atlantic City."

"I found a grand I didn't know I had, thought maybe I'd see if I couldn't turn it into something a little bigger. At this point, what the fuck, right?"

Can't argue with that, Miles thinks.

Jimmy asks if Jack is at his mother's tonight.

"Yeah. Where else would he be?"

"You could pick Jack up, then swing across town to the club. It's probably better if you went there after dark anyway."

"I don't know, man."

"I'll sell the stuff myself and give you half," Jimmy says. "I'm guessing we could get a couple of grand for it, maybe more. Every little bit helps, right?"

All Miles needs to think about his recently agreed upon monthly payment to the IRS.

He glances down at the watch again, then looks back at the people standing on the elevated platform just a few hundred feet from his window.

"Yeah, all right," he says. "I'll swing by. Jack would probably like to see the place one last time."

"Sounds good, man."

"Good luck in Atlantic City."

But by the utter silence coming from his phone, Miles knows that the connection has been lost.

He leaves after six o'clock to avoid rush hour traffic.

Back in the days when the club was generating money, Miles would lease a new vehicle every two years and pay four hundred a month to park it in a garage a block from his apartment in Chelsea. Nothing said luxury like living in Manhattan and owning a vehicle. He did this without even thinking twice about it. He did this even though he rarely ventured outside of Manhattan. There was never a month when he took home less than five grand. There were even months when he took home ten.

Such luxuries, though, were among the first to go when it came time to cut corners. Piece by piece he dismantled his life—moved to a cheaper apartment, began selling possessions on eBay, dropped his health insurance.

Then came the tax bill he couldn't possibly pay. He was already divorced, had been for close to a year when the business first crashed and burned. It didn't take long before it was all he could do to make his child support payments.

And then came the month when he couldn't even make that.

But when Phil, his friend up in South Norwalk—SoNo, the locals call it, perhaps to make it seem like they're living in an extension of New York and not merely in a failed industrial city thirty miles from it—came through with the job and cheap apartment, Miles jumped at it.

Despite the fact that he lived on the train line, he knew life outside the city would require he own some kind of vehicle, so he bought a fifteen-year-old Chevy minivan from the one dealer—way out in Jersey—who would extend him credit. Choosing a vehicle he could use to transport or store things—or live in, if it came to that—seemed like the smart thing to do.

He can't help but hope that his share of the copper wiring and pipe he'll load into the van tonight might actually pay off the loan on the thing.

One less monthly payment would mean one less thing to feed his chronic insomnia, at least potentially.

———— ⌄ ————

Thirty-five minutes after leaving South Norwalk, Miles crosses over the Manhattan Bridge, then follows the West Side Highway south along the Hudson River.

It takes just fifteen minutes to reach the Fourteenth Street exit. A block east on Fourteenth, he turns right onto Washington Street, then left onto Bank, where Julie's apartment—her new husband's apartment—stands just a block shy of the street's end.

It is a quiet West Village neighborhood, secluded and yet only a minute's walk from Greenwich Avenue.

Affluent, exclusive.

Everything Julie wanted but he couldn't give her, even with all his success.

Good for Julie.

Still, not a bad place at all for their kid to grow up.

Passing the long row of four-story brownstones that line the narrow street, Miles spots up ahead a parking space just past Julie's door and pulls into it.

The hooded sweatshirt he is wearing should be enough against the evening chill, so he leaves behind his jacket—bought for five hundred dollars back when five hundred dollars meant nothing—and exits his vehicle.

He climbs the steep steps and then rings the buzzer. The building, a single-family residence, has a vast interior, so it's a good half minute before Julie answers the door.

"Is he ready?"

"He's getting his knapsack."

Julie is tall, and she has long, strawberry-blonde hair and pale skin that quickly flushes whenever she is angry or aroused. A demon for the rigorous daily schedule she sets for herself, she is dressed already for her seven thirty abs class at the Equinox branch just around the corner.

Miles hopes for a quick "prisoner exchange," as they call it. Polite chat as he grabs the kid, then the two of them gone.

In the dark hallway behind Julie, however, Jack is nowhere to be seen. And it is obvious to Miles that his ex has something on her mind now.

Her arms folded across her stomach and the look of confusion on her face are dead giveaways.

Her attention is fixed on the street behind him. Whatever is bothering her is there.

"What?" Miles asks.

"You drove in. I thought you were going to take the train."

"I have to swing by the club to pick something up."

"But Jack was all excited for the big train trip with his father."

"I just got the call before I left. I didn't think it would be a problem."

"What you mean is you forgot."

Miles shrugs. "If it makes you happy to think that, then yeah, I forgot."

In his scramble to earn every cent he can and meet his many obligations, Miles takes any and all shifts his friend offers him. Bar shifts, waiter shifts, even dishwasher shifts. Though virtually unheard of in the restaurant business, Miles has weekends off so he can resume visits with his son, a condition of his divorce he hadn't been able to meet when Jimmy and he had to lay off most of their staff and begin covering all bar shifts themselves.

Less than lucrative shifts, toward the end.

In exchange for this favor, Miles must keep himself on-call during the week. Should someone need a night off or not show up for a shift, a quick call to Miles's cell, even at the last possible minute, is all that is needed.

Therefore, life these days is for him little more than hectic motion.

Do this, go there, be on time for that.

Rush, hurry, accomplish.

An object in motion tends to stay in motion.

What is to him a mad dash to meet all responsibilities is to Julie signs of a man in panic—and in over his head.

"How long will you be at the club?" she says.

"I just have to grab some things. In and out."

"He's going be disappointed."

In Julie's world, disappointment is to be avoided at all costs.

"I'll make it up to him with the weekend I have planned," Miles says. "We're going to the Martine Center in the morning, then a 3-D movie at the IMAX after lunch. On Sunday I'll take him to the beach, and he can collect shells and feed the gulls. Trust me, he'll come back happy. And we'll definitely take the train in on Sunday."

"The train tonight was supposed to be definite." Her face is flushed.

"Look, Jule, I don't want to fight. He'll be okay. I'm sorry, but he rolls with things easier than you do. Or at least he does when he's with me."

"Is your place set?"

"Of course."

"You got his cereal? And his soy milk?"

"Yes." Miles pauses. Something other than the last-minute change in transportation is concerning her. He tilts his head into her line of vision, forcing her to look directly at him. "Jule," he says. "What's going on?"

"You haven't done this for a while, that's all."

"And you think I'd forget that my own son has allergies."

"You forget a lot these days."

"And you worry too much, Jule. He'll be fine."

"It's not him I worried about."

"What does that mean?"

She takes a breath, lets it out. Despite this, her tension remains.

"You look like hell," she says.

"Thanks."

"You're still not sleeping."

"I'm fine."

"You're a bad liar."

"What do you want me to say? I'm doing the best I can here."

"Will you be able to pay child support next month?"

"You'll have it on the first. I promise."

She nods, though clearly still unsatisfied. Whatever is bothering her, *really* bothering her, they haven't addressed it yet.

"How's your thing with the IRS going?"

"I'm back to making monthly payments. It's worked out."

"It was a stupid mistake."

"No argument from me. Look, you don't have to worry about me, okay? I'll get back on my feet. I made something out of nothing before, and I can do it again."

"Yeah, but you didn't owe God-knows-how-much before. There's a big difference between starting from nothing and starting over in debt."

Miles looks down the hallway again, wishing that Jack would arrive and break this up. He doesn't see or hear a thing, however.

A thought suddenly occurs to him. He takes a step toward his ex and says softly, "Wait, are you guys in trouble?"

Julie shakes her head, scoffing as if the question were ridiculous. "*No.*"

"It seemed possible. No one's immune these days, not even bank presidents. *Especially* bank presidents. So what's the problem then, Jule?"

She struggles to find the right words, but then it seems she no longer cares if they are right or not.

"I just didn't think I'd still be worried about you, that's all. I thought I'd be able to let go of that."

Her line of vision drops to the watch on his wrist, and with this, Miles finally understands.

"I'm not my father," he says flatly.

If not for a telegram from a law firm in Geneva, sent a month after the fact, Miles would never have known his long-estranged father was dead, let alone how the man had died.

"All the time we were married that just sat in a box in your sock drawer. Now every time I see you, you have it on."

"I don't wear it because it was his. If anything, I wear it because it was hers. I found it among her things after she died."

"That doesn't make it any better."

He takes another step closer, smells a mix of fresh perfume and shampoo. Julie is the only person he knows of who showers prior to working out.

"Look," he whispers, "I'm not going to kill myself, if that's what this is about. Things can't ever get so bad that I'd even *think* about doing that."

"They say the sons of men who kill themselves also end up killing themselves."

"I don't give a shit about that. My father abandoned me and my mother almost thirty years ago. There's nothing of him in me, good or bad. You know that. And anyway, you think I'd do that to my own son?"

"If I lost everything, killing myself is probably all I'd think about."

He keeps his voice calm; it's his only hope of her actually hearing his words.

"That's you, Jule. That's not me. Listen, if you want to know the truth, I wear the watch because I'm not my own boss anymore. I need to be on time for things. Plus, Jimmy convinced me that women judge a man by the watch he wears. My car's a piece of shit, and I'm living in a crap apartment up in South Norwalk. Basically, I need all the help I can get here."

"I thought you were seeing that artist."

"When I told her I had to move out of the city, she called it off."

Julie nods. His calm is spreading to her. "I'm sorry," she says. "That's cruel."

Miles laughs, wanting to lighten things up. "It's a cruel world."

Julie considers that, then: "Listen, I've been thinking about going to my lawyer."

"What for?"

"Nick says he has no problem taking care of Jack financially. I could go back in front of the judge and officially waive the child support. For now, anyway."

Before Miles can respond, he hears the sound of his son in the long entrance hallway.

Hearing him as well, Julie quickly shifts her posture.

The boy appears beside his mother. They have the same hair and fair skin, and he is tall for a six-year-old, which he also gets from her.

His eyes, though, are sky blue and steady—his father's eyes.

"Here he is." Julie's voice is suddenly cheerful. Crouching down, she has to grab her son to keep him from going out the door. She zips his parka closed; it's just a little bit too big for him. "Do you have everything?"

The boy nods impatiently. "You packed."

"Just making sure you didn't take anything out." She leans close suddenly, taking on a tone of mock-accusation. "Did you?"

He smiles. "No."

"Positive?"

"Yes."

They kiss, and Julie stands. "Behave for your father, okay?"

"I will."

Placing her hand on the boy's shoulder, she passes him through the doorway to Miles.

"You're going to drive to Daddy's new apartment," she says. "He promises to bring you back on the train on Sunday, though, so don't let him forget."

Jack moves to the edge of the top step. He is clearly less interested in modes of transportation than he is in just going.

"See, he's fine," Miles says. He playfully grabs the boy by his knapsack and uses it as a leash to keep him from starting down the stairs.

Jack laughs, and Miles looks at Julie.

"He's my son, Jule." His voice is hushed but firm. "I'll provide for him. I always will, no matter what. Okay?"

Her arms once again folded across her stomach, she nods, but grudgingly.

Never one for leaving well enough alone, she says, "How, Miles? Even if you went back to work as an electrician, you'd have to get your license and rejoin the union, and that costs money. And what if you start falling behind again? Nick says if you miss just one payment, the IRS will send agents out looking for you again. I don't want them knocking on our door like last time. *He* doesn't want that."

So, there it is, Miles thinks.

He says the only thing he can.

"You'll get the money on time from now on, I promise. Everyone will."

"*How*, though?"

Before Miles can respond, Jack says, "Let's *go already*."

"I'll bring him back Sunday night," Miles says.

He turns away, and he and his son walk side by side down the stoop stairs. It isn't till they reach the sidewalk that Miles lets go of the knapsack. Jack runs ahead.

Remaining in the doorway, Julie watches as they head toward the minivan.

"Why don't you have a coat on?" Jack asks his father.

"I left it in the car."

"You're supposed to wear a coat every time you go outside."

"I know, you're right."

Julie is still in the doorway when the Chevy drives past.

Wearing a smile that would only deceive a child, if even that, she waves.

A right turn onto Waverly Place, then another onto Seventh Avenue South, after which Miles says, "Would you like to see your old man's club?"

Buckled into the passenger seat and all but buried inside his oversized parka, Jack shrugs. "Okay."

"After that we'll drive to my new place."

"On the beach?"

"Well, it's not on the actual beach. But it's near enough that we can walk to it. I was thinking we'd go there Sunday morning, see if we can find some seashells. What do you think?"

"Okay."

As Miles steers across town, he asks questions about school, Jack's teacher and friends, everything and anything he can think of.

Jack can be as moody as his mother, but tonight he is chatty, and there is a sparkle in his blue eyes.

Miles always tends to forget his troubles—well, for the most part—when he is with his boy.

Fifteen minutes later they are parked on the north side of Delancey Street, near the entrance to the Williamsburg Bridge.

The club is dark. A casual glance at its two large storefront windows is all one would need to know that the place is empty.

Above the door remains the only indication of what, till recently, it housed.

An unlit neon sign that reads, "Blue Moods." A reference to a Miles Davis album, as well as a promise of what patrons would find upon entering.

Broken by a vandal shortly after the club closed for good, the sign, which had cost four grand, is now worthless. Jimmy said he was considering taking it for himself as a keepsake, but apparently he either forgot or changed his mind.

Walking around the nose of his vehicle to the passenger door, Miles glances down the block toward the Delancey Bar and Grill.

Still open for business, its glowing blue-red neon sign is more than twice the size of Miles's sign.

The only other vehicle parked along the long stretch of the shared block is a black SUV. From what Miles can see, three people are seated inside.

He assumes they are the Delancey's doormen, keeping warm as they wait for the Friday night crowd to arrive.

Miles helps Jack out of the minivan, and the two are approaching the darkened club's entrance when the doors of the SUV suddenly open.

First the driver and passenger doors swing out like wings quickly expanding, and then the passenger-side rear door opens.

The occupants—two men and a woman—emerge and head straight for Miles.

As casually as he can, he puts himself between the approaching strangers and his boy.

"You still aren't wearing your jacket?" Jack says.

Miles nods but doesn't take his eyes off the three people. "It's okay."

"Won't you get sick?"

"Hang on a second, buddy, okay?"

One of the two men calls out.

"Hello there. I was wondering if we could have a moment of your time."

This man, the eldest of the two, is in his late fifties. The other man, walking a step behind, is in his thirties. Though he isn't as tall as the first, he is significantly bigger through the chest and shoulders.

The woman, a step ahead of the men, is in her midtwenties. She moves quickly, has an athlete's spring in her step.

All three are wearing dark coats over dark suits. Expensive shoes flash in the light of the streetlamps.

Their dress, familiar to Miles, leads him to only one conclusion.

The older man has his hands in the pockets of his coat, but the other two keep theirs, clad in black leather gloves, hanging loose at their sides.

When they are close enough that he won't have to raise his voice to be heard, Miles says, "I thought I wasn't supposed to get any more visits from you guys. You might want to check your records; I've been making payments for three months now."

The older man says flatly, "Actually, Miles, we're not with the IRS."

The woman reaches Miles and Jack first. She comes to a stop just a few feet away.

There is something aggressive to her nearness, and she looks Miles up and down, as if sizing him up.

"So who are you, then?" Miles says to the older man.

"My name is Trask. I was a friend of your father's. I was wondering if we could talk."

He reaches Miles next. The second man comes to a stop just behind Trask. He glances at Miles, briefly and a bit dismissively, then proceeds to scan Delancey Street with narrowed eyes.

Miles has seen enough celebrities in his club over the years to recognize the mannerisms of bodyguards.

"Might we go inside?" Trask asks.

"It's probably as cold in there as it is out here."

"Still, it would be better if we were off the street. It's important that we talk; otherwise, we wouldn't be contacting you directly like this."

Miles is uncertain what the man means by that last part, but he doesn't ask for clarification—he has something more important on his mind right now.

"I have my kid."

"It won't take long," Trask says. "And we've come prepared."
He nods toward the woman, who removes from her right overcoat
pocket a small Matchbox car still in its packaging.

Miles looks at her for a moment, then glances at the second
man, still scanning their surroundings with efficient and steady eyes.

Finally Miles turns his attention back to Trask.

"We don't have a lot of time to waste," the older man says. "And
trust me, son, we wouldn't have come if it weren't important." He
smiles warmly, almost fondly.

Still, Miles doesn't move. More than anything, he is a little
caught off guard by the use of the word *son*.

"Please," the man says, "it really would be better if we talked
inside."

Five

The club's cold is cave-like—damp and strangely dormant, as if this space has been unoccupied not for weeks but months—and every sound, from footsteps to the swish of clothing, radiates into emptiness, hits bare wall, and bounces quickly back.

Running the length of the left side of the narrow room is the bar, original to the building, as is the high ceiling of ornately stamped tin.

Behind the bar are bare glass shelves on a wall covered with smoked mirrors, and just past the bar's far end is an open area where two dozen cocktail tables once stood before a small platform that Miles and Jimmy had built in a hurry just hours before they first opened the doors to the public.

A foot high and barely big enough for a quintet plus gear, it had served as a stage for everyone from music majors from Julliard and NYU to nearly every member of the Marsalis family.

Everything else that had once helped fill this space is now gone.

Miles doesn't bother to turn on the lights; the electricity was shut off weeks ago. But between the streetlamps and the light from the Williamsburg Bridge spilling in through the two large windows, there is more than enough to see by.

The younger, larger man remains by the door, positioning himself with his left shoulder to it so he can keep an eye on both the interior and exterior alternately. Trask and the woman stand side by side and face Miles. The woman immediately crouches down and, smiling but not saying a word, holds up the Matchbox car for Jack to see.

She is attractive—curly dark hair, brown eyes, round face with angular features and the slightest overbite. Her smile, all confidence and warmth, is no doubt meant to convey to both the boy and his father that she is to be trusted.

Despite this, Jack isn't quite sure what to make of her. He stands close to his father's leg and does nothing but look warily at the offering.

Bending down, Miles places his hand on Jack's head and says, "These men and I need to talk for a minute, okay?" He looks at the woman and asks her name.

"I'm Angelina," she says. Her accent is French, her voice a soft alto. Miles notices right away that she speaks from her diaphragm—a singer, then, or maybe an actress.

He says to his son, "Why don't you show Angelina here the stage. I think if you do, that car might just be for you."

Jack nods. Angelina stands but bends at the waist so she remains face-to-face with the boy. She holds out her gloved hand, and Jack takes it. Together they walk the length of the bar and out of earshot.

At the end of the room, where the least light reaches, they sit side by side on the edge of the stage. Angelina opens the package and hands the toy to Jack, who takes it with two hands and studies it.

Trask says, "I have to tell you, Miles, you are not any easy man to find all of a sudden."

Though he is immediately made curious by the phrase "all of a sudden," Miles chooses, as he did a moment before, to pursue a greater question.

"You were obviously waiting for me just now. How did you know I was coming here?"

"Your partner was able to help us with that. When we couldn't find you, we went looking for him. He offered to arrange a meeting, for a fee, of course."

"Let me guess. A thousand dollars."

"You really should pick your friends more carefully."

It seems to Miles to be a warning made with the utmost sincerity. He wonders now if the wiring and pipe are actually still in the basement, or if Jimmy had already gotten them out. He wonders, too, if their landlord is really padlocking the place tomorrow.

Jimmy was always crafty, though to Julie the guy was more shady than simply smart. Miles was aware of that side of his old friend but didn't care; Jimmy was skilled at running the business—paying the bills, hiring and firing the staff, dealing with distributors and vendors. This freed Miles to focus on booking the talent and, when necessary, picking them up at the airports and driving them to their hotels.

He knew from the start that his partnership with Jimmy was akin to a deal with the devil, but it was the devil he knew, as opposed to the devil he didn't. Who doesn't always opt for that?

"Why the trick?" Miles asks. "Why not be straightforward?"

"We weren't sure you'd be willing to meet with us, so we asked him to be discreet. And we were hoping for a private place to talk."

Miles glances at the man standing guard by the door, then back at Trask. "You said you knew my father."

"Yes."

"Are you from the law firm?"

"What law firm?"

"I got a telegram informing me he was dead. It came from some law firm in Geneva, about a month after he died."

"No, we're not from that or any law firm."

"So what is it you want?"

"Your help."

Miles knows when he is being baited. His instinct is to resist taking it. Finally, though, he says, "My help with what?"

"Before we get into that, I want you to know that I didn't just know your father. He and I were very close. I'm sorry for your loss, by the way."

"It wasn't a loss."

Trask nods. "I understand that. You were angry with him, for leaving you and your mother like he did. I'm not sure if this will make much sense to you right now, but he wanted you to be angry. Powerful emotions can often motivate a man, drive him to do great things. Your father wanted you motivated." Trask takes a step closer, and yet his hands remain deep in the pockets of his black overcoat. "I'm sure you don't know this, but he kept tabs on you."

Miles says nothing.

"When he learned that your mother was killed, he sent two men to observe you. I was one of them. We spent several weeks watching you and reporting back to him. Naturally, he was very concerned about you. In fact, we had orders to step in and help you if you ever needed it. Money, protection, whatever the situation required."

Miles says flatly, "I don't believe that."

"Which part?'

"All of it. Any of it."

"I'm sorry that you doubt me, Miles. But it's true."

"Prove it."

Trask takes a breath, then nods and says, "You and your mother were living on the Upper East Side. Eighty-First and Second, if I remember correctly. A four-hundred-dollar-a-month studio apartment. After her death you stayed with the parents of a girlfriend for a few weeks, down on Astor Place. You were seventeen. You wore this ratty old blue sweater all the time. Your girlfriend was eighteen and the daughter of a partner in a major law firm. He and his wife seemed to genuinely care about you. Eventually, you and your girl got an apartment of your own on the Upper West Side, not far from Columbia, where she was enrolled as a freshman."

Trask pauses to let all that sink in, then says, "How am I doing so far?"

"Go on."

"I think it was a week after your mother died that you went out and got a job with a contractor. My partner and I always used to wonder about that particular choice of yours. My guess was that because your mother worked day and night you used to spend a lot of time with your building's super, and he got you interested in fixing things. I've always wondered if I got that right."

Miles says nothing.

"Anyway, not long after that you began your apprenticeship as an electrician. Once your father was certain that you were okay, he pulled my partner and me out of New York. He continued to keep tabs on you, though, mainly through a private investigator he kept on retainer. You finished high school, did some college, got your electrician's license, and became an independent contractor. When you had enough money saved, you started this club with your friend. Another choice that I never really understood. All was well—with the exception of your divorce—till the economy took a nosedive. Is that enough proof, or do you need more?"

"No," Miles says. "That should do it."

Trask pauses again, looks Miles up and down once, then: "You should know that your father was pleased you didn't waste time feeling sorry for yourself after your mother's death. You probably could have mooched off your girlfriend's rich parents, but you didn't, you did what had to be done, went out and made your own way. Your father was proud of that, and he had every confidence that this recent setback of yours was only temporary. He knew it wouldn't be long before you got back on your feet again."

Miles waits, saying nothing. It is of course unnerving to learn that for the past two decades he has been watched—or at least kept track of—by the very man he'd been raised to believe was nothing less than a bastard, and had long ago written off as such.

Still, it would take more than a few words from a man Miles has only just met to even begin to ease the ill feelings he has had most of his life to nurture.

"Everything I have, I owe to your father," Trask announces. "Everything I know, he taught me. I worked for him for thirty years.

My entire adult life. I made a promise to him a long time ago that I would look after you and your sister if anything were to happen to him."

"Half sister," Miles corrects.

Trask isn't at all put off by this. If anything, he seems to completely understand.

"Of course. Yes. Sorry. *Half* sister. Which brings us to why I am here. It seems that Elena has gotten herself into some trouble."

Miles has never even heard the woman's name before, and for some reason, hearing it now throws him a little.

A name naturally requires that one have a face to go with it.

He pushes this from his mind and says finally, "I'm sorry to hear that."

"You don't sound all that sorry."

Miles shrugs. "My mother and I were his starter family. We got nothing, and his new family got everything. So no, I don't really feel that much concern for her."

"Regardless of that, you and Elena are his children—his only children. And because of that, you both now share the same burden."

Once more Miles chooses to ignore the obvious question raised by this man's choice of words. To do otherwise would undoubtedly mean having to hear more.

And he has heard enough.

"Look, it's heartwarming that my father meant so much to you. And I'm sorry his daughter is in trouble. But I have my own problems."

Trask nods. "Yes, I know. A sizeable debt to the IRS, not to mention the dozen or so distributors and suppliers you owe. And of course there's that line of credit with the bank and your personal credit cards. Tell me, the lease, the liquor license, nearly everything having to do with this business was in your name, correct? Something to do with your buddy's past problems with the law. So, legally speaking, it's all in your lap, isn't it? You're the one everyone will come after, should your buddy decide to leave you high and dry.

The same buddy who just sold you out to us for a measly grand. He had no idea who I was, only knew that I wanted to talk to you. To be honest with you, Miles, it wouldn't surprise me in the least if he never came back from Atlantic City. Actually, I'd be surprised if he *didn't* disappear on you."

Miles is about to turn and tell Jack that they're leaving, but Trask closes the remaining distance between them before Miles can even move and takes hold of Miles's forearm with a firm hand.

"Do you know what your father did for a living, Miles?"

Glancing down at Trask's gloved hand, Miles repeats the only thing his mother ever said on the subject.

"He was in banking. International banking."

"More specifically, your father was a provider. Do you know what that is?"

"No."

"He provided things, any and all things. Yes, he worked as a private banker, but that was only a front. And, in itself, a lucrative one. Frankly, I'd kill just to get my hands on the money he earned through legitimate means. His real wealth, though, and I'm talking vast sums here, came from other more . . . complicated transactions."

It takes a good moment for Miles to give in and ask what Trask means by "complicated transactions."

"Your father's bank was in Geneva. As in Switzerland. As in a Swiss bank. Are you familiar with Swiss banks, what they're known for?"

"Yeah."

"For the right client, your father was more than willing to go the extra mile. I believe his first job was a simple matter of converting a client's cash into diamonds, having those diamonds smuggled into Paris and then delivered back to the client, who would then have them sold for cash. That's called money laundering. Over the years your father built a network of connections and couriers, and it wasn't long before he realized that he could get his hands on pretty much anything. More importantly, he could get anything into any country. And when I say anything, I mean *anything*.

"Eventually, laundering money for clients was the least profitable part of his business. As his reputation grew, so did the size of the fees he could demand. Even certain governments came to him from time to time, when they needed something—or something done—but couldn't risk direct involvement. Toward the end there, it was even alleged that your father was working for known terrorist organizations, helping them hide and move their money. Word is, he was helping one particularly bad guy bring certain materials and components into the United States. He was obsessed with amassing more and more wealth and didn't care who might get hurt down the road."

Trask pauses, then: "And I'm sorry to say, but it seems that obsession is hereditary."

Miles asks what that means.

"I've known Elena all her life," Trask answers. "She and your father were inseparable. Whenever possible, he took her with him on his many business trips. Sometimes he'd even pull her out of school so she could travel with him. She got the best education money could buy—the best boarding schools, and on top of that, everything he had to teach. Her mother was an Israeli national, so when Elena turned eighteen, she returned to Israel to do her stint in the army. Every Israeli citizen, male or female, is required to serve at least two years. She did three. I doubt, though, there was anything the army taught her that your father hadn't already. After she got out, she fell in love with a man named Pavol Jelinek. Jelinek had been in the special forces for eight years. The two of them settled in Haifa, and through him her very specific education no doubt continued."

"This is all very interesting, but what does it have to do with me?"

"The law firm that contacted you informed you of the nature of your father's death, correct?"

"Yeah. They said he killed himself."

"Elena believes otherwise. She has been on a rampage, traveling all over the world, trying to dig up proof. What she expects to do, should she actually find any proof, is anyone's guess. But considering everything she has been taught, and the company she kept—meaning Jelinek—I think it's safe to assume the worst. Add to that her tendency toward obsessive behavior, and what we have here are the makings of a disaster."

"I still don't see what any of this has to do with me."

"Right before he died, your father transferred all his assets to Elena. They were . . . considerable assets. No one knows for certain just how considerable. I don't even know. But it's easily in the tens of millions, probably more. Euros, of course, not dollars."

Trask once more pauses so that the information can sink in.

"One thing we do know is that Elena is willing to spare no expense in the pursuit of her obsession. We know this because we've been chasing her for the past ten months. In doing this, I've burned through quite a bit of my own money. Money I had set aside for my retirement. You see, your father taught me everything I know, but not everything he knew. Certain skills, it seems, he chose to only pass on to his daughter. She's impossible to catch, even when she's standing right there in front of you. She's like a rabbit. So not only is she skilled, but her resources are virtually unlimited. She could keep this up for years—decades—and not even come close to running out of funds."

"I'm still not sure how I can help you."

"We managed to catch up with Elena a month ago in Amsterdam."

"How exactly did you manage that? I mean, if she's so hard to find."

"She has three passports, that we know of, and she used one of them to enter Amsterdam."

"How do you know she has three passports?"

"Because I'm the one who provided them. Obtaining fake passports is one of the things I did for your father."

"So what happened? In Amsterdam, I mean."

"I tried to talk sense into her. Like I said, I've known her all her life—I'm family to her. I told her what I believe to be true, that this isn't what her father would have wanted her to do with her life. She clearly disagreed. Though she promised to meet with me the next day so we could talk some more, she didn't show. She left Amsterdam shortly after out meeting, using the passport she had come in on. She did not, however, enter another country, which can only mean she managed to get her hands on a fourth passport. I feared we had lost her for good, but two nights ago some men were killed up in Montreal. One of them, it turns out, was Jelinek. The other, I believe, was someone who worked for your father."

"You believe? You don't know for certain?"

"Your father's network employed a cellular structure. Everyone who worked for him had a code name, and no one but your father knew who anyone really was. The man who was killed fits the description of the kind of man your father might make good use of. But it's Jelinek's presence that seals the deal and, frankly, causes me concern."

"Why?"

"She got the person closest to her killed," Trask says. "Obviously, she's willing to sacrifice the man she loved, and for what? Proof that her father didn't kill himself, when everyone, including the authorities in Geneva, says he did? And if he didn't kill himself, then she's risking the wrath of those who did kill him. Again, your father worked for some very dangerous people. She's her father's daughter, yes, there's no doubting that. I wouldn't want to be the one she was after. But this, what she's doing now, it's just . . . dangerous. Worse than that, it's reckless. I fear she is out of control, a danger to herself and to others. I want to keep the promise I made to your father. I owe him that much, but I can't do this forever. I can't keep following her around the world. My resources are by no means unlimited. In fact, they're on the verge of drying up. And I'm too old to start all over again."

Dried-up resources is something Miles can definitely identify with.

Still . . .

"I'm not really following," he says.

"I'm asking you to come to Montreal with us."

"What for?"

"In case we find her."

"I've never met her. I've never even seen a picture of her. You think *I'd* be able to talk sense into her?"

"At this point, no, I don't think anyone can do that. But because you are family, there are certain things you can do legally that we cannot."

"What things?"

"It will be easier for us to get her into the States from Canada. There are several ways of doing that. But we need to find her while she's still there. Once back here, you could file for conservatorship. I've had a lawyer draw up all the necessary papers. I also have two prominent New York City psychiatrists ready to testify that she's a threat to herself and others. I know this sounds unpleasant—involuntary commitment—but it's important to me that we get her the care she needs, and while we have the chance. If we still have a chance. Once she's out of Canada, things get much more complicated. So, as I said, we don't have a lot of time to waste here. And by helping me, you'll of course be helping yourself."

"How?"

"While Elena's getting the care she needs, your father's money will be safe. This will allow you take steps of your own. My lawyers can help you with that, too."

"It's not his money anymore, it's hers. He obviously wanted her to have it."

"That's not necessarily true. Your father's will has yet to be found. Maybe Elena knows where it is, maybe she doesn't. What was found among his things, however, were a bank routing number and checking account number. *Your* bank's routing number and *your* checking account, it turns out. Your father had the means of transferring funds to you anytime he wanted. Naturally, it took some effort for him to obtain that information without your knowledge, which means he must have gone to that trouble for a reason."

"Yet he sent all his money to her."

"Aren't you curious why?"

"No."

"It's possible that she's holding out on you, Miles. Heirs screw each other all the time. I don't need to tell you what your fair share of his money could do for you. No more debts. Financial security for life. I understand that while your club was in business you were living quite the life. You could have all that back—that and much more."

Miles shakes his head. "I'm sorry, but my hands are full right now. And anyway, the whole point is moot. The IRS flagged my passport. I'm not supposed to leave the country without first notifying them."

"That wouldn't be a problem," Trask says assuredly.

"Maybe not, but I can't just leave work." He turns toward the back of the room and calls, "Jack, we're leaving now."

The boy and the woman stand.

Trask, in his quietest voice yet, says, "I'll pay you twenty thousand dollars. In cash, up front. Yours to keep even if we don't find her. We'll call it a consultant fee. A tax-free consultant fee."

Miles pauses.

"The offer's good till tomorrow morning," Trask says. "Elena has a two-day start on us, so that's as long as we can wait. At least think about it. You'll do that much, right? For an old friend of your father's?"

It takes a moment—a long moment—for Miles to pass for a second time.

"No, thanks."

"Like I said, Miles, I've known your father all of my adult life. I find it difficult to believe that he didn't make some kind of provision for you in his will. Your son seems like a bright kid. In case you haven't noticed, college is expensive these days, and it's only getting more so. I'm sure you don't want him to have to work his way through it rewiring buildings like you did. Crawling through walls, getting covered with asbestos. If not for me or your sister or yourself, then consider doing this for him. A few days in Montreal seems to me a small sacrifice to make, no? Considering what you might gain from it. And if the worst that comes of it is twenty grand, it's twenty grand you didn't have before. Twenty grand no one, not even the IRS, knows about."

Jack reaches his father side. As she passes Miles, Angelina smiles and says, "He's a very polite boy."

Then she joins the large man standing by the door. Miles takes a second look at her. It is then that he notices the large man is staring at him with what can only be read as hostile eyes.

Trask removes a business card from his overcoat pocket with his gloved hand.

"This is Cohn's number." Trask gestures toward the man by the door. "He's Cohn. If you change your mind, please call. If you don't, well, good luck with everything."

He offers the card, and Miles takes it.

"I'm glad we finally got to meet face-to-face," Trask says. "And I'm sure your father was right, you'll end up on your feet again, sooner or later. You are, after all, an Aureli. They're hard to keep down."

Six

Once he gets Jack to fall asleep in the back room, Miles stands at the living room window.

No train is due, so the well-lit platform a hundred feet away is empty. A straight line into the city from there, just an hour's ride—not bad as far as exiles go. Still, he has never lived anywhere other than the city before. Even in the early days, when he had nothing and was scrambling just to get by, he always managed to find a place somewhere in Manhattan.

Or at least someone who already had a place there and wanted him to move in.

He thinks of the apartments he has known, and the women he shared them with. Some relationships lasted years while others just fell apart within the span of a single season. Ally, the Columbia student with whom he lived on the Upper West Side after his mother was killed, was the woman he was with the longest. That was so long ago, though, that he can't even remember why it ultimately ended. Was there one thing that caused the failure, or many? Were they just kids who in the process of growing up had simply grown apart?

After that, who? Marianne, a dance major at NYU with a small two-room in a rent-controlled building down on Leroy Street. Then Suzanne, who moved into Miles's apartment, a sublet as small as a ship's cabin on MacDougal Street, and the first place he found for himself. She made jewelry by day and tended bar at night, smoked clove cigarettes, wore only black, and was as emotionally elusive as a housecat. Remembering her—the things he willingly put up with from her—makes him laugh at himself.

Then who? Annie on East Thirty-Fourth, Christine on West Forty-Eighth, Lori just two blocks north of where he had lived with his mother.

All the while, working as a contractor, making money and saving what he could. Moving in with someone, then moving out; or having someone move in with him, then that person moving out.

He even once moved into a woman's place only to take over the lease when their relationship fell to pieces and she moved out.

It went like this till he met Julie. Each place he lived, every woman he loved, or tried to—all just steps in the journey leading him to her.

And to Jack.

But now what? A cheap apartment out of the city and back to scrounging again—no, worse than scrounging. Moving as he had from place to place for all those years, he only ever carried with him clothes and essentials.

But these days, with every step he takes, he drags with him a monstrous debt, as well as the shock of having been a fool, of having believed that the good times would simply never end.

It isn't long before he is looking at the number on the card Trask had given him.

I find it difficult to believe your father didn't make some provision for you in his will.

Heirs screw each other all the time.

Miles has thought of himself as many things, but never an heir.

But then:

And if the worst that comes of it is twenty grand, it's twenty grand you didn't have before. Twenty grand no one, not even the IRS, knows about.

He tells himself that he will be doing only what needs to be done.

For Jack, and for Julie, too.

Who would do less?

Picking up his cell phone, Miles first calls the restaurant where he works. The hostess answers. He asks for Phil and is put on hold. A half minute later Phil picks up.

"It's Miles."

"What's up?"

"I need a favor. I was hoping someone could cover my shifts next week."

"What's going on?"

"Family stuff."

"How many shifts are we talking about?"

"I'm not sure. Monday and Tuesday, at least."

"I'm sure I can find someone. You'll be back by Thursday, though, right?"

"Probably. Why, what's Thursday."

"It's Thanksgiving, remember? We're booked up, three full seatings."

"I forgot."

"I need you behind the bar, man. And anyway, it's a five-hundred-dollar day. You don't want to miss out on that."

"You're right."

"I've been good to you, man, giving you weekends off so you can have your kid. Try to find someone else who'll work with you like that."

"I appreciate everything you've done, you know that."

"I'll find someone to cover your shifts through Wednesday, but I need you here on Thursday. Deal?"

"Yeah."

"We start setting up at nine."

"I'll be there."

Miles ends the call, then enters the number off the business card.

A male voice answers after the second ring. Deep, emotionless, abrupt. "Miles?"

"Yeah."

"Are you in?"

"Yeah, but I have a few conditions."

"Go ahead."

"Trask said I can get the money up front."

"That's right."

"After you give it to me, I'll need fifteen minutes to run an errand."

"Okay. What else?"

"All I can give you is three days. Tomorrow is Saturday, so if we don't find her by, say, Tuesday night, I'm gone. I have a job I can't afford to lose."

"The sooner we get started, the better."

"I can meet you first thing in the morning. I have my kid till then."

"What time tomorrow?"

"We can catch the early train. It gets into Grand Central at seven thirty. But it'd be better if we met downtown."

"Just tell me where."

"There's a vintage clothing shop in the West Village called Starstruck. It's on Greenwich Avenue. That part of the street is metered, so you won't have any problem finding parking there on a Saturday morning."

Cohn is silent for a moment. Miles begins to think the call has been dropped.

Finally, though, Cohn says, "Starstruck on Greenwich Avenue. That should be fine."

Miles wonders what Cohn's delay could mean, but only briefly.

"We should be there by a quarter to eight," Miles says.

"We'll be waiting."

Miles closes the phone. It is the last movement he makes for a long time.

Finally, he opens the phone again and places the call he wishes he didn't have to make.

Julie answers after the third ring.

Saturday

Seven

Catching the 6:35 train means that Miles has kept at least one of his promises to his son.

Sitting by the window, he pulls Jack onto his lap so the boy can have a clear view of the scenery rushing past.

Predawn when they stepped onto the train, it is full morning when they emerge from the Grand Central Terminal.

A cab takes them to Greenwich Avenue. After paying the fare, Miles is left with only a few singles. He stuffs them into the pocket of his hooded sweatshirt. It is cold, and he should be wearing something more, but he left his jacket in his minivan last night, and there simply wasn't time to grab it this morning as they rushed to catch the train.

A black Audi A4 is the only vehicle parked on the south side of Greenwich Avenue. As Miles and his son approach it from behind— Miles carrying the boy's backpack—Cohn and Angelina emerge, Cohn from the passenger side, Angelina from the driver's.

Cohn looks the same—he is dressed as he was last night, in a black coat over a black suit, and has the same harshness to his eyes— but Angelina is dressed very differently.

Green army field jacket over a dark turtleneck sweater made of densely woven wool, faded jeans, and black leather boots. Her curly hair is down, and a black cotton scarf hangs loose around her neck.

Cohn approaches Miles quickly, walking on the balls of his feet like a boxer. He hands Miles an envelope.

"You've got fifteen minutes," he says.

Julie's place is less than a five-minute walk away.

As father and son make their way, Miles opens the envelope and sees the promised cash inside.

Four stacks of fifties, each one surrounded with a paper bank band.

Printed on each band: *$5,000.*

He removes one of the stacks from the envelope and, looking around—there is no one around to watch him at this hour—stuffs it into the hip pocket of his jeans.

The other three stacks he leaves in the envelope, which he holds in one hand as he takes Jack's hand with the other.

Even before they are halfway up the stoop, the front door opens, and Julie, wearing a long cardigan-coat, is standing in the doorway like a guardian.

She is smiling, but Miles knows that the smile is both forced and for Jack's sake.

He tells his son once more that he's sorry about the weekend and that he'll make it up to him next time. They hug, and then Miles hands the boy his backpack. Jack drags it behind him as he hurries past his mother.

Once he disappears down the long entranceway, so does Julie's smile.

"Nick and I had things we were going to do today," she says. "We were counting on this."

"I know, I'm sorry. Like I said, though, it's important."

"What's more important than your son?"

"Nothing," Miles says. "That's the point." He hands her the envelope.

She takes it. The look on her face tells him that she knows by the shape and weight of the envelope what it contains.

Still, she opens it to have a look.

"What's going on?"

"It's Jack's child support for the next year. Well, almost."

She has thumbed through all three stacks. "This is fifteen thousand dollars, Miles. Where did you get this?"

"It doesn't matter. I'm going away for a few days, but I'll be back in plenty of time for Friday night."

"Where are you going?"

He shakes his head and repeats that it doesn't matter. "Someone's waiting for me. I'll explain everything when I get back."

"Who's waiting for you?"

Miles nods toward the envelope and says, "You might want to put that somewhere other than the bank. For now, at least."

He turns and starts down the stairs, is on the sidewalk and heading back toward Greenwich when he hears Julie say, "Just tell me you know what you're doing."

"Don't worry, Jule. Okay? I'll see you in a few days, I promise."

Back at the black Audi, with several minutes to spare, Miles is handed a second envelope.

This one contains a US passport and New York State driver's license.

He examines them, sees his photo on both—the same photos, in fact, that appear on his legitimate passport and driver's license.

He recalls having to send a duplicate photo when he applied for his passport. And the DMV certainly has digital copies of his driver's license photo.

Though the photos are of him, the name printed on each document is not.

Johnson, John Joseph.

"Why this name?" Miles asks.

Cohn ignores the question. "Trask has gone up ahead. You'll be driving up with Angelina."

"Wait. We're driving there?"

Opening the driver's door, Angelina says, "It's only a five-hour ride. If you add in the time it takes to get to and from the airport, plus all the waiting around before you even take off, it's actually faster to drive there than to fly. Plus, there's a storm moving across upstate."

Cohn says, "You're going to want to memorize the address on your new ID. The border guards going into Canada are more lax than the border guards you'll encounter when you're coming back to the States, but you'll still need to be prepared. They'll ask you questions, and you'll need to answer quickly and naturally, no hesitation."

Miles has never crossed the border into Canada before, so he has no idea what to expect. Still, he knows that the system is computerized, so information is not only instantly recorded but instantly shared as well.

"You're sure this passport is going to work?" he asks.

Again, Cohn ignores the question. "If you run into any trouble, do exactly what Angelina tells you to, the moment she tells you to do it. Do you understand?"

Miles doesn't bother with the question on his mind now.

Exactly what kind of trouble might we run into?

"We'll be fine," Angelina says.

Miles looks at her, then back at Cohn—or rather where Cohn had been standing a second ago.

The man is walking away.

Moving fast.

Miles steps to the passenger side of the Audi.

Angelina smiles at him over the vehicle's roof. "He's not very personable, is he?"

"No."

"Fortunately for him, we don't pay him for his company." Her eyes go to Miles's hooded sweatshirt. "You're going to need a little more than that up there."

"I don't think we'll find any stores open right now."

"It's okay. We'll get you situated once we're there."

She climbs in behind the wheel. Miles slides into the passenger seat. The car's interior, sleek and sculpted, is warm.

Starting the engine, Angelina shifts into gear and makes a U-turn, heading west on Greenwich. A right onto Eighth Avenue, then a quick left onto West Fourteenth, and within a minute they are turning onto the West Side Highway and heading north.

It is only then that Miles notices the sky directly ahead.

Gray clouds with blackish centers crowding together from one end of the horizon to the other.

"Snowstorm?" he asks.

"Yeah."

"How bad?"

"Bad enough. We don't have much choice, though, do we?"

Miles says nothing.

Smiling again, Angelina says, "Don't worry, we'll be fine."

As they approach the toll at the Henry Hudson Bridge, Angelina pulls the E-ZPass transponder from the Velcro strips holding it to the windshield.

She tells Miles that he'll find a silver-colored Mylar bag in the glove compartment. He pulls it out, and she hands the transponder to him, telling him to place it inside the bag.

"Won't the bag block the signal?" he asks.

Opening the console between them, she says, "That's the idea," and grabs a five-dollar bill.

Miles slips the transponder into the bag and seals it just as they reach the tollbooth.

"What's the point of having this if you don't use it?"

"For the next few days we don't exist," she explains.

"What does that mean?"

She tells him that they only use cash from now on. No credit cards, nothing that can be used to track them.

"Understand?"

Miles does, at least to a degree, so he nods.

Once clear of the toll, they cross over the Manhattan River and into the Bronx.

It is then that Miles smells her perfume.

Every woman has her own scent.

Angelina's is a potent mix of jasmine and peppermint. It is a combination that for some reason triggers in Miles thoughts of warm summer nights.

Eight

In a large and unfamiliar bed, Elena wakes.

Through the tears in her eyes—it is like looking through a distorting glass with a continually shifting thickness—she sees the curtains that hang along both sides of the window she had opened prior to finally climbing into bed just a few hours before. White, elegantly laced, and long, they billow, twist, and flutter like twin ghosts.

The air moving them comes from the river. After blowing past quai King-Edward and whipping across rue de la Commune, a journey of only a few hundred feet with little to nothing along the way to block or slow it, the wind enters her hotel room as steady gusts of raw dampness.

By three a.m. she knew that she needed to get some rest, but she didn't want to sleep so deeply for fear that Pavol, not just her father, would be waiting for her in her dreams.

To see him—to relive his death with any kind of detail, and how could that not happen?—would, she knew, break her.

But she had come too far to risk letting that happen.

Come too far with farther left to go.

Surrounding herself with a punishing cold seemed the best deterrent to sound slumber.

And anyway, there will be plenty of time to mourn once this is over. She will have the rest of her life to feel the full weight of anguish and loss and shock. When she finally returns to their home near the sea, she can let the pain have its way with her, tear her to pieces, and, if required, drive her mad.

Still, the presence of tears in her eyes tells her that something must have found her in that semiconsciousness. She is lucky enough, however, not to remember it now.

Crawling out from under the blankets, she crosses to the window, shutting it.

The cold has served its purpose; it is time to work now, and she'll need warmth for that.

She has taken this room for a week, paying for it in full. Auberge du Vieux-Port is a luxury hotel that offers from all its spacious rooms—brick walls, wood floors polished to a shine, exposed timber beams that are so weathered they could have come from a shipwreck—clear views of rue de la Commune and the Saint Lawrence River beyond.

But location, not scenery, is her concern. Being only nine doors down from the building Jean-Claude had provided means she can see over the bare trees that line the promenade and divide the street from the river's edge to the hangar on quai de l'Horloge, now at least a quarter of a mile away. Despite the distance, she can still make out the word "Labyrinthe" spelled out in white letters on the orange awning.

It is important for her to keep this place within sight, to remind herself of the men who have fallen, the high price paid so far.

She looks at the clock on the bedside table.

Eight a.m.

It takes a moment, though, for her to remember that is it Saturday.

So, that makes it sixty hours, roughly, since the batteries in the tracer bills were activated. And sixty more, give or take, till they're dead.

But subtract another twenty-four hours from that to compensate for the start of their slow death.

So forty-six hours till the signal will begin to steadily fade.

Late Monday morning, then.

Not long, and yet, at the same time, somehow forever.

The tracking device, set on standby and plugged into the wall socket so its own battery would recharge, is silent. It has been since she fled the apartment in the Latin Quarter two nights ago.

Pressing the button marked "Test," she sees all ten LED lights spike, then go dark. The battery indicator glows bright green, indicating a full charge.

The device is in working order. Its silence means there is no signal to detect

Pavol's killer is beyond the mile radius. But how far beyond? Would he soon return, or was he gone for good?

There is another possibility. He could have discovered and destroyed the tracer bills. If that is the case, she will never find him. And if he comes to find her, she will have no warning of his approach.

This is too much to consider in her state—exhausted from lack of sleep, alternately numb from shock and sick with grief.

With the room quickly warming around her, she decides to resume the tasks that have consumed her since checking in on Thursday.

What else can she do?

———

Once she had settled into this room Thursday morning, she called for a cab and had the driver take her up the hill to Chinatown, where she purchased an Epson printer, document shredder, and four reams of paper from an office supply store.

On the way up, and on the way back down, she kept a careful eye out for any indication of a tail. But she saw none. Exiting the cab and entering the hotel lobby, she paused just inside and to the left of the door, pretending to wait for someone.

The three plastic bags, two oversized, the third smaller but heavy, hung from her left hand. Her right she kept free in case she needed to reach for the CZ-75 resting in the inside pocket of her coat.

The two front desk clerks, though busy, each took a moment to smile at her as she waited. One was an older man with neat, dark hair, the other a young woman who wore her thick blonde hair pinned up in a bun. Both were dressed in dark, expensive suits. Smiling back at them, Elena was confident that nothing about her expression would betray what was really inside her. A soldier once, she could, when required, smile through agony.

When a long enough moment had passed and no one came through the front entrance, Elena stepped to the elevator. Next to it was a stand with complimentary newspapers. The *Gazette* and the *Globe and Mail.* Grabbing a copy of each, she rode to the third floor, where she exited the elevator and walked up the stairs to the fourth.

Once back in her room, she set up the Epson, connecting it to the notebook computer containing the downloaded files, and began printing out hard copies.

It was slow work, painstaking—she had to open each document, select "Print," close that document, open the next, and then repeat the process. As the Epson worked on those first few pages, she checked the newspapers.

To her surprise, the previous night's killings weren't either paper's headline. And though an article covering it was on the front page of the *Globe and Mail,* it was located below the fold and next to a piece about a Canadian journalist's time in a Tehran jail and how the verses of songwriter and poet Leonard Cohen, a Montreal native, brought him comfort during his captivity.

Elena skimmed the article in the *Globe* quickly, looking at first for names. Only two were mentioned: Frank Tyler, an American, and Jean-Claude Gilroy of Montreal. Pavol's name was nowhere to be seen. A search for the phrase "as of yet unidentified male" brought immediate results.

For the newspaper to identify Jean-Claude by name meant that his wife had to have been already notified of his death. Elena made a note to transfer the money she owed him to his offshore account as soon as she was done here. It would be the right thing to do, considering. After all, Jean-Claude had children—Elena knew at least that much about him.

Returning to the top of the article, she began to actually read it and learned by the second paragraph that only Tyler and the unidentified male were listed as dead. Jean-Claude, it turned out, was "shot twice and in critical condition at Montreal General Hospital."

All other details as reported didn't interest Elena; she had, after all, witnessed the whole thing. Turning to the *Gazette* and searching through it, she found the article on the fourth page and under the banner "Shooting in Vieux-Port."

This report was more or less identical to the one in the *Globe*, the only exceptions being that the unidentified male was "believed to be a foreigner," and the American was "a retired United States government employee."

So, the *Gazette* reporter knew something the *Globe* reporter didn't, Elena thought. She wondered how long before Tyler's former employer would be identified. The fact that he worked for the American government came as no surprise to her; the machinations of her father's business were a mystery to her, but the nature of it was not.

The fact that the articles were below the fold on one paper and on the fourth page of another made sense to Elena. Montreal—particularly Old Montreal and the port area—relied heavily on tourism. Murders had to be underplayed in the press as much as possible. And the mention of foreigners implied that the city was at its heart a safe place and that, if not for a few bad apples who strayed in from elsewhere, there would be no danger for anyone wishing to visit.

Done, she tossed the papers aside, checked the Epson, and saw that the tenth page was printing. After going through the process of queuing up another ten, she powered up the second computer and went online via the hotel's free Wi-Fi.

Accessing the online banking service of Banque Genevoise de Gestion in Geneva, she entered her account number on the bank's login form, at which point the bank's server displayed a "challenge" and asked for "the matching response."

She removed the titanium flash drive from around her neck and inserted it into the USB port. Within seconds the program stored in the drive opened and requested her ten-digit PIN, which she entered. The program on the drive then "read" the challenge sent by the bank's server and responded with the appropriate encrypted response.

Without the communication between the flash drive and the bank's server, accessing her account via the Internet would be impossible. The variation of challenges and matching responses were in the millions. And if an incorrect ten-digit PIN were to be entered more than three times once the flash drive was connected and the program activated, online access to the account would be automatically blocked, requiring Elena to travel to Geneva and secure a new flash drive from her banker in person.

Grabbing her backpack, she removed the Moleskine notebook and flipped through its pages till she found the account number of the Cayman Islands bank belonging to Jean-Claude, which was on the page opposite the list of the serial numbers copied from the fifty grand in American bills that were taken by the bearded panhandler.

Initiating a wire transfer of one hundred thousand euros, she entered Jean-Claude's account number and finalized the transaction.

She glanced at the balance of her account.

€49,543,919.00.

Her father had wired just over fifty million two days before his death.

No, she corrected herself, *before his murder.* The man who called himself Mephistopheles had said he was murdered. And not by a man but by men. She hung onto that fact as if to let go of it would mean a fall from some great height.

How much had she gone through already? A half million euros, give or take, including the one hundred thousand she just wired to Jean-Claude.

It didn't matter to her. She'd burn through it all if she had to.

Logging off, she pulled the flash drive from the USB port and hung it around her neck again, feeling the cold of its protective metal case between her breasts.

Removing the printed pages from the tray of the Epson, she queued up another ten documents, then, sitting in the chair by the window, began to read her father's files.

Much of what she read she didn't understand—many files were simple invoices, others just notes and memos. Others still looked to be what amounted to action plans.

These could be the internal documents of any corporation—well, if not for all the code names.

Mephistopheles was one of the first she came across. There were other names, each a literary reference, but soon enough she noticed that four names appeared more frequently than others: Mephistopheles, Faust, Don Quixote, and Hamlet.

Because she did not fully understand what she was reading, and because she was required to pause every few minutes to queue up more pages, Elena was quickly growing more and more frustrated. Still, she continued to read, absorbing every word, no matter if seemingly meaningless, hoping that in some later document another piece of minutiae she might happen to come across would combine with a previous detail and suddenly enlighten her.

But that didn't happen. Thursday turned into Thursday night, and Thursday night into Friday morning. With only four hundred pages printed out and read, she gave up and slept for a few hours with the window open.

Friday was only more of the same. She was beginning to fear that the files that had cost her so dearly wouldn't lead her anywhere. In the morning, an edition of the *Globe* was delivered to her room, along with a half dozen small chocolate croissants in a baker's box wound in blue and white string. Though she had no appetite, she forced herself to eat a few bites. As she did, she looked at the paper and found that the follow-up to yesterday's article was not only on the front page, it was the headline: "Shooting in Vieux-Port."

Tyler's former employer was identified as the United States Department of Defense. Jean-Claude was described as a "career criminal," and his status was upgraded to "stable."

And there, in print, was Pavol's name.

She stopped eating then and went back to work.

It took all of Friday, and much of Friday night, to print out the remaining pages. Over twelve hundred in total. Reading, stopping to tend to the printer, then reading some more—tedious work, and, as far as finding what she needed, getting nowhere. Her fear increased, and when exhaustion finally drove her under the blankets at three a.m., Elena felt her frustration about to explode into despair.

Obsession, and the river air pouring in through the open window, kept her from deep sleep. She fell into a light unconsciousness at times, but unconsciousness wasn't rest. And every time consciousness would resume, the first thing it brought was an awareness of the strange bed and the emptiness beside her.

———

No pages to print today, but one last task before reading what remains.

Opening the surveillance program on the other notebook computer, she locates the footage recorded from the two buttonhole cameras.

From her backpack she removes a second flash drive. It is made of a silver-colored metal and, though not titanium, is nearly identical to the one hanging around her neck. Currently empty, it is capable of storing 8 gigs. More than enough.

Connecting it to the computer, she drags and drops copies of both WMV files to the flash drive. When the transfer is complete, she closes the surveillance program and disconnects the flash drive, inserts it into the first computer's port, and transfers to it the folder containing the digital copies of her father's files.

Disconnecting the flash drive once more, she ties the string from the bakery box to the key-chain loop at the drive's butt-end. With a small Gerber hand tool she carries with her always, she walks to a wall socket and removes the single screw holding the cover in place.

With the cover off, she ties the free end of the string to the mounting X-bracket, triple-knotting it, then slips the flash drive past the bracket and carefully lowers it down behind the wall.

She replaces the cover, tightens the screw, and, back at the notebook computer, deletes all the files from the hard drive of the first computer, then opens and initiates the scrubber program to wipe the hard drive clean of any "ghost" images.

Once that is done, the only copies in existence are the twelve-hundred-plus pages she has printed out and the digital copies stored on that flash drive hidden behind the wall.

The hard copies she can shred if it becomes necessary. And the flash drive she can simply leave where it is—there if she needs it, safe if she doesn't. Chances are it would never be found. And if it is, all this certainly would be long over, one way or another, and so it simply wouldn't matter.

Sitting in the chair by the closed window, where the light is best, she begins again to read.

Nine

Miles, his eyes closed, hears a rubbery thud.

He hears it again, and then again, each sound identical but evenly spaced and quick.

His first thought is that it's the sound of a flat tire. Opening his eyes and hearing the thud again, he realizes that it's only the blades of the windshield wipers reaching the apex of their arcs, then changing direction and rapidly descending.

He realizes, too, that he has slept, knows this by the heaviness of his limbs and the slowness of his mind.

For how long, though? he wonders.

Angelina, her attention fixed on the road ahead, has both gloved hands on the steering wheel. It takes Miles, still groggy, a moment to see that beyond the windows of the Audi is a frantically swirling snow squall.

The pavement is still visible under a dusting of snow that rises and floats like white smoke, but the terrain along both sides of the highway is already completely covered in white.

"You're awake," Angelina says.

Miles, slouching, sits up. "Yeah. How long was I out?"

"Three hours, maybe."

"You're kidding."

"No."

"Jesus. That's a record for me."

"What do you mean?"

"I don't sleep much."

"Insomniac?"

Miles nods, blinking against all the harsh white. He feels, as always, more drunk than refreshed.

"A fellow sufferer," Angelina says. "For me, the moment my head hits the pillow, my mind starts racing. I'm lucky if I get two hours a night."

"Really?"

"Yeah."

"How long has it been like that for you?" Miles asks.

"All my life."

"Shit."

"You?"

"About a year now."

"So what happened a year ago?" Angelina asks.

Miles shrugs as if to say that it's a long story.

Angelina keeps her eyes on the road. She has the manner of someone who is expecting what they are watching very well might disappear at any moment. "They say lack of sleep can drive a person insane."

Miles says he believes it. "But you seem pretty okay to me."

"Oh, trust me, I'm psychotic." Taking her right hand off the wheel, she reaches for the left breast pocket of her army field jacket. Miles can tell by the condition of the garment—frayed cuffs and collar, a sewn-up tear here, a faded spot on the shoulder where a patch had once been—that it is old. A hand-me-down, or maybe a thrift shop find. At Starstruck, the vintage clothing store on Greenwich Avenue, older military gear can easily cost triple what new gear costs.

Clawing deep into the pocket with her index and middle fingers, she removes a small, silvery cylinder and offers it to Miles.

He takes it and says, "What's this?"

Printed along the cylinder in green lettering is "Migrastick."

Below that, in smaller letters Miles can only barely read: "Rollerstick 3ml/0.1fl.oz."

"It's supposed to help with migraines," Angelina explains. "You rub it on your temples and forehead and the back of your neck. It's basically peppermint oil in a little roll-on thing. I find it relaxes me, sometimes even actually makes me drowsy. Try it out."

Miles unscrews the cap, and instantly his nose is filled with the smell of peppermint. He applies the tip to his right temple, rolls it around for a second, and then does the same to his left. The smell of peppermint is suddenly overwhelming, and within a few seconds he can feel a strange cooling sensation in both his eyes, as if he has looked straight into a steady and chilly breeze.

This, he thinks, explains the smell of peppermint when he first got into the car, and his thoughts of summer nights.

"Put a dab on your forehead and the back of your neck," Angelina suggests.

Miles does. The sensation of cooling air increases.

And then, suddenly, he feels himself relaxing.

"Wow," he says.

"The peppermint oil is in a base of isopropyl, which is alcohol, so as it evaporates off your skin, this little cloud of refreshing cool surrounds your head. Plus, the temples and forehead and back of your neck are pressure points, so rubbing them, even for a few seconds, is supposed to trigger the release of chemicals in your brain that alleviate stress."

"Wow," Miles says again.

"Nice, huh?"

He feels not only relaxed but somehow clean.

Recapping the cylinder, he offers it back to her, but she tells him to keep it.

"You sure?"

"I have another one in my bag." She nods toward the backseat.

Looking back, Miles sees a messenger bag made of black ballistic nylon.

He slips the Migrastick into the left hip pocket of his jeans, and in doing so he is reminded of the stack of five grand jammed in the right.

He remembers, too, the fake passport and driver's license in the pocket of his hooded sweatshirt.

Who am I again? That's right—John Joseph Johnson.

And who the hell is that? Sounds like the name of some porn star.

Am I Johnny to my friends? Or maybe J.J.? For that matter, I could be Jack. That would, of course, be the easiest name for him to remember.

After all, it's the reason he's doing this.

He nods toward the chaos beyond the windshield. "Has it been snowing like this for long?"

"No. We're just heading into it, I think."

"You can turn on the radio if you want to listen to the weather."

"No, that's okay. Would you mind some music?" Angelina asks.

"No."

She turns on the dashboard-mounted CD player. Miles hears from the multispeaker sound system a brief spatter of applause, then, suddenly, a trumpet fitted with a Harmon mute running upward in triplets.

A pause, then a muffled bass drum and a single chord stuck on a piano. Another pause, and then the trumpet resumes.

The tune is instantly familiar to him. "Autumn Leaves." The exact recording, however, takes him a moment to recognize.

"That's Miles Davis," he says after a few measures.

Angelina nods.

Another moment, and Miles asks, "Which record is that?"

"At the Olympia, 1960."

"Him and Sonny Sitt in Paris."

"Right."

"That's an obscure recording."

"It's one of my favorites," Angelina says. "He's playing hard, spends a lot of time in the upper register—well, a lot of time for him. It's the most aggressive I've ever heard him."

"So you know jazz."

"I'd go insane without it."

Listening, Miles looks out the passenger window. Through the falling snow he sees a mountain. Or maybe just a hill. Or maybe just a rock formation. To him, a lifetime New Yorker, though, it is a mountain.

"You know, I was named after Miles Davis," he says. "My mother used to be a jazz singer. Then all the jazz clubs in New York went out of business, and her career was over."

"What did she do then?"

He pauses, shrugs: "Whatever she could. Mainly she cleaned other people's apartments and a few businesses."

"Tough."

Miles nods, decides to change the subject to something more pressing. "How long till we get to the border?"

"About two hours. But probably longer now because of the storm."

Glancing at the speedometer, he sees that the Audi is moving at just over forty miles an hour.

Within a matter of minutes, the snowfall increases from a swirling squall to almost blizzard conditions.

The smoky-white pavement ahead simply disappears entirely behind a furiously shifting wall of white, and the speed of the Audi drops down to less than twenty.

Crawling northward.

Only occasionally can Miles see anything other than white outside his passenger window. An exit sign here—for the town of

Chesterfield—and a mile marker there—131. The chaos is at times more than his tired eyes can take. Whatever release the peppermint oil offered is now gone, replaced by the tension of moving so slowly through dangerous weather and strange terrain.

At one point Angelina announces that she needs to concentrate and switches off the CD player, after which the only sounds to be heard are the hum of the engine, the crunch of snow beneath the tires, and the familiar thumping of the windshield wipers.

This far north, traffic on I-87 is sparse, so there is little danger of colliding with another vehicle in this whiteout. Miles, in fact, has yet to even see one since waking. But there are moments—long moments—when both edges of the road can no longer be seen, and all that is left to guide Angelina is the vague difference to be heard between a paved highway beneath mounting snow and the uneven surface of the highway's shoulder beneath mounting snow.

Miles watches out his window, ready to warn her the instant he detects that they are straying too far to the right. Having nothing more to do than that is a helpless feeling, but would he feel any better if he were behind the wheel right now?

An hour, and then an hour more.

Conditions improve slightly, then deteriorate, improve again, and deteriorate once more.

Outside his window, when the snow allows, Miles sees tall evergreens, narrow birch trees, and more rock formations. At one point they cross over a river—the Ausable River, according to a sign he glimpses briefly.

It is here that they finally leave the worst of the storm. Soon enough the Audi is to forty, then fifty. Ten minutes after crossing the river it is up to sixty-five, and there is very little indication anywhere but behind them of the freak storm.

Outside the town of Peru the mountains—or hills, or whatever the hell they are—drop off, and all that can be seen to the east and west is an endless plain.

To the north, barely visible over the horizon, is a ridge. Blue, and no taller, really, than the teeth of a saw.

Angelina pulls off at exit 35 and heads for a Mobil station visible from the exit ramp. Next to it is a Subway restaurant.

"How far from here?" Miles asks.

"It's an hour to the border. From there it's another hour to Montreal."

Miles looks at his watch; it's just past two. "We should probably get something to eat."

Angelina nods. "We'll have to get it to go."

Parking at the pump, Angelina grabs her bag from the backseat and places it on her lap. Though most of it is rugged ballistic nylon, it has leather accents—two thick patches at the bottom corners and two leather straps to hold the flap closed. The shoulder strap is made of the same fabric as a car's seat belt. A small rectangle of metal on one of the two outside pockets reads "Belstaff."

Unbuckling the two leather straps, Angelina opens the flap and reaches into the main compartment, which is crammed full of things. Before Miles can get a good look at any of them, she removes what she was looking for and closes the flap again, then tosses the bag into the backseat.

In her hand is a baseball cap with a long bill. Putting it on, with the bill pulled so low it all but obscures her face, she says to Miles, "Ready?"

"Want me to pump it for you?"

She smiles. "Sure. Thanks. Make sure you touch metal and discharge any static before you start. And don't use your cell phone near the pump. Don't want you bursting into flames."

"Does that actually happen?"

"That's what they say, no?"

They exit the vehicle. She walks into the station and hands the cashier a twenty. As she does this, Miles touches the metal frame of the pump and feels the snap of a tiny shock. He waits till the pump is activated by the cashier, then begins. Walking out of the station, Angelina pauses to compose and send a text—to Trask, Miles assumes, informing him that they are running late.

As Miles tops off the tank, he looks up and sees several surveillance cameras mounted on the overhang above the pumps.

Thus the baseball cap with the bill pulled low, he thinks.

In the Subway shop, as the cashier rings up their sandwiches, Miles reaches into his pocket for the stack of fifties—the only money he has, aside from a few singles. Angelina gestures for him not to bother and pays for both orders.

"It's on Trask," she says.

As they leave, he sees yet another surveillance camera above the shop door.

A sign up ahead: "Canada Customs 5 Miles."

The sight of it causes Miles's gut to tighten.

As though she senses this, Angelina, her eyes forward, says, "Don't worry."

"The passport is going to work, right?"

She smiles and repeats, "Don't worry."

The baseball cap is back in her messenger bag, the ringlets of her dark hair hanging loose once again and framing her face. Miles can barely think of a time in his life without also thinking of the woman associated with it—the woman, and the neighborhood in which they lived. Most of his adult life—since his mother's death—there was hardly a night when he wasn't sleeping next to someone—till recently, that is. His exile in Connecticut seems to have stripped him of the confidence he once possessed—the very same confidence to which many New York women are seemingly drawn.

He can't help but wonder if he will in the future associate the time he went to Montreal with the dark-haired woman now beside him.

The dark-haired woman with the French accent and sharp features and slight overbite wearing a faded army field jacket, scarf, jeans, and black leather boots.

Soon enough the border comes into view, and Angelina reaches into her left breast pocket and removes a Canadian passport. Miles takes out the one Cohn gave him. Though there is a long line of vehicles waiting to enter the States from the Canadian side, the six booths leading into Canada are all free. Turning and looking through the rear window, Miles sees only two vehicles on the long stretch of otherwise empty road behind them.

Pulling into a booth, Angelina brings the Audi to a stop and shifts into park. The uniformed customs guard is a stoic-looking woman in her midforties. She asks for their passports. Angelina hands over hers, then takes Miles's passport and hands it over as well.

The customs guard opens both, glancing at the respective photos before turning each passport sideways and sliding them one by one under an infrared scanner. Watching a computer screen, she says to Angelina, "Are you bringing in any food or plants?"

"No."

"What was the reason for your visit to the United States?"

"Social."

The woman turns away from the computer screen and tilts her head downward so she can look past Angelina to the man beside her.

"What is the reason for your visit to Canada, sir?" she asks.

Stumped, Miles looks at Angelina.

After a pause, Angelina turns to the border guard and says with a giddy laugh, "Me!"

The guard isn't amused, but she isn't angry, either. Miles gets the sense that part of her training involves learning to act as if no answer to any of the questions she asks satisfies her.

"How long do you intend on staying in Canada?" the guard says to Miles.

"A few days. I have to be back at work on Thursday."

"Where will you be staying?"

Mile again defers Angelina.

"I live in Montreal," she says to the woman. "He'll be staying with me."

The customs guard pauses, then nods and hands both passports to Angelina.

"Enjoy your stay," the woman says.

Angelina passes the books to Miles, then shifts into gear and pulls out of the booth.

Miles is curious as to the name on Angelina's passport. Surely if they aren't supposed to exist for the next few days—cash for the tolls, gasoline, and food, and Angelina's baseball cap worn to obscure her face from gas station security cameras—then wouldn't the use of her own passport negate that?

As Angelina works up through the gears, Miles opens her passport enough for a quick glimpse inside.

The photo is of her, but the name printed below it is Angier, Catherine Anne.

A fake passport for her as well?

Once the Audi is up to speed, Angelina holds out her right hand. Miles places her passport in it. She returns the passport to her left breast pocket, and Miles stuffs his into the pocket of his hooded sweatshirt.

———

A long straightaway to Montreal.

Bare trees line the highway, beyond which are fields of tall, grassy reeds with bushy brown feathers swaying at their tops.

The bluish ridgeline in the distance grows a bit larger as the Audi moves northward.

A few miles of road construction slows their approach still more, causing them to lose close to a half hour, but then, just after four o'clock, Miles sees through the windshield the first hints of a city skyline.

A long bridge carries them over the Saint Lawrence River, which, Miles notes, is as wide as the Hudson. A series of turns and they are heading eastward.

"We'll be there in about twenty minutes," Angelina says.

Miles sees a port area, complete with docked freighters and a framework of giant cranes and booms and several immense and weathered warehouses. He is, for some reason, surprised by this.

"Are you from here?" he asks.

Angelina nods. "Yes. I think you'll like it; it's a very special place."

So far, for Miles, there is nothing all that special about it. The skyline to his left looks like any city skyline: a crowded nest of steel and glass towers. Stale and gray and cold. And the shipyards to his right look like standard industrial blight.

But then Angelina steers the Audi off the freeway and, after several turns, onto a street called rue Notre-Dame. She tells Miles that this is downtown Montreal, and again, to him, it looks quite ordinary.

It takes, though, just a little over a mile for that change. The buildings, in a matter of a few blocks, become shorter and less modern. White-gray facades full of tall windows—banks and shops and restaurants and boutique hotels. He is reminded of photographs and movies of Paris. *Montreal is, after all, a French city, isn't it?* he thinks.

And then, to his right, appears a large cathedral—the Basilique Notre-Dame. It is now four thirty, and, to his surprise, twilight has fallen. The cathedral is already lit up, its three tall archways glowing yellow. A line of people extend from its wide stairs and along the block.

Before Miles can ask what those people are waiting for, Angelina makes a right turn onto rue Saint-Sulpice.

It is a narrow, one-way street, not paved but cobbled, that slopes down toward the river. To the left is a row of five-story buildings that look as if they were built hundreds of years ago. A series of shops occupy the ground floors: Bastille Souvenirs, Noel Eternal, Lotus Boutique, a bakery called simply Cupcake.

The front windows of each shop are lit with strings of light. It's as though Miles has turned a corner into a Christmas village.

And with the exception of the half dozen or so vehicles parked on the street, it is as though he has stepped back at least a century, maybe two.

The cathedral fills the entire right side of the block. As wide as the building's front is, it is at least three times as deep.

Massive, hulking, made of gray stones—a fortress, really.

It ends finally at a small alleyway, after which another ancient-looking building begins, this one, though, five stories tall and narrow, the first in a block that leads down to a wide boulevard beyond which is a more picturesque waterfront than the one Miles viewed just twenty minutes before.

Here is where Angelina pulls the Audi to the curb and parks.

"Home," she says, pulling up the lever of the parking brake.

Getting out, Miles studies the scene.

It is maybe a few degrees above freezing, but there is no wind, so the cold doesn't really feel cold but somehow strangely serene, like a pleasant void.

A void, perhaps, in which nothing matters.

Dusk is quickly deepening as they enter through the street door. A brass plate marks the address and the name of the business that occupies the ground floor:

418 Saint-Sulpice.

Bureau des Ventes.

By the time they reach Angelina's apartment, which is clearly a converted attic and takes up the entire narrow top floor, it is more or less night outside.

Stepping to a window in the living room, standing on a floor of wide wooden planks joined not with nails or spikes but round pegs, Miles looks down at the canyon-like street below.

A couple in long coats, walking hand in hand along the opposing sidewalk, turn and pass through a wrought iron gate and into a courtyard directly across from Angelina's building. Miles watches as they make it through to the next block, then turn right toward the river and disappear from his sight.

A vehicle moves slowly down Saint-Sulpice then, the sound of its tires on the cobblestones echoing off the buildings on both sides of the street and rising upward.

The sound is a series of rapid rubbery thuds, not unlike the sound to which Miles awoke just hours before.

Ten

In her darkening hotel room, reaching for the reading lamp standing beside the chair, Elena suddenly hears the tracking device beep.

The room, even with the light still off, isn't completely dark; rue de la Commune, and quai King-Edward beyond it, are so well lit that she could make her way around at night without ever having to switch on a lamp.

Looking toward the device—its beeps are soft but steady—she sees at first that two of the LED lights are glowing. That number quickly rises to three, then four, then finally peak at five.

She immediately wonders if this means that the tracer bills—and the man who took them from Pavol—are within a half mile.

The tracking device did not come with a set of instructions, and Jean-Claude did not show her anything more than how to turn it on and off and set it to standby so that when the device wasn't plugged in, the drain on the battery would be less.

Does each light represent a tenth of a mile?

She is suddenly uncertain what to do. Frozen, still in her chair, she stares at the unit. Should she continue with her reading? Could she actually do that? Or should she leave right now and make an effort to determine the exact location of the signal's origin?

But then what? Wait around for the chance to kill the man who killed Pavol? Or somehow *make* that happen? Find a way to gain entrance to wherever that man is and gun him down? And after that, could she simply make her way back to her comfortable hotel room and resume studying her father's papers?

What was it Pavol had said?

Killing a man isn't easy.

And what if something went wrong? What if she got herself killed in the process of avenging Pavol? What if she didn't succeed at all? Or if she did succeed, what if she didn't make a clean getaway? Who, then, would care that her father hadn't killed himself? Who else would pursue the men who had murdered him and made his death look like a suicide?

Finally standing, she crosses to the device and stares at the five lights, hears the steady, metronome-like beeps.

Holding at five, never more, never less.

So definitely not in motion at this moment. Could he be at his home? At a restaurant? She could always just go and try to get a look at him, see who the man behind the beard and the smudged dirt was.

But why nothing for days and then, suddenly, five lights? He could have been out of town all this time.

Or maybe he had discovered the tracer bills immediately after taking them into his possession and he needed this long to set up a trap, using the transmitted signal as bait.

She knows that she has no choice, that she must, for now, switch the device off.

The risk of failure is just too great.

First things first.

Knowing and doing, however, are two different things.

Finally, though, she reaches down and moves the switch from standby to the off position.

The lights go dark, and the beeping ceases.

The silence is nothing less than haunting.

She has to trust that she will find a way to hunt and kill the man who murdered Pavol. Even as the minutes count down and she slips closer and closer to time running out, she has to believe she can accomplish the impossible.

She had been, after all, bred for this.

Returning to her chair and turning on the reading lamp, she gets back to her reading.

First things first, she reminds herself.

Just a hundred or so pages to go.

She had discovered during Saturday's reading a few key facts about her father's pipeline.

Montreal was the city through which items heading from Europe to the United States, and to Europe from the United States, passed. That, to her, made sense. Montreal was a port city, and only an hour north of a "friendly" border. Crossing into Canada by car, particularly with a US or Canadian passport, was both quick and easy. Crossing into the States from Canada was perhaps not as quick but still easy; the many questions asked by the immigration officers were usually the same, and though the "interview" at the border could sometimes take ten minutes and include a casual search of the vehicle's trunk, it would not be difficult to transfer things like cash or precious stones hidden within clothing or luggage, or information stored on an encrypted notebook computer.

And with access to fake passports, a courier could cross over any number of times without being flagged by Immigration's computerized system.

The code names Elena had noted earlier continued to dominate her father's papers.

Mephistopheles, Faust, Hamlet, and Don Quixote.

And since her father never referred to himself anywhere in his papers, if he had a code name, she quickly realized she wasn't likely to learn of it here.

There were many sentences—notes written in his own regal handwriting on the edges of otherwise typed-up pages—that read: "Meet with Don Quixote at 7:30," and "Mephistopheles to make drop-off with Faust at noon; Faust to deliver here by 3:00."

The fact that addresses were never mentioned probably meant that only the times at which he met with his numerous associates varied while the locations remained always the same.

She was able to determine by the invoices that Don Quixote, whoever he was, acted as her father's local scout, just as Jean-Claude served as hers. Mephistopheles, whom the newspaper identified as a retired DOD employee, seemed to be the link to the States, while Faust and Hamlet traveled back and forth from Europe and Asia.

She began to keep notes in the Moleskine notebook, writing down names and dates in hopes that, once gathered, they would add up to something.

There had been maybe a hundred pages left when sundown had caused her to reach out for the nearby lamp, only to be stopped by the sound of the tracking device.

Now, reading through these last pages, she sees by the dates listed that she is getting closer, page by page, to the night her father's life was ended.

* * *

She comes across an invoice for surveillance equipment—micro-video cameras with wireless transmitters and a receiver-equipped notebook computer to record what the cameras capture. At first she thinks it is a duplicate of the very first file she had printed out and read days ago. A closer look, however, tells her that it is dated just three days prior to her father's death.

Going back to the stack of pages on the floor, she looks at that first file again. This one indicates that Don Quixote had delivered similar equipment to a "Montreal address." This second file, however, indicates that surveillance equipment was delivered and set up at a "Geneva address."

There is no indication on this second document, though, who made the delivery or who installed the gear.

It was in his Geneva apartment that her father's body was found. Elena, with Pavol at her side, arrived twelve hours after having been notified. The local police did a thorough search of the crime scene but did not mention in their reports anything about surveillance equipment.

When she and Pavol were finally allowed to enter, Elena, knowing her father's penchant for security, not to mention documentation, conducted her own search, with Pavol's expert help, and found nothing.

Yet here in her hand is proof that some kind of equipment had been installed at a "Geneva address." If that did not mean her father's own home, then where else could it have been installed?

And if it did mean his home, then where had the equipment— and what it recorded—gone?

Who had taken it?

The last fifty or so pages begin to show indications that an otherwise well-oiled machine was beginning to break down. There are mentions of "Hamlet late for meeting" and "Faust a no-show."

In the final twenty pages, she finds more and more entries like that. It is within the last ten pages that she finds a note indicating that Don Quixote, just days before her father's death, was expected in Geneva.

What was his Montreal scout doing there? she wonders.

Then, on the next to last page, written in the margins in the same regal hand, Elena finds: "DQ, Hades Club, Mon."

"Mon" for Monday?

Or "Mon" for Montreal?

It is the only mention of any specific location in all twelve-hundred-plus pages.

Going online, she enters "Hades Club Montreal" into a search engine and gets no results. After a moment, she enters "Hades Club Geneva," just to be thorough, and also gets no hits.

Opening the drawers of the desk on the other side of the room, she finds a phone book and looks for a listing for "Hades Club" but again comes up with nothing.

She knows precious little about the city in which she has lived for the past month. Hiding does that. To her, the Hades Club sounds like the name of a men's club. There is such a club in the Latin Quarter, just two blocks from the apartment. Though she can't remember what it's called, she is certain it isn't that name.

There is only one person to whom she can turn now.

What had the newspaper reported this morning? Stable condition? And in yesterday's paper? Montreal General Hospital.

She gets the address of the hospital from the phone book, then unplugs the tracking device and packs it into her backpack. Grabbing the Moleskine notebook, she tosses that in as well. She hesitates, though, over whether or not to carry the CZ-75, then finally decides not to. If she were to be somehow caught with it, all her efforts up to now—all that she has lost in pursuit of her cause—will have been in vain.

To accomplish what she must, she needs to be free.

Gathering together the thick stack of pages and placing them on top of her only functioning notebook computer, she puts them into one of the plastic shopping bags, which she brings with her as she exits her room, backpack over her shoulder.

At the front desk she asks the clerk—the same young woman she saw Thursday morning—if it would be possible to have something of value secured in the hotel's safe. The woman says that she would be happy to take care of that. Elena hands her the bag, along with ten dollars, Canadian, then crosses the lobby and steps out into the night, unarmed and alone.

Across rue de la Commune a cab is dropping off a couple. It is red, not yellow, as most of the other cabs she has seen have been.

Crossing the wide street and getting into the vacant backseat, Elena gives the driver the hospital's address. He heads west.

Opening the backpack, she removes the tracking device and switches it to standby. It immediately starts beeping—more rapidly than before, and louder, too.

Six, then seven of its ten lights illuminate.

So these are *indications of distance,* she thinks. And the closer to the signal she is, the faster and louder the beeping gets.

The driver looks in the rearview mirror, his eyes fixed on Elena. "Everything okay?" he asks.

Elena nods. "Yes."

Finding a small dial marked "Volume," she rolls it with her thumb till the beeping is silenced. She keeps her eyes on the LED lights, though.

For about a half minute the number of glowing lights peaks at eight, then drops down to seven, then six, then five.

It is as the cab leaves Old Montreal and enters the downtown area that the lights drop to four, three, two, one, then finally go and remain dark.

Miles is shown his room, which is just large enough for a single bed and bureau with a little space left for one person to move around in.

The ceiling slopes sharply to the floor, and the only window looks out over the buildings that make up the rest of this block, each roof just slightly lower than the one before it, like a set of stairs. Beyond these rooftops is a well-lit, tree-lined promenade, a long pier upon which stands a large modern-looking building, and the Saint Lawrence River.

Miles finds this scene appealing. His eyes are accustomed to a New York view—even "SoNo" looks like New York, or tries to—so to have something else to behold, something dramatically different to take in, is to his eyes and mind what a burst of fresh air would be to his nose and lungs.

So bright, this city is, made even more so by an overcast sky that keeps the white lights from dissipating. And so old, these buildings, weatherworn and yet clean and well maintained.

He finds the size of this room appealing as well. More than appealing, he finds it *soothing*. The best hiding places are small, and even after millennia of evolution and civilization, a person, when danger is sensed, can still give in to the ancient instinct to climb high. Miles can't imagine a safer place than this tiny room so high above everything like a gargoyle's perch.

He has found his home for the next few days, and if he were to be honest, he would admit that he wouldn't mind spending every moment here, standing at this window or stretched out on that single bed, untouched by all those responsibilities and failures he has, for now at least, left far behind.

Who even knew he was here? Who could hope to find him?

Hell, he wasn't even himself; he was some guy named Jack Johnson.

And what, if anything, did Jack Johnson owe anyone?

Angelina, still in her army field jacket, the Belstaff bag hanging off her shoulder, is standing in the doorway.

"I hope this will do," she says.

Miles looks over his shoulder at her. "This is perfect."

Now that he has his safe place, he thinks of the five grand in his pocket. It deserves a safe place as well.

"Is there somewhere I can stash my money?" he asks.

"The money Cohn gave you?"

"Yeah."

"You'd better hang onto that, just in case."

"Really?"

"We may have to leave here and not come back at some point, and without any warning. Besides, this is Montreal, not New York City. The worst we have here is an abundance of panhandlers. And anyway, you're safe as long as you're with me."

She smiles confidently, even boldly. Dressed as she is in a combat jacket, and considering the athlete's spring in her step, he sees no reason to really doubt her.

She shows him the rest of the apartment: her dark bedroom in the rear, the single bathroom that stands between her room and his, and the large kitchen. Returning to the living room, she tosses her bag onto a chair, unwinds the scarf from around her neck, and then unzips and removes her field jacket.

Crossing her back, in contrast to her bone-white sweater made of thick wool, is the black leather strap of a shoulder holster.

As Angelina faces him again, Miles sees that a pistol is tucked snugly below her left armpit. Hanging from the holster is a small rectangular compartment, from which hangs an identical compartment, both containing, Miles assumes, extra ammo clips.

"Jesus," he says. "You had that when we crossed the border?"

"Of course."

"What if they had stopped us?"

She smiles assuredly. "They never do."

"And what if the cops stop us while we're here?"

Again, an assuring smile—or rather, one that is meant to be assuring. "They won't," she says.

Despite Angelina's confident manner, Miles now feels a little uneasy. The idea of remaining in that tiny room for the next few days suddenly seems more than simply appealing. It just might be, in fact, the thing for him to do.

Shrugging one shoulder and then the next, Angelina slips free of the holster and tosses it on top of her bag. Last night she was wearing a long overcoat, and she kept her army jacket on, for reasons that are now obvious, during the entire trip north, so this is Miles's first look at her frame, which, no surprise, is that of an athlete as well: round shoulders pulled back like a cadet's, flat stomach, small breasts.

Sleek but sturdy.

She pulls up the left sleeve of her sweater, folding the cuff over twice so it will stay up, and then does the same with her right. Her forearms, lined with strands of flexing muscles, are vascular, as are her hands.

Miles is reminded of the artist—a sculptor—he was dating when his life came crashing down around him.

"Are you hungry?" Angelina asks.

"Yeah."

"I have to check in with Trask, and then I'll make us something to eat. Okay?"

Miles nods, then glances down at her blue jeans. Two thick seams surround each pant leg, one above the knees and the other below. When he worked as an electrician, he used to wear Carhartt carpenter jeans, which had an extra layer of denim running down the front of both legs, from the thigh to the shins, like chaps. He has never before, though, seen pants like the ones she is wearing.

"What's up with your jeans?"

Angelina looks down. "The knees?"

"Yeah."

"They're motorcycle jeans. There's a layer of Kevlar woven around the knees and across the butt, for extra protection."

"You ride?"

"No. It's all just part of the gear."

"Gear?"

"You'll see—or maybe you won't, if we're lucky." She takes out her cell phone and flips it open. Turning away, she presses a single button.

Waiting for Trask to answer, Angelina wanders into the kitchen. Miles returns to the same living room window he stood at moments ago.

Below, another couple is strolling along Saint-Sulpice. He watches them as they pause in front of Eternal Noel to look in the window.

Following the narrow street downward with his eyes, Miles sees in the opening between the buildings that line both sides of Saint-Sulpice no signs of traffic on the wide boulevard below, which strikes him as slightly strange since a street like this in New York, particularly at this hour, would be full of speeding cars.

He watches it for a moment, sees nothing, and begins to wonder if the street might be closed to vehicles.

Finally, though, he spots a single red-colored taxicab roll past, then quickly disappear from his sight. It is another moment before another vehicle, heading in the opposite direction, passes by.

After that Angelina returns from the kitchen.

Her demeanor has changed—Miles senses that right away. She grabs her shoulder holster and puts it back on, expertly, then winds the scarf around her neck and reaches for her jacket.

"We have to move," she says.

"What's going on?"

"Your sister has a partner who's in a hospital not far from here. Trask wants us to ask him a few questions. We have to hurry, though; visiting hours end soon."

She puts on her jacket, then picks up the messenger bag and pulls the strap over her head so it crosses her torso diagonally with the bag hanging securely against the opposite hip.

Miles thinks first of correcting Angelina—Elena is his half sister, not sister—but doesn't.

The urgency with which she is moving now tells him that this isn't the time for that.

It tells him, too, that when Trask speaks, Angelina, like a good soldier, flies into determined action.

Eleven

From the far edge of a crowded parking lot, Elena watches the main entrance of Montreal General Hospital.

A mix of staff and visitors enter and exit in more or less a steady stream. Scanning the lot, she can see dozens of vehicles—far too many for her to study each one for a suspicious occupant seated either behind the wheel or, as a professional would do, in the passenger seat. For that matter, anyone hoping that she might arrive at the hospital—anyone posted here to watch for her, just in case—could easily be waiting inside.

But she needs what she needs, so taking a breath and keeping her head down, with eyes on the lookout for sudden motion, she follows the perimeter of the lot to the main entrance. It takes all she has to maintain a casual pace—as she had leaving Vieux-Port three nights ago, she half expects to be shot down at any moment. Finally, though, she reaches the door and enters.

Immediately inside is a security checkpoint manned by two uniformed guards—a man and woman, both black and in their midtwenties, both wearing blue-colored latex gloves.

The woman is holding a bottle of hand sanitizer, which she distributes to each visitor who passes through the checkpoint.

A sign posted nearby is in French, a language Elena only barely knows. She recognizes, though, "Grippe H1N1." Swine flu. And she sees the word *prevenir*, knows this means "to prevent."

The female guard looks Elena in the eyes as she pumps the clear gel into Elena's palm. The male guard, his hands on his hips, doesn't even look at Elena once.

The female guard says something to Elena in French.

"*Poly vous Englese?*" Elena asks. Her accent, she knows, is terrible; what little she knows was taught to her by a Czech.

"Visiting hours end in fifteen minutes," the guard tells her. "For dinner service. It resumes again at seven."

Elena nods and, rubbing her hands together till the gel evaporates, moves into the lobby.

To the left is a bank of elevators and a doorway to a stairwell. To the right is an information desk. Elena stops at the desk, and the attendant gives her Jean-Claude's room number.

Waiting at the elevators, Elena glances around, at those next to her, also waiting for the next elevator, and those in the lobby. The only two people anywhere near the main entrance—and not in motion—are the guards; everyone else is either passing through or coming in.

No one anywhere—near the door or gathered beside her—seems to be paying her any undue attention.

The elevator arrives. Inside, with five strangers crowded around her, one of whom has already pressed the button for the fifth floor—Jean-Claude's floor—Elena tells herself to breathe. Strangely, she feels safer in the confined space than she did in the open lobby. What are the chances, after all, of all five of these strangers being in collusion? And if one or two of them had been sent here to wait for her, and had somehow managed to join her as she waited for the elevator without raising her suspicions, it is unlikely that any action will be taken while so many witnesses are present.

Another reason for her momentary sense of security is that Krav Maga, the system of unarmed fighting taught to members of the Israeli military, addresses close-quarter combat quite effectively. Palm strikes, groin attacks, head-butts, elbow and knee strikes, fingers or thumbs into the eyes—whatever it takes to disable quickly. And the closer the attacker is the better. Since a male, when attacking a female, instinctively grabs instead of strikes, what a woman will likely need to know to defend herself is contained within the Krav Maga system.

Her training during her three years in the military, though efficient, had only scratched the surface. Her years with Pavol—the hours they'd devoted to her study of hand-to-hand fighting—was what had burned her skills deep into her muscle memory.

The elevator stops at every floor, and one by one its riders exit. By the time it reaches the fourth floor, Elena and one other person— a man roughly her father's age, standing ahead of her—are the only passengers remaining.

In silence they ride to the fifth floor. As the doors open again, the man steps out and immediately turns left. Elena listens to his footsteps on the linoleum, and once she is convinced he is moving off, and therefore no threat to her, she, too, exits.

A sign on the wall straight ahead tells her that Jean-Claude's room is somewhere to the right. Walking down the hallway, she passes an orderly pushing a tall, wheeled rack filled with food trays. He looks at her and nods once. When she reaches Jean-Claude's room at the very end of the hall, she pauses for a moment, listening for any sound coming from behind it.

Hearing nothing, she glances down the long hallway. Seeing no one there but the orderly, his back to her as he removes a dinner tray from the top of the rolling rack, she pushes the door open and slips inside.

⁀

Miles watches the strange city from the passenger seat of the Audi.

Montreal seems to be a hill city—moving through it is to climb upward from the river's edge to one plateau and then, from there, to another. Sometimes the climb is subtle, but often enough it is steep—steeper, anyway, than any incline in Manhattan.

He sees outside the window a series of chain clothing shops: Urban Outfitters, the Gap, H&M, J.Crew. An upscale shopping district, the buildings new and clean, the sidewalks crowded with people in long coats.

Looking for a street sign, he spots one. Rue Peel, the steepest street so far. A department store called Harry Rosen's catches his eye—outside Angelina's window, not his own. Its two front windows display male mannequins handsomely dressed for the season.

Miles takes another look out his window at the pedestrians and says, "I'll probably need to pick up a jacket or something."

Angelina nods. "We should have time after."

Within a moment the Audi is clear of the shopping district and moving through a more residential area, Miles is reminded of Harlem—older looking buildings, some in disrepair, small neighborhood markets and shops.

At one point Angelina steers the Audi to the curb and parks outside a corner market.

"We'll need flowers or something," she explains.

"Why?"

"So we look like we're visiting someone."

Inside the market, she selects from a plastic bucket in front of the register a bouquet of yellow Asiatic lilies and blue delphinium wrapped in a cone of white paper.

Miles spots the last copy of a newspaper on an otherwise empty rack not far from the door.

The *Globe and Mail.*

The headline reads, "Shooting in Vieux-Port."

He grabs it and joins Angelina at the register.

Seeing what's in his hand, she says with a smile, "What do you want that for?"

He shows her the headline. Her smile fades slightly.

"What's wrong?" he asks.

She shakes her head, the smile quickly returning. "Nothing." She turns to the cashier and says, "The paper, too, please."

Back in the Audi, they continue uphill. Miles has time to read only the first few lines of the article before Angelina announces, "We're here."

Through the windshield, the large hospital looms.

———

There are two beds in the room, but only one, the bed farthest from the door, is occupied.

Moving closer to it, Elena first pauses to make certain no one is in the bathroom.

As she steps closer still to the bed, the man in it appears to her as one ensnared in a web of tubing and wires. An oxygen feed is draped beneath his nose like a thin snake, and white surgical tape in the vague shape of an X across his mouth holds in place an endotracheal tube that is attached to a respirator. Two intravenous lines feed into his forearm, and another, a catheter line, rises from beneath his blankets. A monitor on a stand beside his bed shows on its digital display his basic vital signs—heart and respiration rates, blood pressure, and temperature.

Reaching the foot of the bed, Elena pauses for another moment, keeping silent and still. It is difficult for her to see Jean-Claude like this—to see what her actions have wrought. It is impossible to see her scout and not think of the last time they were together—in the dark office of that derelict building, Pavol standing beside him.

It is difficult, too, not to see in her mind those two men being shot.

Or the panhandler standing over Pavol and firing.

All caught on videotape—a tape she has not yet been able to view.

She closes her eyes and takes a long, cleansing breath. When she opens her eyes again, she sees that Jean-Claude's are not only open now but looking straight at her.

Moving around to the side of the bed, putting it between herself and the door, she leans down. His eyes, which have followed her, are glassy and dull.

"Are you in pain?" she whispers. It is the first thing she can think to ask.

He rocks his head slightly from side to side.

One of the intravenous tubes feeds him glucose, while the other no doubt provides him with a steady supply of morphine.

Her voice still a whisper, she says, "I wired the money to your account. I sent more than we agreed upon, to cover your medical expenses. Your wife knows how to access it, correct?"

A single nod.

Elena smiles as best she can. "Good." She pauses, then: "I need something else, though. I need your help with something. Will you help me?"

Jean-Claude's eyes close for a moment, then reopen. He nods again.

"Can you write?" she asks.

His right arm, above the blankets for the sake of the intravenous lines, rises to his chest, then rests there. Half open and looking like a claw, it awaits something with which to write.

Elena quickly takes off the backpack. Opening it, she reaches in and grabs the Moleskine notebook. Clipped to its hard cover is a pen, which she pulls free and places as carefully as she can into Jean-Claude's hand.

Flipping to the last page of the notebook, she holds it close to his right hand and says, "Is there a place in Montreal called the Hades Club?"

Jean-Claude's eyes narrow, as if to ask, "*Why?*"

"Please. Is there a place here called the Hades Club?"

He nods, and Elena's heart races.

"Do you know where it is?"

He presses the tip of the pen against the paper and writes with a trembling hand, "North of Parc du Mont-Royal."

His handwriting is a messy scrawl, but she can read his words well enough.

"There's no listing for it in the phone book," she says.

Jean-Claude writes, "Underground club."

"What does that mean?"

He writes again, "Members only."

His scrawl is getting even messier, and the pressure he applies to the notebook is lighter than it was just a moment before. He is getting weak, fading fast.

"A men's club?" she asks. "Is that what you mean?"

Jean-Claude nods.

"Do you know the exact address?"

Again, Jean-Claude writes. It is taking much longer for him to form each letter. He has made barely three or four strokes when the door suddenly opens.

Elena rises, the notebook in her hand.

A nurse, middle-aged and heavyset, wearing a uniform that is neat and tidy, enters the room.

Seeing Elena—seeing that she is startled—the nurse, immediately suspicious and protective of her patient, heads straight toward the bed. As she moves, she demands something, but does so in French.

Elena recognizes enough of the words to get the gist. "*What are you doing?*"

The nurse's eyes go to the notebook in Elena's hand. She speaks again, but it is another string of French, rapidly spoken. Elena recognizes among them the words for "disturb" and "rest."

Glancing down at the notebook in her hand, Elena sees that Jean-Claude has only managed to write a three-digit number.

Ignoring the nurse, Elena leans down again and holds the notebook in front of his hand.

"Finish," she says softly. "Please."

The nurse has reached the bed. Only it is between her and Elena now. Obviously the nurse heard what Elena had said because she has quickly abandoned French for English.

"Visiting hours are over," she commands. "I need you to leave."

Jean-Claude begins writing again.

"Ma'am," the nurse says. "Ma'am."

Elena can tell Jean-Claude is writing as quickly as he can. His knuckles are white from holding the pen.

"*Ma'am!*" the nurse snaps.

Jean-Claude continues to write.

"*Ma'am!*"

Jean-Claude drops his hand to his chest.

Elena looks at what he has written to make sure she can in fact read it, then eases the pen from his twisted hand and whispers, "Thank you."

"Who do you think are you?" the nurse demands.

Without looking at the woman, Elena grabs her backpack and opens it, ready to toss the notebook inside.

It is then that she sees something she doesn't at first understand.

Inside the pack is a flickering light.

The tracking device.

Dropping the notebook inside, she grabs the device.

Nine of its ten LED lights are glowing.

She knows by the wideness of Jean-Claude's eyes that he sees it, too.

Sees it and understands.

They look at each other, and he immediately nods once more, this time as if to say, "*Go.*"

Miles follows Angelina through the hospital's main entrance.

A female security guard in blue gloves says something to them in French.

"What did she say?" he asks.

"Visiting hours are over in a few minutes."

"Sorry," the guard says in English. "You'll have to come back at seven."

Angelina tells her that they have just gotten out of work and won't be able to make it later on. "We just want to drop off these flowers. I swear, we'll put them in his room and leave."

The guard nods. "Yeah, okay. Hurry, though, please." She holds out a dispenser of clear gel.

Miles is uncertain what to make of this.

"Protection against the swine flu," Angelina explains. She is wearing black leather gloves, which she begins to pull off. As she does, Miles extends his bare hands.

Holding the nozzle above his palm, the guard presses the pump once, then again.

Miles rubs his hands together as Angelina receives her dose of the cold gel.

As they head toward the bank of elevators, Miles asks, "How do you know what room he's in?"

"Trask told me."

As they approach the bank, an elevator arrives. After its half dozen or so passengers exit, Miles and Angelina step inside.

Closing and shouldering the pack, Elena moves quickly toward the door.

The nurse follows her, saying in an angry and accusing tone, "Who are you?"

Ignoring the woman, Elena opens the door. Instead of entering the hallway, however, she peeks her head out and looks to her right.

Down the hallway a group of departing visitors are waiting by the bank of elevators.

"The nearest stairs?" Elena asks the nurse.

"You can't bother our critical patients like this."

"The stairs!"

"I'm calling security."

"Good, do that," Elena snaps. "Tell them to hurry."

She hopes that between this protective nurse and hospital security, Jean-Claude will be safe.

The nurse retreats into the room, heading for the phone on the table between the two beds. Elena spots an illuminated sign hanging from the ceiling midway down the hall.

"*Sortie.*"

She bolts for it, moving as quickly as she can without reaching an all-out run. As she arrives at the door, she can hear the elevator doors opening.

She runs down the first flight of stairs, then pauses on the landing to check the device again.

She can't help herself.

Ten out of ten lights now.

Right above her.

She considers returning up the stairs and opening the door just enough to allow her a glimpse of the person who possesses the tracer bills as he heads for Jean-Claude's room.

It is doubtful he would come to the hospital wearing his panhandler disguise.

Would she ever get this chance again?

But other questions crowd her mind like a panicked mob.

Does he know I am here somehow? Has he somehow followed me? Could his arrival at this moment really be a mere coincidence?

There is, she knows, no risking a look.

More than that, there is no risking what the sight of him might unleash within her.

First things first.

She clears her mind, focusing on what must be done next.

She will need to make it downstairs and through the lobby before the nurse can notify the two guards at the door.

If I am lucky, the nurse will call a supervisor first, who will then either call the two guards or, if I am really lucky, rush to notify them in person.

Even the best-case scenario leaves her little time.

She breaks into an all-out run down the stairs. By the time she passes from the third floor to the second, her quads are already burning.

Too much inactivity in the past month, too much waiting and hiding.

Finally reaching the ground floor, she pauses to compose herself. All she has is seconds, if that.

Opening the door, she enters the lobby. Since this is the end of visiting hours, the area is even more crowded than when she had arrived.

As she heads for the main entrance, she fixes her eyes on the two guards ahead. Since no one is arriving, the female is no longer dispensing hand sanitizer. She has placed the bottle on a nearby table and is removing her blue latex gloves.

The male guard, still with his hands on his hips, is facing his partner, talking and smiling.

These are not the mannerisms of professionals who have been informed of a crazy woman attempting to flee the building.

Elena, within a cluster of slow-moving people, passes the guards without either of them noticing her.

As she moves through the entrance, she hears behind her the sound of a radio squawking, then words in French. Urgent words. But she doesn't look back, just keeps moving.

Peeling away from the cluster, she tears off across the parking lot, half listening once again for the crack of a gunshot.

Within less than a minute, though, she has cleared the lot and is making her way down rue Cedar.

Still running, legs burning—so still alive.

She had paid the driver of the red-colored cab to wait for her at the end of this street, and the sight of his vehicle waiting for her there is nothing short of thrilling.

Climbing into the backseat is sudden relief from a wild and almost blinding fear.

The door to the room they are looking for is open.

Of all the doors lining this hallway, it is the only one that is.

Angelina steps through it, followed by Miles, who sees in the only occupied bed a man who is clearly very badly messed up.

A startling sight, to say the least.

Together they approach the foot of the man's bed.

"What happened to him?" Miles whispers.

Angelina tells him that he was shot.

Miles blurts out the first question that comes to his mind. "By who?"

He has never before seen a person who has been shot.

Before Angelina can respond, though, a male security guard rushes into the room, followed closely by an agitated nurse.

Miles notices that Angelina instantly puts herself between him and these two people.

The guard is not the one from downstairs. This man is Caucasian and large through the chest and shoulders. Easily the tallest person—or thing—in the room, he moves fast for his size. He and the nurse are already halfway across the room when the nurse suddenly stops.

A look of doubt drains the anger from her face. "Wait," she says. "That's not her."

The guard slows to a stop. Miles notices that his hand is hovering above the grip of the pistol in his leather holster.

"She's not the one," the nurse says. "It was another woman."

Angelina shows immediate interest.

"What other woman?" she asks quickly.

There is in her voice a tone of authority, and for some reason, the nurse responds to it.

"Another woman was just here," she reports. "She was making him write something in a notebook. When I called security, she took off."

"Took off where?"

"Down the stairs."

Angelina says to Miles, "C'mon," then starts toward the door. She tosses the bouquet of flowers onto the empty bed as she passes it.

Miles, however, doesn't move. He looks first at the uniformed guard and nurse, then at the badly wounded man on the bed. For some reason he thinks of the only dead body he has ever seen—that of his mother.

He snaps from that memory when he notices that the man's eyes are open and looking at him.

To Miles's surprise, the man's right hand moves.

It rises a few inches and then hovers.

Making first a fist, the man extends his middle finger.

Looking at the man's face, crisscrossed with white tape and tubes, Miles sees a grim and yet defiant smile.

In the doorway, Angelina says again, "C'mon."

The nurse is checking the intravenous feeds connected to the man's arm, and the security guard is barking French into a handheld radio.

Confusion and chaos, everyone, including Angelina, scrambling to do his or her job.

Miles, however, is just an observer here—or so he tells himself. What had Trask said? *A consultant.*

No need for him, then, even standing this close to a man who has been shot, to care enough to give in to the sense of urgency around him.

He remembers what Cohn had said.

When Angelina says move, you move.

It seems taking this advice is the thing to do right now, so Miles turns and follows Angelina into the hallway. Halfway down it she leads him through a door marked "*Sortie.*"

He can barely keep up with her as they rush down four flights of stairs. He has the same difficulty as they cross the lobby and exit the hospital.

Walking fast once in public, he notes, but never running.

Stopping just outside the main door, she scans the large parking lot with determined eyes.

Miles gives her a moment, then says, "You think it was her?" He pauses before saying her name. "Elena, I mean." He realizes he has never said it aloud before.

Angelina nods decisively. "Yeah. It was her. At least we know she's still in Montreal. But why'd she come here? What did her friend up there know?"

It seems to Miles that she is thinking out loud, so he waits another moment, during which he feels the night cold seeping through his cotton sweatshirt.

What had felt strangely comfortable just an hour ago, when he'd first emerged from the Audi outside Angelina's building, is suddenly anything but.

He slips his hands into his pockets and raises his shoulders against the chill. He is, he knows, on the verge of shivering.

"I'm definitely going to need a jacket," he says.

Angelina, still scanning, doesn't respond.

"Maybe we can stop at one of those stores we passed on the way here," he suggests.

"We need to get back to my place. Then we'll figure it out."

"It'll only take me a minute to run in and run out. I'm not picky about what I wear."

Angelina looks back at him. "You're here to help us find your sister, aren't you?"

This time Miles can't help but correct her. "Half sister."

Angelina turns and says, a bit dismissively, "We're paying you good money. And considering what's at stake, you might want to think about taking this more seriously."

She steps away, heading toward the Audi.

It takes another moment, but Miles follows her.

What other choice does he have?

Twelve

Back in her hotel room, Elena stands at her window and looks diagonally across rue de la Commune to the converted warehouse on quai de l'Horloge.

She can see clearly enough the white letters on the shed's orange awning, and the single word they spell out: "Labyrinthe."

When she has stared at that for long enough, she glances down at her hands, which are shaking less now than they were when she had returned a half hour ago. Shaking less, yes, but still shaking.

Her entire life she has had men beside her. Growing up, her father was a steady presence. Though he traveled often, he would frequently take her along. By the time she was ten, she had seen every major European city. Recalling any one of them is to recall her father—the feeling of his strong hand holding hers, the safety his size and smarts and money promised.

Her three years in the army were spent surrounded by men—fellow soldiers and officers. And just days after her service was up, she met Pavol. Within a matter of another few days, they were in love and from then on together day and night.

She has always preferred the company of men. More than that, she thrived in a world that traditionally belonged to them. Her mother, who died when Elena was young, tried to discourage that, but Elena would have none of it.

She cannot remember more than a few days in her life—those times when her father couldn't take her with him, and that short span between the end of her military service and finding Pavol—when a strong male wasn't present, or when the absence of one would last only a matter of hours.

A teacher, a protector, a guide, an anchor—various men at various times filled these roles.

Now, though, this room echoes with the absence of the one thing she has always known.

No man beside her now.

And none to arrive within a few hours.

A man had raised her. Men had taught and trained her.

Men had loved her—well, one man, for certain.

Men, too, had killed her father.

And one man in particular, disguised as a panhandler . . .

She knows what she needs to do. And she tells herself that she has what it takes to do it.

The tracking device is on the bed, beside her backpack. Upon her return she rolled the volume control to its highest level so she would not miss it when the beeping ultimately resumed.

And now it does, a single beep followed by a few seconds of silence. Then another beep followed by another few seconds of silence.

And finally, a series of steady tones, at first hushed and intermittent.

It doesn't take long, however, for the beeps to get louder and the gaps between them to shorten.

By the time she actually looks at the unit, five of its ten lights are lit.

The tracer bills are once again a half mile away. She waits a few moments, but the lights hold at five.

So, a half mile away and at rest, just like before. If whoever possesses those bills knows where she is, wouldn't that person—or persons—want to get closer than a half mile? Wouldn't they want to monitor her actions? Identify which building she currently occupies?

Hard to know for certain, but those things are what she would do. She begins to sense that she isn't the hunted but rather the hunter. If so, the hunter invariably has the advantage, no?

But this doesn't make sense to her.

Why did they go to the hospital? Why did they arrive while she was there?

What are they up to?

What will they—what should she—do next?

She quickly tires of the steady beeping and turns the volume down again. Next to that control is a headphone jack. She grabs the backpack, which has three outside pockets that Pavol always kept full of necessary items: first aid and sewing kits, matches, a small flashlight, water purification tablets, extra cell phone chargers, snack foods, and so on.

The main compartment was always kept empty so it could be filled at the last minute with whatever was needed should a "bug-out" suddenly become necessary. But these three outer pockets, once packed tight, were left alone.

She searches through the first pocket and finds what she is looking for.

A clear plastic Baggie containing a single earbud with microphone attached—for hands-free talking on a cell phone. Also in the Baggie are several universal jack adaptors. Finding the right one—for a 35 mm jack—she inserts it into the device, connects the earbud to it, places the earbud into her ear, and then rolls the volume up till she can hear the beeping again.

Now she can monitor it while in public without drawing attention to herself, as she had done in the cab to the hospital.

She came close to being caught off guard once already, when the device was in her backpack with the volume down and her enemies were just floors away.

Once is one time too many.

Opening the Moleskine notebook, she reads the address Jean-Claude had struggled to write. Once she has memorized it, she pulls the page from the binding. She had him write on the last page in the book so there would be no pages beneath to leave an impression on. After wiping the back cover clean, she tears up the page and flushes it down the toilet, waiting to make sure every scrap of it is swallowed down.

Going to the hospital unarmed was a necessity, but she doesn't dare go where she is heading now without protection.

She checks, then pockets, the CZ-75, and does the same with the two loaded ammo clips.

Among the gear she brought with her from their apartment is a lock-pick kit, which she puts into the main compartment of the knapsack. The tracking device goes into the outer left pocket of her coat. With the single earbud snug in her ear, she leaves the room.

On the front desk in the lobby is a small rack with several copies of a tourist's map of Montreal. Taking one, she finds on it Parc du Mont-Royal, a large park at the very top of the map. The small compass icon in the upper right corner tells her that the top of the map is west, not north. Jean-Claude had said the club was north of the park. Searching the right area, she quickly finds the street.

She sees no cabs anywhere on Commune and decides to walk up to rue Notre-Dame, where three night ago cabs waited in a rank outside the Palais de Justice.

Climbing boulevard Saint-Laurent, she listens to the beeping. The volume and tempo remain unchanged for the entire three-minute journey.

So movement from east to west doesn't change her relative distance from the tracer bills, at least not by a half mile.

The bills, then, are located somewhere to the north or south of her.

She makes a note to determine as soon as she can which direction will increase the beeping.

First things first, one step at a time.

Once she is in the backseat of a cab and heading away from Old Port, the beeping begins to steadily fade.

By the time the cab passes into Chinatown, the beeping ceases entirely.

———⌣———

In his room in Angelina's apartment, Miles glances again at the headline of the edition of the *Globe and Mail* he bought at the corner market.

Though he is half interested at best, he decides to skim the rest of the article. What he reads, however, tells him nothing that Trask hadn't already explained or at least alluded to.

The only detail that catches Miles's eye is the fact that one of the two men who were killed had worked for the Department of Defense. But Trask said his father had done work for governments as well as individual clients, and the fact that that included the United States government isn't really surprising at all.

What was it Trask had called his father? A provider?

Yeah, well, Miles thinks, *the man didn't provide me or my mother with shit.*

Tossing the newspaper aside, he looks at his Rolex and sees that it is seven p.m. He decides that there has got to be something better to do in this city on a Saturday night than chase after someone who doesn't want to be found.

He can still smell the peppermint he had applied to his head and the back of his neck a few hours before. Every woman has her distinct scent, and this is Angelina's—or part of hers, at least. Miles decides to seek her out, see if maybe they can go out and do something, either see the sights or get some drinks.

Better that than sit around and wait.

An object in motion tends to stay in motion.

Leaving his room, he makes his way down the short hallway and into the large living room, where Angelina, still wearing her field jacket, is composing a text on her cell phone.

Miles waits for her to finish, then asks what the plan is.

"I'm finding that out now."

Though he barely knows her, he can gather from her tone that she is concerned about something. His first guess, based on how quickly she had jumped into action when she got the call from Trask earlier, is that what she is worried about is her boss's reaction to what happened at the hospital.

"It wasn't your fault," he offers.

"What wasn't?"

"The hospital. I mean, how could you have known she'd be there? If in fact it even was her."

"It was."

"You see my point, though, right? It's not like you were sent there to get her and she got away."

"It won't matter to Trask."

"That doesn't sound very fair."

"It's not about being fair. He pays us well and expects results."

"Us? You and Cohn."

She nods.

"How long have you worked for Trask?"

"Awhile."

"And what is it you do for him exactly?"

This time she shakes her head. Miles knows she is not only telling him that she won't answer that question but that he should stop asking her questions altogether—at least questions along those lines.

He decides then to change the subject to what it was he came out here to ask in the first place.

"So, are there any good jazz clubs in town? I mean, there has to be, right? This is a French city."

"I don't think we'll have time for that."

"We wouldn't have to stay for long. One drink, a couple of songs."

She shakes her head again. Her cell rings, and she quickly looks at the display.

"Trask?"

She nods, reading the text. Within seconds she is composing a response, her thumbs moving swiftly.

When her reply is on its way, Miles says, "Do you have anything to drink here?"

"In my apartment?"

"Yeah."

"No." A quick shrug, then: "Reformed drunk."

"I noticed while we were out that there aren't any liquor stores around. At least I didn't see any. Don't people in this city drink at home? Alone and in the dark, the way you're supposed to?"

His joke fails to inspire even a smile. She tells him that food markets sell beer and wine, but only certain licensed stores called SAQs can sell liquor. "Why? Do you need something?"

Miles shrugs. "Sometimes a shot or two before bed can be the difference between two hours of bad sleep and three or four hours of bad sleep. If you don't drink, what helps you sleep?"

"Nothing."

"There has to be something."

Before Angelina can respond, her cell phone rings again.

"That's Trask calling," she says. "Please excuse me."

She walks down the hallway to the back bedroom, answering the phone as she goes. Her tone is hushed, and upon entering her room, she closes the heavy door.

Though Miles can barely hear her voice, he can tell she is speaking French.

He steps to the living room window and looks down. The view is the same as the view from his bedroom—a better one, certainly, than the view from his apartment in South Norwalk, and one he could get used to.

A foreign city, filled with strangers who know nothing about him or his failures.

There is a part of him, he must admit, that wishes he were exiled here.

He studies the courtyard directly across Saint-Sulpice. Its entrance is a tall wrought iron fence and gate, which is open, and its surface is cobblestone. There are several long rows of what look like cement flower beds with benches attached lining the wide passage. At the far end it is a similar fence and gate and then a narrow street across which stands a brick building, itself looking as solid as a fortress.

A strolling couple enters the empty courtyard from the far end. They cross through it and reach Saint-Sulpice, and by the time they are halfway down that narrow street, Angelina has returned to the living room.

She is moving with her now-familiar sense of urgency.

"What's up?" Miles asks.

"We have an hour till Trask gets here. We should use it wisely."

"Okay."

"I'm going to the *marché* to pick up some food, and you need to get yourself a warm jacket. There's a men's clothing shop a few blocks from here. It's Cohn's tailor, actually. I'll write down directions, and we'll meet back here in a half hour."

Angelina takes a pad of paper and pen from the end table beside the couch. As fast as she can, she writes out directions.

Miles realizes that if Cohn has a tailor here, he must also live here. If that is the case, then why did he stay behind in NYC? And if he didn't stay behind, then why didn't he ride up with them in Angelina's Audi? There was, after all, plenty of room.

But Miles ignores those questions in favor of a more pressing one.

"You aren't by any chance going past the . . . what are liquor stores called again?"

"SAQ. I am, yes. What would you like?"

"Some kind of Irish crème. Bailey's, if you have that up here. I know, it's not the most manly thing I could have asked for, but something about the combination of cream and whiskey does the trick."

Angelina smiles. "Is being manly important to you?"

He tries for another joke. "Shouldn't it be?"

Tearing the paper from the pad, she hands it to Miles, doing so, he notices, without meeting his eyes.

For the next few moments, in fact, she does everything she can to avoid looking at him directly.

He wonders if he has somehow offended her.

Or are his jokes that bad?

Angelina says, "It can be pretty easy to get turned around down here, so stick to the map on your way there and on your way back. Seriously, I don't want to have to go looking for you."

Miles looks at the paper and notices that she has written a phone number at the bottom. "That's your cell?"

"Yes."

"If I get lost, I can just call, no?"

"Just stick to the map, please. If anything were to happen to you, Trask will have my ass. Do you hear me?"

Miles nods, then folds and pockets the paper.

"I called ahead and told the tailor you were coming. He was just closing up, but he's keeping the store open for you, so go straight there. I'll meet you back here right after. A half hour, tops."

He nods. "And you'll swing by the SAQ."

"Yes."

"Thanks."

She grabs her scarf and winds it around her neck, then zips up her field jacket. But instead of grabbing the rugged-looking messenger bag hanging on the back of a chair, she lifts its flap and, reaching inside, quickly removes something.

Miles only glimpses the item as she slips it into one of her jacket's large cargo pockets.

It looks to be a black metal rod about six inches long. Before Miles can ask what it is, Angelina, moving again with determination, is heading for the door.

Trask gives orders, and she moves.

Down on the street, Angelina says, "Be careful."

Then they part—Angelina heading up toward rue Notre-Dame, Miles, as instructed, passing through the wrought iron gates and into the empty garden courtyard he had seen from the window.

A street sign on the gate reads: "Rue le Royer."

Feeling the deepening cold as he moves, he hears only the sounds of his own footsteps echoing off the block-long buildings between which the courtyard cuts.

Then he hears another pair of footsteps coming from somewhere up ahead. He looks in time to see a man pass in and out of sight at the far end of the courtyard.

A man with long hair and a beard, dressed in a ratty old overcoat.

He remembers what Angelina had said about an abundance of panhandlers in Montreal, so he thinks nothing of what he has just glimpsed and continues following the route laid out for him.

Elena has the cabbie drop her off on a street that, according to her map, is a dozen or so blocks from her destination

Instead of asking him to wait, she pauses as he drives away, beginning her journey only when the vehicle is gone from sight.

The map has also provided her with an alternate escape route— the orange Metro line at Beaubien or Rosemont will take her straight down Saint-Denis to place d'Armes, just blocks from her hotel.

Should she not want to risk another cab ride—drivers keep records, and most seem to take several long looks at her in the mirror and would therefore be likely to recall her face enough to describe it—then this will be her way out.

Whenever possible, her father had often told her, never enter a place—building or neighborhood or city—without first determining more than one way out. One of the first things she and Pavol did when they arrived in Montreal was locate the train station and memorize the departure times and destinations of every train that left it.

This area of Montreal is nothing like the Latin Quarter or Vieux-Port. The neighborhood closest to the wooded park is a mix of residential and business. All of the stores and offices she passes are closed, only the restaurants, of which there are many, remain open.

She walks for a good half hour, through neighborhoods of varying affluence, then finally reaches rue Napoleon, a side street that starts at rue Saint-Hubert and runs northeast for four blocks. Just past the corner of rue Saint-André is her destination, a three-story building in what strikes her as an entirely residential neighborhood.

There is no sign identifying this place as a club, but there wouldn't be, would there? What did Jean-Claude write? "Underground."

Narrow driveways separate each building from its neighbor, and the driveway that runs past this building to its small back lot is empty.

The windows on every floor are curtained, but there is no hint of light coming from beyond any of them. Even the heaviest curtain, Elena thinks, would let some light show.

Too early for someone to be asleep. No one home, maybe?

She doesn't pause in front of the building but passes it, continuing to the end of the block and taking a right, then another at the end of that block so she can survey the building from the rear as she completes her surveillance circle.

Another right followed by another brings her back to the building of interest. As she made her circuit she noticed there was no street traffic at all, and she saw only one fellow pedestrian—an old woman walking a miniature poodle.

As she reaches the driveway again, Elena turns into it and walks alongside the house, pausing only when she has passed it and is standing on the edge of the small rear lot.

It is barely big enough for three vehicles. Not the kind of parking area one would expect for a club. But perhaps this club isn't the kind of club one drives to; perhaps one is driven here, either by town car or taxi. The residential tone of the neighborhood supports her theory; a driveway lined with vehicles—along with vehicles curbed nose-to-bumper along the length of the street—would simply call too much attention.

At the back of the building is a fire escape—a possible second way out, should she need it.

But what Elena requires now is a way in.

Thirteen

Miles reaches the men's clothing shop on rue Saint-Paul, just a few doors down from the corner of rue Saint-Gabriel.

The narrow, gently curving cobblestone street is a mix of galleries and restaurants. Miles can see at the far end a touristy souvenir shop, and across from it another high-end clothing store that appears to be already closed. Apartments comprise the four stories above the street-level businesses, and Miles can't help but wonder about the people who live in them.

How do they make their living? What drew them to make their homes in such a storybook place?

An older man with a full head of soft white hair greets Miles as he enters the men's shop. The man is dressed in a three-piece suit and shiny black shoes. Around his neck hangs a long, well-worn measuring tape. He smiles, displaying teeth that strike Miles as too white and perfectly aligned to be real.

The shop is small, with two long racks of suits and trousers along one wall and shelves of neatly folded shirts along the other. Some of the shirts are bright white, others varying shades of blue.

At the end of the room is a three-sided mirror and a tie rack from which hangs no more than a dozen ties. Beside the tie rack is a curtained doorway leading to a back room.

The man has large hands, and his handshake is fast and firm. Since Angelina called him with what Miles needs—and since it is already past closing time—he wastes no time and leads Miles past the racks of suit jackets and trousers to a small section in the back corner reserved for a dozen or so outer coats.

Most of them appear to be London Fog raincoats, tan-colored, though one is a dark blue. Not Miles's style. More than that, he has only one memory of his father, and in it the man is wearing such a raincoat.

A tall man standing in an apartment hallway.

Then, turning and heading out the door.

The other coats are black and more rugged looking—similar in style, in fact, to Angelina's army field jacket, the only difference being that the material is black.

He asks the man what those jackets are.

"Those are Barbour. They're made of waxed cotton—very durable and completely waterproof."

One of those dark jackets—that last one on the rack, in fact—has something the others don't: a gold emblem on its sleeve that catches Miles's eye because it is identical to the emblem on Angelina's bag.

"What's that one?" he asks.

———⌣———

Elena stands within the grid of shadows cast by the overhead fire escape and studies the back door.

The lock is a standard deadbolt—no problem there—but she needs to determine whether or not the door is connected to an alarm system.

Placing the backpack at her feet, she opens the flap and reaches in for her leather gloves. Once they are on, she grabs the small flashlight and the case containing the lock-pick gun and goes to work.

Within less than thirty seconds she has spun the deadbolt. Only then does she try the sturdy brass knob and finds that is locked as well. Another thirty seconds and that, too, is turning freely.

She returns the kit to the backpack, which she keeps balanced against her leg. Turning the knob, she eases the heavy steel door forward a fraction of an inch and with the flashlight examines the space where the door has cleared the upper frame, looking for indications of magnetic sensors, the most common type of alarm. Seeing none, she eases the door open just a little bit more and repeats her search.

Nothing.

She continues this process till the door is open wide enough for her to slip through. Turning sideways and holding the door firmly to keep it from opening any farther, she makes it inside, then, grabbing her bag and dragging it in behind her, closes the door quickly and throws both locks.

Turning the light toward the center of the dark, windowless room, she realizes quickly that she has entered a storage area: rows of metal shelves, crowded with everything from paint cans to toolboxes to cardboard boxes of various sizes, line both walls.

On the floor is a portable generator, next to which is a red jerry can. The pungent odor of gasoline fills the small room.

Several steps later she reaches yet another locked door. Checking this one for sensors and finding none, she picks the lock and, repeating her careful process, opens this door just enough to slip through, pulling her backpack with her and closing and relocking this door as well.

Doing so may slow her exit should she need to flee quickly, but leaving these doors unlocked would certainly announce her presence to anyone who might arrive while she is inside.

And should she need a quick escape, there is always the fire escape.

She sweeps this room with her flashlight. Along the far wall is a bar. Behind it are several shelves stocked with liquor bottles. Between her and that bar is a sitting room with a dozen antique sofas, each one plush and covered with velvet. Lots of dark reds and purples so deep they appear almost black. Instead of being arranged in a horseshoe or circle so they face each other, however, these sofas are scattered and placed so they are facing away from each other.

She only now remembers that it is Saturday night; if this is a club, shouldn't someone be here now setting up?

Maybe it's an after-hours club, a midnight-to-dawn kind of place. Maybe employees don't begin arriving till later. Ten or maybe even eleven.

At first she doesn't understand why the owner of this place wouldn't rig its doors with some kind of security system, but then it comes to her: any system worth having, if someone were to break in, would notify the police, or at least alert the neighbors. If this is an underground club as Jean-Claude indicated, then the last thing its owner would want is for the authorities to be summoned or the neighbors to be bothered.

Sweeping her flashlight around the room, Elena spots in a corner past the end of the bar two doorways, both curtained. Pausing first to listen for any sounds coming from the floor above, and hearing none, she moves down the long bar, checking as she goes all four upper corners of the room for motion detectors or cameras. She sees none. It's reasonable to assume that the patrons of such an establishment would wish to remain anonymous, and the presence of security cameras would obviously be a threat to their anonymity.

Reaching the two curtained doorways, she checks one and sees that it leads to a small back room furnished with only a few sofas. Through the other curtain is a set of steep stairs. After shining the light upward, she begins to climb, stepping as lightly as she can on the worn planks.

An old wooden door, open, awaits her. Reaching the top step, she pauses to listen once more, then proceeds into the doorway.

This room, as dark as the one below, is an open space with yet more sofas, these arranged in a horseshoe and facing a small riser on which stand two metallic poles. Stripper poles, no doubt about that. The wall beyond the riser is a smoked mirror, and hanging from a framework of metal tubing directly above are several theater lights painted flat black and fitted with colored gel lenses: blue, red, and green.

Past the stage is yet another curtained doorway. Walking to it, Elena parts the curtain—heavy velvet, like all the others—and sees a narrow hallway with a dozen doors, six to each side. At the far end of the hall is an empty wooden stool. The doors are numbered, and she doesn't feel the need to glance into any of them; it is obvious what those rooms contain.

The air is stale and cold, and all the windows are curtained with the same dramatic fabric. Bohemian, baroque, old world, gypsy. Moving to the rear of the room and pushing one of the curtains aside, she sees that both the wooden frames and the glass panes are painted black. There is no gap between the bottom edge of the frame and the sill, which means this window is painted shut. She checks another and finds that it is painted shut as well.

So much for access to the fire escape and the second way out.

Still, Elena pushes on and heads for a door she assumes will lead to the next set of stairs.

This one, metal like the outer back door, is fitted with not one but two deadbolt locks. With the backpack at her feet again, she takes out the lock-pick gun and goes to work.

Less than two minutes later she is through and climbing another set of stairs.

Reaching the top step, she enters what is obviously an attic converted into someone's living space.

A large unmade bed stands at the far end, and two sofas, significantly less elaborate than the ones downstairs, face each other. Three of the four walls have windows that aren't curtained or painted, and along the windowless wall is a long workbench upon which sit two notebook computers and several model spaceships in various degrees of completion.

She smells glue and paint. A number of shelves display completed models—spaceships, airplanes, automobiles—as well as what she can only assume are action figures from comic books and movies.

There is only one hint that this isn't the playroom of some teenage boy.

Two video cameras mounted on tripods are aimed at one of the sofas.

Positioned in a way that would allow each camera two distinct angles of that sofa—and whatever action took place upon it—makes their specific purpose obvious.

Whether or not this is in fact the home of the man code-named Don Quixote is the question she needs to answer now. With that in mind, she moves to the workbench and touches the spacebars of both computers, awakening them from sleep mode.

It is then that she sees to the right of the workbench yet another door.

Heavy steel and double-bolted, with not one but two magnetic sensors mounted on the upper frame.

———

The old tailor takes the jacket from the rack and holds it up for Miles to see.

"This is a Belstaff," he says, almost proudly.

"You're kidding."

"You know the label?"

"The person who sent me here has a Belstaff bag."

"Ah, the beautiful Angelina." The man nods and goes into a well-rehearsed sales pitch. "Belstaff was a British company that manufactured motorcycle jackets starting back before the Second World War. They were acquired by an Italian company a number of years ago and are quite fashionable these days—a little too fashionable for my taste. But they make reproductions of the old British jackets, and those are just top-notch. Like the Barbour, the cotton is waxed to keep out the rain and the wind. The tartan lining is cotton as well, so it helps keep you warm when you need to be but breathes when you need to cool down. As you can see, the shoulders and elbows are reinforced with extra layers of canvas, which is about as close to leather as you can get. Of course, leather isn't waterproof, and it doesn't breathe."

"What size is it?"

The man pulls the jacket from its hanger and holds it up for Miles to try on. "The label says it's an extra-large, but because they're Italian-made, the sizes tend to run on the small side."

Miles removes his hooded sweatshirt and lays it over the rack. As he does, the tailor's eyes quickly go to the Rolex on his wrist.

Once he has slipped into the jacket, Miles steps to the mirror, pulls the zipper closed, snaps the four brass buttons of the wind flap, and tightens the attached waist belt.

"It fits you very well," the tailor observes.

Miles nods. He likes the way it makes him look, but it's the promise of durability that appeals the most.

He thinks of Angelina's motorcycle jeans. If she wears such gear, and if he's going to spend the next few days following her around, then maybe his wearing similar gear wouldn't be such a bad idea.

Not only that, when was the last time he bought something? Or had the money to buy something? And winter *is* coming, so . . .

"How much?"

Neither notebook computer is equipped with security protocols, so Elena easily accesses and searches their hard drives.

All she finds on either are photographs and videos, hundreds and hundreds of the former, dozens of the later. No documents, no e-mail accounts, nothing that would be of use to her.

In fact, the very lack of anything but photos and videos tells her that what she has come for is most likely behind the secure door to her right.

And the presence of the two video cameras aimed at one of the sofas, along with the fact that the only programs she can find on either computer are video editing programs, is a pretty good indication that the face of whoever lives here just might be visible in some of these many photographs.

If all she comes away with is a good look at Don Quixote's face, then that's at least something.

She opens a random photograph about midway down the list and instantly recognizes in it one of the two sofas behind her. The quality of the photo—just a little grainy, the two figures it shows slightly blurred—tells her that this photo is likely a still-capture from a video.

The two figures are a man and a woman. The man, standing, in nothing but a pair of jeans that are unbuttoned, has the woman bent over the arm of the couch and is taking her from behind. She is dressed in only a black garter belt and torn fishnet stockings. The man is slender like a teenage boy, but by the dark stubble on his chin, which is the only part of his face that is visible thanks to his long black hair, it is clear that he is a man.

Elena quickly closes the photo, then pauses before opening another one farther on down the long list.

The angle in this photo is different, so it is a still-capture from the other camera, but the action is the same.

And as before, the man's dark hair masks much of his face.

Elena quickly closes that photo and decides to try one more. She selects one closer to the top of the list, thinking it might be a still-capture from earlier in the "session" and allow her a view of his face.

What she finds is a shot of the man, still in jeans only, though buttoned up now, cutting the woman's shirt—a white dress shirt—with a knife. She is wearing over her torn fishnet stockings a plaid schoolgirl's shirt.

Whether this is role-playing or something more troubling, Elena can't tell. And though the man's face is still not visible, she does see in this photo something that wasn't visible in the previous two.

A tattoo on the man's left shoulder of Picasso's *Don Quixote.*

Elongated man holding a lance and seated upon elongated horse, both barely more than stick figures. Tiny windmills in the background and a childlike rendering of the sun in the sky above them.

Nothing more than a sketch Picasso reportedly dashed off in minutes, but accurately recreated in black ink on this man's shoulder.

Who else could this be but the colleague her father referred to as Don Quixote?

Closing this photo, she steps away from the workbench and studies the door to the right. Opening her backpack, she removes her lock-pick kit and finds inside it several strips of silver foil the size of chewing gum wrappers.

Placing the foil between the sensors should reflect the electromagnetic current and prevent the alarm from being triggered once the door is opened and the sensors are separated.

Should being the operative word here.

Pavol explained the technique to her once, when Jean-Claude first delivered the lock-pick kit to them days after their arrival in Montreal. But that was a month ago, and to remember it is to remember Pavol.

She has, though, no choice but to try the procedure.

Before she does, however, she hears from outside the muffled thud of a car door closing, followed seconds later by another muffled thud. Checking the window that overlooks the driveway, she sees parked in it now a Mercedes SUV.

Moving away from the vehicle and toward the back door is a man and woman, huddled close together.

More than huddled, the man—his hair, whoever he is, hidden under a knit cap—has his arm around the woman's shoulder and seems to be as much holding her up as helping her along.

By the time Elena hears from below the sound of the back door closing, she is inside a crowded closet not far from the unmade bed, listening as the man and the woman make their way up the first set of stairs.

"I can let you have this jacket for six hundred," the tailor says.

Miles knows he shouldn't be surprised by the price but nonetheless is.

Reading his customer's reaction, the tailor, back in sales mode, says, "All the other jackets I carry will cost about the same. But you must believe me, a jacket like this is built to last. You'll have it for the rest of your life. And it's my last one because I simply can't keep them in stock."

Miles knows he has no choice; the only other clothing store he has seen is closed, and even if it weren't, its merchandise would certainly be similarly priced.

He wonders how he is going to pay for it. He has three credit cards with him, two of which are maxed. The third card is maybe a hundred dollars, tops, shy of its limit. But then he remembers what Angelina said about paying only with cash.

And he has plenty of that.

He tells the man that all he has are American bills.

"American would be fine with me. If you're paying in cash, I'll waive the tax."

Using a small pair of scissors he pulls from his jacket pocket, the tailor cuts the price tag from the collar and hands it to Miles. Attached to it is a small paper packet containing spare brass buttons. The tag identifies this jacket's model: "Tourist Trophy."

Miles places the tag into one of the cargo pockets, then removes the five grand from his jeans. Without breaking the paper band surrounding it, he counts out twelve fifties from the top of the stack and pulls them free.

He gives the man the cash, and the man gives him a shopping bag containing his hooded sweatshirt.

Instead of returning his stack to his jeans pocket, Miles puts it in the left breast pocket of his jacket.

They shake hands again, and Miles leaves. Turning to close the door, he looks through the glass, expecting to see the man counting the bills, or placing them in the register or even pocketing them.

What he sees instead is the man holding one of the fifties up to the overhead light and studying it. Putting that bill down on the counter, he holds up the next and studies it in the same careful manner.

Pulling the door closed, Miles is curious why the hell the man would be doing that. The only reason he can think of is that the man is checking for counterfeits.

Miles, warm at last inside his well-fitting jacket, starts to backtrack toward Angelina's apartment.

He considers taking a different route from the one she laid out for him. He'd like to see more of this place, maybe take a quick tour of the waterfront area below. Wandering these scenic old streets is close enough to a distraction from the many troubles he has left four hundred miles to the south.

But he decides against deviation and follows the exact route he took to get here, as instructed by his host.

The host he is eager to see again.

Eventually Miles sees the entrance to rue le Royer up ahead.

A dozen or so strides in front of him, moving arm-in-arm, is a couple. They stop at the wrought iron gate suddenly, as if surprised. After a pause, they continue walking, but a little faster than they were before, their rushed footsteps echoing.

It is only after they have taken several steps away that Miles understands what caused them to halt in the first place.

Standing in the gateway, wavering just a little like a drunk, is the man in a tattered overcoat.

The man he had glimpsed earlier.

As Miles approaches, the man seems to zero in on him.

Only his eyes are visible, the rest of his face lost behind long, dirty hair, a scraggly beard, and smudged dirt.

Even though Miles is still half a block away, the man calls to him.

He speaks English, not French.

"Can you spare some change?"

Fourteen

With her CZ-75 drawn and ready, Elena listens as the footsteps below grow louder.

The closet door is slightly ajar, much of the attic room visible through that inch-wide crack. What part of that room she can't see from this angle can be brought into view by simply shifting slightly to her right or left.

She hears a voice, but only one—the man's. It is only after he and the woman reach the stairs directly below the attic that Elena can make out his words.

He is coaching the woman, saying to her, "One more step. Okay, another step. Now another. There you go."

Finally they begin to emerge through the opening in the floor. The man's right arm is still around the woman, and with his left he is holding her left forearm, from which her hand dangles limply.

The woman—young, and, Elena quickly determines, not the woman from the still-captures she viewed—is clearly drunk, or maybe stoned.

As they reach the top step, the man directs the woman toward the sofas. Elena concludes by the appearance of the woman's half-closed eyes that she isn't drunk but drugged; a drunk stumbles and wavers on weak legs, while this woman—slender, with short blonde hair and a narrow face—moves more like someone exhausted being half led, half dragged off to bed. Her head rests upon the man's shoulder, and she smiles as if she is dreaming.

He eases the blonde down onto the sofa at which the two video cameras are aimed. She doesn't slump into a slouch but rather reclines comfortably, opening her eyes for long enough to look up at the man. She does so with gratitude and trust.

"Just relax," he whispers.

She nods and closes her eyes, the tranquil smile lingering.

The man watches her for a moment, and when her eyes do not open again, he steps away and goes to work.

Powering up the cameras, he does a quick last-minute check through the viewfinders, checking each camera's alignment. Once he is satisfied with the framing, he moves to a dimmer switch on the wall beside his workbench, activating a ceiling light mounted directly above the sofa.

When the light is just right—not too bright, not too dim—he kneels down and opens the bottom drawer of a small cabinet beneath the workbench. Reaching in carefully, he removes a knife that is identical to the one he used to cut the white shirt off the woman in the photos.

Before he can even close the drawer, Elena is behind him and pressing the muzzle of the CZ-75 against the back of his head.

"You can feel that, right?" she says.

The man freezes. "Yes."

"Drop the knife."

He does as he is told.

Elena pulls the knit cap from his head, allowing his long black hair to fall free. "You're going to do something for me," she says.

"You have a slight Middle-Eastern accent," he observes. "Israeli, perhaps?"

Elena responds by pressing the muzzle more firmly against his skull and ordering him to pull up his left sleeve.

The man is wearing a short-sleeved black T-shirt, tight on his narrow frame. He moves his right hand toward his left arm with an exaggerated slowness, then pulls up his sleeve.

All Elena needs to see are the feet of the horse and the low horizon of windmills.

"That's enough," she says.

Backing away till she is well beyond his reach, the gun trained on the back of his head, Elena glances quickly at the woman on the sofa to make certain she is still unconscious. Looking back at the tattooed man, she says, "Put your hands on top of your head and interlock your fingers."

He does this.

"Stand up and turn around. Slowly."

The man rises and turns.

Elena takes a long look at his face. She sees in it no hint of fear or worry.

"Do you know who I am?" she says.

He nods. "He never told me your name, of course. But yeah, I know who you are."

"You worked for my father. You provided him with equipment, correct?"

"Yes."

"You delivered surveillance gear to him in Geneva three days before his death. And you installed it in his apartment."

"First of all, you can put the gun down because you aren't going to kill me. You came here to find out what I know. If you kill me, I can't really answer your questions, can I?"

Elena keeps the CZ-75 level with his head. "Shooting a man doesn't necessarily mean killing him."

"You have what it takes to do that, do you? Hurt someone without mercy. Cries of pain can be very . . . distracting, trust me."

Elena glances again at the woman on the sofa. "Try me and see."

"You found your father's files. That's the only way you could have tracked me down." He pauses. "I read about the men who were killed the other night. Let me guess: Mephistopheles, right? That's the man who gave you the files. Or, knowing him, he's the one who sold them to you."

Elena says nothing.

"Did you kill him? Mephistopheles?"

"No."

"Did you see who did?"

"All I saw was a man in disguise."

"Long hair and beard, dressed up to look like a panhandler. Correct? Drunk one minute, moving like fucking Muhammad Ali the next."

"So you know him."

"Why don't you put down the gun so we can have a talk like civilized people?"

Elena keeps the CZ-75 aimed at his head and says, "Who is he?"

"The word is he was a member of your father's security team. A particularly nasty bastard, I'm told."

"He worked for my father."

"Yes."

"So why would he kill Mephistopheles?"

"You'd have to ask him that."

Elena pauses to think about this, then gestures toward the door to the right of the workbench.

"That's the only secured door in this entire building. What's behind it?"

"What you came here for."

She hesitates. "That easy, huh?"

"You're the one with the gun. And anyway, I want what you want."

"Which is?"

"To find your father's killer."

"Why?"

"Pure selfishness, I assure you."

"You think you might be next."

The man nods.

Elena gestures toward the heavy steel door. "All right."

The tattooed man lowers his hands and digs into his hip pocket, removing a ring of keys.

He unlocks the two deadbolts with two separate keys, then opens the door and steps through. As he does, a bright overhead light comes on automatically.

Elena, stepping to the doorway to keep him in her line of sight, stops short of entering. The tattooed man turns and punches an eight-digit code into a keypad on the wall just inside and to the left of the door.

At last, a security system, Elena thinks. But she doubts it is the kind to sound an alarm or bring the police.

When the tattooed man has entered the code, Elena tells him to move away from the door. He complies, backing into the room.

Only then does Elena step into the doorway, and what she sees is a room that is the complete opposite of the attic bedroom.

Clean and uncluttered to the point of seeming sterile, it is empty save for a small cage-like enclosure of chain-link fence inside which stands only two things: a draftsman table and, beside it, a bank of servers encased in a heavy metal frame bolted to the floor.

On the table is a desktop computer, a large widescreen monitor, and a printer. The computer tower is connected by several USB wires to the servers.

The next thing Elena notices is that the walls and ceiling of this small room are lined with a silvery insulating material she knows to be flame retardant. And the floor is painted flat black, most likely the heat-resistant paint with which barbecues are painted. It appears to be many coats thick.

A precaution, she concludes quickly, not to keep these items in this room safe from fire but rather to prevent, or at least slow, a fire started in this room from spreading to the rest of the house.

She infers from this that the magnetic sensors above the door are connected to some kind of incendiary device located somewhere in this room. Maybe even more than one. Opening the doors and not entering the proper code in a timely manner is likely what triggers the device or devices.

If destroying this computer and bank of servers is that important, then so must be the information stored on them.

Files, maybe, containing identities and addresses.

Places for her to go next, and the people to track down once there.

———

As Miles approaches the gate, he says to the panhandler, "Sorry, I don't have any change."

The panhandler holds out a gloved hand and says, "I could really use a drink." His words are slurred, his French accent heavy. His eyes, the only part of his face really visible, are narrowed but alert.

"Like I said, man, I don't have anything to give."

He reaches the man, then passes him. Stepping through the gate, Miles looks down the long courtyard to the gate at the other end. Through it, directly across rue Saint-Sulpice, stands Angelina's building.

"I'll take coins," the panhandler says. "Whatever you have. All I need is one more drink. I have trouble sleeping, you know. Drinking helps."

Miles looks over his shoulder at the man. Despite his curiosity— what were the chances of a stranger saying that to him just now—all he offers is a polite smile and a friendly, "Sorry."

Turning to face the empty courtyard ahead, he continues walking.

"That's a nice coat," the man says. "It looks warm."

Miles looks over his shoulder again but is surprised to see that the man has followed him. He is, in fact, standing a mere foot away.

How did he do that without me hearing?

"You sound like an American," the man says. "To tell you the truth, I don't really like Americans."

Fifteen

Still facing her, the tattooed man says, "The fact that your father had me rig his apartment with surveillance meant he knew something was about to happen. I got the sense that he was letting it play out so he could lure whoever was about to betray him out into the open."

"So what went wrong?"

"That's the question, isn't it?"

"Several names showed up in his files more than others. Yours was one. Faust and Hamlet were two others. Who are they? Where can I find them?"

"No one knew who anyone else was. All we ever had were those code names your father assigned. Handoffs were face-to-face, but your father had all these elaborate routes figured out to prevent any one courier from following the other. It also prevented anyone who may have followed the first courier to a location where a handoff was to take place from tailing the second to his drop-off, and from there on to the next, and from there to your father. But the thing is, we were all making way too much money. Easy money. Betrayal of anyone within the pipeline would screw that up. And betrayal of your father would shut it down for good."

"You believe my father was killed by someone who worked for him."

"I don't know how anyone else could have gotten to him. For that matter, I don't know how anyone who worked for him could have gotten to him, either."

"You could have. You were in his apartment three days before he was murdered. You could have passed his address on to someone."

"I was picked up at the airport by some badass dude I'd never met and have not seen since. I had a hood over my head the entire ride into the city. And when the ride ended and the hood was removed, I was in an underground parking garage. An elevator ride later and I was inside an apartment. Every curtain was drawn, so I couldn't even see what was outside."

"Why didn't he have someone local install the equipment?"

He shrugs. "It's easier to disorient a visitor than a resident. A local asset might have been able to determine his address. Plus, I was the best, and your father always wanted the best. Mostly, though, he had me do it because he trusted me."

"It's often the very people we trust who end up betraying us," Elena says.

"In your father's case, it was *only* the people he trusted who could have betrayed him. I know that he used Hamlet and Faust more than any of the other couriers. I know they were with him when he founded the pipeline."

"But you have no idea where they are or how to contact them."

"I never met Faust face-to-face, only Hamlet. There was a cell phone number I'd send one of a number of coded texts to. The text was a signal for him to meet me at the predetermined time and location."

"I want that information."

"No problem."

The door to the cage is secured with a padlock, and the tattooed man unlocks it with a third key from his ring. Opening the chain-link door, he steps to the draftsman's desk and touches the spacebar on the computer's keyboard. The widescreen monitor blinks on and shows a four-way split screen. In each screen are views from surveillance cameras of the floors below.

The bar, the hallway leading to the backrooms, and the two couch areas.

After a few seconds the images automatically rotate to views of other locations throughout this building's interior, including what Elena assumes are some of the rooms behind those numbered doors down that narrow hallway beyond the riser with the stripper poles.

Multiple cameras hidden throughout.

An active surveillance system constantly recording, or maybe triggered by motion.

Either way, Elena knows now that there is video of her entering and making her way around—video that is stored somewhere in those banks of secured servers bolted to the floor.

Unlike like the two computers in the attic room, this one is protected by security protocols.

Elena watches as the tattooed man presses his thumb to a postage stamp–sized scanner beside the keyboard.

Once his thumbprint is read, identified, and accepted, a prompt screen appears on the widescreen monitor, requesting that a username and password be entered. He types them in, and instantly the four-way split screen is replaced with a large folder containing a long list of folder-shaped icons.

The file he opens is labeled "Hamlet" and contains a single phone number, below which is a list of a dozen six-letter words, all in caps. Code words. Across from each one is the location and time that corresponds with that word.

Elena quickly reads and memorizes as many as she can.

Parc La Fontaine, 9:00 p.m.

Olympic Park, 10:00 a.m.

quai King-Edward, midnight.

From a dropdown menu the tattooed man selects "Print." After a brief lag, the high-speed printer begins working. The single sheet is spit out in a matter of seconds.

The tattooed man, however, makes no move toward removing the paper from the tray.

"These might not even work anymore. After all, it has been a year. In all likelihood, Hamlet destroyed his phone. I destroyed mine the moment I heard your father was dead." He pauses to think for a moment, then says: "I take it you were in contact with the Geneva police during their so-called investigation."

"Yes."

"I'm assuming they didn't find the surveillance equipment I had installed in his apartment. If they had, it would have shown his killer."

"No equipment was found. Not by them, and not by me."

"So whoever killed him took the equipment with them when they left."

"That's right."

"How then did Mephistopheles come into possession of your father's files? They had to have been taken the same time as the equipment, no? Unless he was the man who killed him."

"If he were, then why would he want to sell the files to me?"

"Why does anyone do anything? Why do I have this place? Why do I sell hidden-camera sex videos on the Internet? The problem with making a lot of money is you tend to spend it. I squandered every cent I made from your father. I wouldn't be surprised if Mephistopheles did the same."

"He knows I have access to my father's money. He would have asked for a lot more than he did if all he was after was cash."

"Was there anything in those files that identified any of his couriers? I mean, your father had to have written that information down somewhere."

"I went through every page. Nothing."

"Mephistopheles could have taken those particular pages out before handing the files over to you."

"Why would he do that?"

The tattooed man shrugs. He pauses, then says: "Hold it a minute. If there were no personal records in those files, then how exactly did you find me?"

"There was a mention of your name and this place."

"My real name?"

"No."

"I don't understand. There was a file on me but no one else?"

"No. I found a handwritten note on the edges of one of the pages."

"What did it say?"

She quotes the note word for word.

"That's a little . . . convenient, don't you think?"

"I know my father's handwriting."

"So do a lot of people."

"What are you saying?"

"Someone could have written that note because they wanted you to find me."

"Why would anyone want that?"

"So you could lead them to me. Could you have been followed here?"

"No."

"Are you sure?"

"Positive. If my father didn't write that note, then who did?"

"I'm not planning on sticking around to find out. And I don't think you should, either. We need to get out of here." He nods behind Elena, toward the woman on the couch. "And I'll need help getting her down to my car. Will you help me with that?"

Elena glances over her shoulder at the unconscious blonde on the sofa, and instantly realizes the terrible mistake she has made.

She hears the sound of movement and turns back to face the tattooed man, but he has already closed the distance between them with a speed she would not have thought him capable of.

Grabbing the barrel of the CZ-75, he twists the weapon so it is aimed at the ceiling, then ducks slightly and plows his right shoulder into her chest, driving her back through the doorway and out into the open attic bedroom.

———

Miles turns away from the panhandler and says over his shoulder, "Don't blame you. I kind of hate Americans, too."

It seems the thing to say, and ignoring the man without actually ignoring him seems the thing to do.

But before Miles can take more than a few steps, the panhandler quickly closes the little distance that remains. Instinctively, Miles turns to face the man.

He doesn't have time to complete his turn, or even register the fist's flight toward him. It slams hard into his solar plexus, and the next thing he knows, he is falling like dead weight down to the cobblestones.

He lands on his left side, and the force of his impact on the solid stones sends a jolt that echoes down his legs like electricity.

He has a vague memory of his head bouncing once off the uneven stones—but that's all it is, a vague memory. The wind has been knocked out of him, and as he struggles to reinflate his paralyzed lungs, he senses the panhandler striding over him. A second later the panhandler has crouched down and is sitting on Miles's hip like a schoolyard bully.

From there it takes a few seconds more for Miles to comprehend what is going on.

The man first grabs Miles's right arm, tugs the cuff of the jacket sleeve downward to expose Miles's wrist, then drops that arm and grabs the other, tugging that sleeve down as well.

When Miles finally realizes that the man is going for his watch, he struggles to pull his hand free of the man's grip, but the instant he does, the man palm-strikes the side of his head—once, twice, then again. Miles's head bounces off the cobblestones with each blow, but unlike a few seconds ago, he feels it each time.

Rattled now, and gasping to breathe, Miles is unable to prevent his attacker from releasing the clasp of the metal band and slipping the watch off.

Just like that, the thing is gone.

Miles can feel the full weight of the man still pressing down upon him. Despite the chaos in his mind—a mix of fear and panic and pain, not to mention the effects of the first blow to his head and the subsequent ones—Miles has clarity enough to wonder why the hell this man doesn't just take the watch and run.

Does he plan on causing more pain and humiliation, for the sport of it, maybe?

Or does he intend on searching his victim's pockets for even more valuables?

Miles thinks instantly of the money in the breast pocket of his brand-new jacket.

The idea of losing that cash is more than he can bear.

In his panic he tries to scramble free, but the man is just too heavy—and too skilled. Out of desperation, Miles strains to turn his head and look down the length of the courtyard, hoping he might see someone—anyone—he could call to for help.

He sees no one, then quickly focuses his attention on the entrance to Angelina's building through the distant gate.

What he sees doesn't make any sense to him at first.

Two brown paper grocery bags are standing unattended by the street door, which is half open, the light from the hallway spilling out onto the street.

A picture postcard, almost.

After few seconds of staring at this, Miles's attention is caught by something else.

Something—someone—is in the courtyard, moving not down the center of it but along one of its shadowed edges.

And not just moving but moving fast.

No, more than fast—moving with determination, on what is clearly an intercept course.

Unrelenting and silent.

And then this person emerges from the shadows. As she does, she makes a downward snapping motion with her right hand.

The six-inch rod in her hand suddenly expands another foot and locks into place with a solid click.

A telescopic baton—Miles remembers the bouncers at the Delancey Bar and Grill carrying ones just like it.

He remembers, too, what Angelina had grabbed from her bag prior to their leaving her apartment.

The panhandler also hears the click and looks toward it, but too late; Angelina is already upon him.

———

Elena outruns the tattooed man's momentum till she senses his forward motion diminishing, and the instant it does, she goes to work.

While he is focused on the gun they both still grip—focused on pulling it from her hand or at least gaining some measure of control on it—Elena applies just enough attention and energy to keep the barrel pointed up at the ceiling, diverting the rest of her will and strength to better use.

As with a tree, Pavol had once told her, it generally takes more than a single blow to bring a man down.

Elena opens with a stomp-kick to the top of the tattooed man's foot, landing the heel of her combat boot squarely on her intended target. Without missing a beat, she turns her head sideways and, bending forward at the waist suddenly as though from a powerful sneeze, launches a head-butt toward the bridge of the man's nose.

Though she misses that exact target, her parietal bone connects with his cheekbone, and she understands by the loosening of his grip on the CZ-75 that she has stunned him.

But before she can launch the next move in her well-practiced combination—a knee thrust to the groin—the man pivots and steps to the side, pressing his hip against hers and executing a hip throw.

As she did with his charge, Elena doesn't bother to resist his strength, knows that doing so will cause the tattooed man to apply more power than needed to lever her off her feet and therefore over-commit to the throw. As he drops her toward the floor, he will lose his own balance and allow her the chance to pull him down with her.

And this is exactly what happens.

Unlike hers, the tattooed man's landing is hard. But he has enough skill to counter her counter by rolling with her momentum, just as she did with his. Pulling her with him, he rolls Elena onto her back and mounts her.

And without hesitation, he resumes his struggle for control of the gun.

What Miles witnesses as he lies on his side on the cobblestones is nothing short of amazing.

Angelina's first blow with the telescopic baton is to the target closest to her: the elbow of the panhandler's right arm, which the man has raised to begin yet another series of blows to Miles's head.

The baton connects with a solid thud, and before the man even has time to cry out, Angelina drops quickly into a crouch and goes straight for the next target: the man's right knee.

Being in a squat over Miles means that the man's kneecap is fully exposed.

The popping sound of the metal rod striking the bone is quickly drowned out by the panhandler's cry.

Despite these two blows, the man rises off Miles and into a crouch of his own—a first step in his attempt to get out of his armed attacker's reach as quickly as possible.

But he can't move fast enough.

Dropping her knee to the pavement and stepping forward with the other foot, Angelina, keeping low, gets even closer to the man and strikes his knee a second time, then, in a backhand motion, hits it again from the other direction an instant later.

Each swing she makes is a blur to Miles's eyes.

The man manages to stand and take a step backward, but he is obviously injured. Elena rises to her feet and, standing tall now, closes in even more, aiming this time for the man's skull.

He raises his arms to protect his head, but the weapon simply connects with his forearm instead, and he is forced to stagger backward even farther.

To Miles, it is a bit like watching a lumbering bear being driven back by a single furious bee.

Angelina drops yet again to the other knee and repeats the forehand-backhand sequence to the man's leg, only this time she misses his knee and connects with his upper shin, causing the man to cry out, "Fuck!"

Stepping forward and rising to her feet again, she goes once more for his skull. His arms are still raised, and she only grazes his elbow, but it is more than enough to cause the man to turn and stumble in clumsy retreat through the gate.

The throw, followed by their rolling, has brought Elena and the tattooed man closer to the long workbench on which sits the two notebook computers.

More important than that, is has brought them nearer to the knife the tattooed man had dropped to the floor.

Though Elena sees it first—it is just two feet away—the man quickly follows her line of vision and spots the blade as well.

For now, though, both their hands are occupied with the struggle over the deadlier of those two weapons.

The man again attempts to pry the gun from her hand with brute force, but she has the advantage of holding it close to her chest—pulling down on something requires less strength than pulling up on it, and this negates the slight advantage his being a man affords him.

In an effort to get more leverage, he lifts his right knee and places his foot squarely on the floor, then pulls up again on the gun. His new position takes some of his weight off Elena, and she responds to it by pivoting in a counterclockwise motion beneath him. Being perpendicular beneath him allows her to lift her own right leg over his head and place it between their chests like a lever. A scissor-like motion is all it takes to force him off his balance.

As he falls onto his back, maintaining his two-handed grip on the gun, he pulls Elena up into a seated position, which allows her to quickly mount him. The muzzle of the gun brushes for a split second against her ribs, but by pressing down on him with all her weight she is able to direct the weapon's aim away.

Still, this close call causes her already rushing heart to pound even harder.

Pure fear crashes through her like a wave.

This maneuver has brought them even closer to the knife, and sensing the futility of their struggle for the gun, the tattooed man wastes no time and lunges for the other weapon.

It is a gamble that pays off because the knife is angled perfectly beside him, allowing him to grab hold of the handle without any fuss and thrust the four-inch blade without hesitation toward Elena's side.

Taking her left hand off the gun, Elena bends forward and lies over him like a lover. His forearm strikes her ribs as the knife in his hand only stabs the empty air behind her. Coiling her arm around his elbow like a snake, she traps his arm against her, rendering the knife, for now, useless.

Face-to-face, she can feel his breath on her skin. The struggle for control of the gun continues, but Elena has no intention of attempting to pull it from his hand. Since she is the one with a finger on the trigger, all she needs to do is angle the weapon so it is directed at him—any part of him at this point—and then squeeze.

Because he has a firm grasp of the barrel and she is holding the grip, however, he has leverage on his side. She knows she'll need something other than strength to break the standoff.

And she realizes suddenly just what it is she has to do.

The next thing Miles knows, Angelina is crouched above him and pulling on his arm with two hands.

"Can you stand?" she says. "I need you to stand, Miles. Okay? I need you to get up right now."

It takes all he has, plus a great deal of help from her, but he gets to his feet.

She winds his arm around the back of her neck, making herself into a crutch, then guides him through the empty courtyard.

He focuses through the distant gate and the half-opened door directly across the street beyond it.

"Who the fuck was that?" he mutters.

"I don't know."

Angelina is moving fast, as much pulling Miles along as helping him remain upright. It is a struggle for him to match her pace, and more than once he stumbles over his own feet and almost falls.

Each time he does, Angelina, like some drill sergeant, urges him to keep moving, just keep moving

"He took my watch," Miles says.

Angelina doesn't reply. Turning her head sharply, she looks behind them, checking, Miles assumes, to make certain they aren't being followed.

Passing through the tall wrought iron gate, they cross Saint-Sulpice and half burst, half fall through the door she left partially open.

Just barely able to control him in the confined space of the narrow foyer, Angelina all but drops Miles onto the bottom step, where he sits as she turns and heads back outside to retrieve the two bags of groceries on the sidewalk.

As she does this, Miles looks toward the courtyard beyond.

But he sees not a soul there.

Bringing the two bags inside, Angelina places them on the floor and closes the heavy door.

———⌣———

Locked in the strangely intimate embrace with the tattooed man, Elena squeezes the trigger.

As the gun, aimed at the wall above the workbench, fires, the recoil action causes the barrel to slide backward to eject the spent bullet casing, then spring forward a fraction of a second later as the next round is loaded into the chamber.

The tattooed man's reaction to the unexpected movement of the weapon in his grip is exactly what she hoped it would be.

He quickly releases the barrel and pulls his hand away as if the gun were some wild animal that suddenly tried to bite him.

Elena now has sole control of the weapon, and it takes only a split second for her to turn it and press the muzzle against the tattooed man's sternum and fire a second shot.

He goes instantly limp beneath her, and the knife falls from his hand and lands with a solid thud on the floorboards beside them.

She pushes the knife away, just in case, then scrambles to her feet and, taking a step back, assumes a shooter's stance and aims the CZ-75 at the prostrate man's head.

Her hands are shaking, but the man does not move. His eyes are open and staring blankly upward. Beneath him the blood pouring from the large hole made by the shattered bullet as it exited his body, then lodged into the floor plank, begins to spread.

How can she see this and not think of her father?

Or Pavol?

And the question—one in a dream, the other in bed beside her—that they each had asked.

What will you do?

It takes Elena a moment to remember the blonde lying on the nearby sofa. She welcomes the realization in the way one caught in a bad dream would welcome a first thought upon waking.

It takes yet a moment more for Elena to actually check on the woman, who is still unconscious.

The fact that the scuffle—not to mention the gunshots—didn't stir the blonde is for Elena yet another indication that she has been drugged.

She knows what she needs to do next, and gets to it without hesitation.

Digging the ring of keys from the man's pocket, she returns to the secured room, enters the chain-link enclosure, and grabs the single sheet of paper from the printer tray. Folding and pocketing it, she looks behind the metal case containing the servers and spots the incendiary device.

Exposing these servers and the computer linked to them to fire would certainly destroy all the information they contained, including the surveillance video showing her entering and moving through the building floor by floor.

But how to trigger the device?

Pavol would know. And so, probably, would Jean-Claude.

But it is only her now.

She can think of only one thing to try.

Stepping through the door and closing it, she waits for as long as she can bear, then opens it again. As before, the overhead light flickers on automatically. Inside the room, she glances at the keypad and sees a blinking red light, then looks at the servers—four of them stacked together, each one the size of stereo components—and waits.

It takes a full thirty seconds, and then she hears the unmistakable sound of a fuse igniting. Almost immediately she smells burning sulfur.

Smoke rises and hovers above the servers, and seconds later sparks flicker into flames that strobe inside the rising smoke like lightning pulsing within the core of a dark cloud.

Of course, Elena wants the fire to spread beyond this room, so she wedges the door open with the knife and, with her backpack on, hurries to the couch, pulling the woman into a seated position. Kneeling just as Pavol had taught her, she lifts the woman via the "fireman carry" and heads for the stairs.

The attic bedroom is already filling with smoke, and one last look back at the open door tells Elena that the server is already in flames.

The muscles in her legs are burning from fatigue by the time she reaches the bottom of the first flight of stairs. Halfway down the second, her legs almost give out entirely. Finding herself on the verge of taking what could only be a bad fall, she catches her balance at the last moment and continues to the bottom floor.

Moving past the bar and sofas and entering the storage room, she smells again the pungent odor of gasoline. As she opens the heavy steel door, she pauses to make a quick check of her surroundings, then crosses the small back lot to the passenger side of the Mercedes SUV, unlocking the doors with the key on the tattooed man's ring.

As carefully and quickly as she can, she places the woman in the rear seat and quietly closes the door. Then, after checking her surroundings yet again, she returns to the storage room and goes straight for the canister of gasoline.

She checks the paint cans on the shelves and determines that two of them contain linseed oil. Clutching those cans in one arm and carrying the canister of gasoline with the other hand, she hurries into the bar area. After setting it on the floor and unscrewing the cap, she kicks the canister over. As the gasoline spills out, she pulls off the lids of the cans of paint and pours their contents onto the nearest sofa.

From her pocket she removes the box of waterproof matches, from which she digs out a single match. Striking it, she waits till the head is fully aflame, then tosses the match onto the still-flowing gasoline.

With a loud whooshing sound, fire bursts instantly to life.

Closing the heavy steel door behind her, Elena hurries to the SUV and climbs in behind the wheel. As she pulls out of the driveway, she looks back at the building via the side view mirror mounted on the driver's door.

The top-floor windows are already filled with a dancing yellow light.

———

Angelina, a crutch again, helps Miles up the three flights of stairs to her apartment.

Back in his room—his safe gargoyle's perch—he sits motionless on his bed as she carefully examines the abrasions on the side of his head.

"You've got blood on your new coat," she observes.

He says nothing, and when she leaves the room to get a damp cloth, he takes off the jacket and lays it across the bed. Remembering the money in the breast pocket, he removes it and returns it to the front pocket of his jeans, vowing to leave it there from now on.

He notices a worn spot in his jeans, on his left outer thigh, no doubt made when he fell to the hard cobblestones.

He notices something else. A damp stain. Blood? He touches it and looks at his fingertip. It is clear, not red. Bringing his finger to his nose, he smells peppermint.

The Migrastick Angelina had given him must have been smashed at some point during the scuffle.

He wipes the stain with his hand and remembers Angelina's actions down in the courtyard—dropping to her knees, then standing again only to drop down once more, picking and choosing her targets with remarkable skill.

He now understands why she wears motorcycle jeans with Kevlar-reinforced knees.

All just part of the gear, she had said.

Miles can't help but wonder how much worse his own injuries would be had he not been inspired by her to purchase such a durable jacket.

From the other room he hears Angelina speaking softly. French, not English. When she returns with a first aid kit and a damp cloth, she tells Miles that she just called Trask and he is on his way over.

Miles wants to say that he thought Trask was already on his way, and this was what created that free hour that Angelina wanted to use wisely.

But he doesn't bother. His head is aching, both inside and out, and his body is sore. These things—combined with the tenderness with which Angelina tends to him and the deep humiliation he now feels—chase the question away.

———

Elena steers the SUV into a large open parking lot behind a pub called Sir Winston Churchill.

Before exiting the vehicle, she finds a blanket under the backseat, unfolds it, and lays it over the woman. Lowering the driver's window an inch, she switches off the motor and takes the ring of keys with her as she gets out. After locking the door, she slides the key ring through the partially open window.

The ring lands on the driver's seat.

The locked doors should keep this woman safe, and though it is cold out tonight, it isn't so cold that she will freeze to death before whatever drug the tattooed man had slipped her wears off.

As she hurries from the lot, mindful not to break into a run, Elena glances in all directions. Seeing no one doesn't necessarily mean no one sees her, she knows this, but there is nothing she can do about that except keep her head low and do all she can to avoid drawing attention to herself.

She knows from studying the map earlier that Gare Centrale, Montreal's train station, is just a few blocks away. Entering it, she finds the ladies' room and checks her reflection in the mirror.

She sees no blood on her clothing or abrasions on her face.

No indications of violence.

What she does see is a look in her eyes that she has never known before.

Pavol had said killing a man wasn't an easy thing to do.

The look in her eyes is in itself a confirmation of that fact.

But hiding that look from anyone who might see her as she passes through the lobby of her hotel won't be a problem.

Hiding—from others as well as herself—is what she is best at.

Sixteen

Sitting alone in his dark room, Miles listens to Angelina talking with Trask out in the living room.

In English this time, not French.

He finds a mirror and glances at his wounds. Superficial, all of them. It is, in fact, the wound to his ego that bothers him the most.

A terrible thing to be helpless.

Pinned to the cobblestones and beaten by a bum.

But it wasn't just helplessness, it was fear, too. Terror. Panic.

Despite having grown up in the city—despite having run a bar for years—Miles has never been in a fight.

This was hardly a fight, though. A beating, yes; a fight, no.

He has to admit that a part of him wants leave Montreal, head back home, throw himself back into his life of momentum and promises.

Picking up any and all shifts at his friend's restaurant, weekends spent with his kid—hour-long train ride in, hour-long train ride out, nothing to fear there. Just debts and the need to figure out a way to rebuild.

Nothing but the *familiar*.

When Angelina finishes making her report, Miles rises from his bed and, walking on shaky legs, steps out to join them. Maybe he can find a way to break his promise and take off without actually having to break it.

To his surprise, Miles sees that Trask hasn't come alone. Standing by one of the front windows, his left shoulder to the glass and his right to the room, is Cohn.

Miles notes that this is the very same stance Cohn had assumed back in the empty club on Delancey. After glancing at Miles briefly, the man, as serious looking as ever, turns back to the window and surveys the street four stories below.

"I understand you've had a bit of a rude welcome to our city," Trask says. "Glad you weren't too badly injured."

"Thanks to Wonder Woman here." It is the least Miles could do, considering all she has done for him. Anything to keep Trask from *having her ass*.

"And your attacker took your watch. A Rolex, wasn't it?"

"Yeah."

"In a few days' time you might be able to buy a thousand just like it without batting an eye." Trask thinks for a moment, then says, "You know, Vieux-Montreal and Vieux-Port are two of the safest places one could hope to find. I can't remember the last time there was a mugging here. I don't want lie to you, Miles, though. There's a chance this wasn't just random street violence."

Miles glances at Angelina, then looks back at Trask. "What else could it have been?"

"There's a man who used to work for your father. He's a very dangerous man, a very capable man. I'm afraid this man might be working for your sister."

"I don't understand."

Angelina says, "It's possible Elena knows you're here and sent this man after you."

"To mug me?"

"To scare you off," Trask corrects. "That's the best-case scenario. The worst is that she sent him to kill you. The mugging would have been a cover, in case there were witnesses. Word is this man favors a particular disguise, and based on what Angelina has told me, we can't rule out that it was him."

It takes Miles a moment to process this. His hosts seem more than content to give him the time he needs.

"How would she even know I was here?" Miles says finally.

"When you have money and connections, you can buy information. We know Elena has the money, and she could have allied herself with any one of the men around the world your father employed. I'm not the only one who feels a sense of loyalty to him. It's possible Elena made contact with the very man I got your passport from. He could have easily confirmed that you crossed the border with it today and then passed that information on to her."

"Why would he do work for you and then turn around and do work for her?"

"For the money, Miles. The collapse of your father's business left a lot people without an income. But she also could have told him some tale of woe about me and turned him to her side. She can be very manipulative."

"But how would she know where exactly in Montreal I was?"

"Like I said, when you have money . . ." Trask leaves it at that.

"Why would she want to have me killed, though?"

"You still don't get it, do you? Heirs screw each other all the time. You don't know Elena like I do. She's ruthless. Your father made her that way. She cares about no one but herself and her crusade."

An image of his half sister is beginning to take shape in Miles's mind. He used to know nothing about her but disliked her simply for what she represented—rejection by his father, of himself and his mother. Now, the more he knows about Elena, the more his general dislike is honed into a more specific feeling of contempt.

Miles shrugs. "It just doesn't make any sense to me."

Trask pauses, then says, "Listen, it's your choice whether to stay on or not. Considering what just happened, I won't hold you to our deal. If you do stay, though, I can promise that Angelina won't leave your side. You've seen what she can do. And Cohn here will be a constant presence from now on. You might not always see him, but trust me, he's there. I can guarantee you that whoever attacked you won't get a second chance. But if you feel that you're in over your head and want to go back home, I'll understand."

Miles glances at Angelina. He is suddenly reluctant to take the chance he was hoping would be offered.

Would he feel differently about what Trask has just said if she weren't standing right there?

Still, he has a son, one he promised he would come home to.

Miles glances from Angelina to Cohn, then looks at Trask again. "Maybe I should head back. Finding her seems like a long shot anyway."

"I need you to be sure."

"I'm sure."

Trask nods. "It'll have to wait till tomorrow. You'll have to take the train back, and that doesn't leave till the morning. You'll be safe here tonight." He looks at Angelina. "If you need anything, tell me now and I'll send Cohn out to get it."

"We've got everything we need."

Trask looks at Miles and pauses once more, then says, "Just so you know, about an hour ago someone set fire to a house up in Parc du Mont-Royal. I have reason to believe Elena was involved. My police connection is meeting with me to fill me in."

"Why are you telling me this?"

"Like I said before, your sister is a danger to herself and others. And it looks like she has gotten another person killed. I was hoping that knowing this might make a difference, that you might change your mind about leaving."

"I'm sorry, it doesn't."

Trask nods again. His disappointment is obvious. "Just do everything Angelina tells you to. In the morning she and Cohn will escort you to the train station, make sure you get on the train. After that you're on your own, though. Do you understand?"

Miles nods. "Yeah."

———

Back in his room, Miles sips from a tumbler filled with Bailey's Irish Cream and crushed ice.

It is his second glass of the sweet and boozy slush.

He feels, though, no hint of drowsiness, only the lingering sting of the scrapes on his head and the growing soreness in the parts of his body that made contact with the cobblestones when he fell.

Shoulder, elbow, hip.

And, too, the dead center of his chest, where his attacker had struck him.

For a while he has no idea where Angelina is or what she is doing. He tells himself that he doesn't care. He tells himself that it doesn't matter if he looked like a coward. He *was* in over his head, and there is no shame in knowing that. Cohn, Angelina, even the man who had beaten him, if he was in fact what Trask said he was— they were all trained and armed, heavily armed in Angelina's case.

This was my father's world, Miles thinks.

What the hell was I doing in it?

Curious about the time, Miles looks for a watch that is no longer there. Checking the small digital clock on the table beside the bed, he sees that it is only half past nine.

After a while he hears the sound of the shower running coming from the bathroom between his tiny room and the back bedroom. Several minutes later that sound ceases, and minutes after that Miles hears other sounds, these coming from the back bedroom.

Drawers opening and closing, a closet door being shut. Then the steady whine of a blow-dryer, and then silence.

Miles thinks of the women he has known—the women he has listened to as they bathed and dressed.

Each step he has taken, a woman has been beside him. His mother first, then girlfriends, then a wife, then another string of girlfriends.

And each step with one woman, for one reason or another, has been one more step in the direction of the next woman. And the next. And the next.

Owning and running a bar helped him meet women, but not keep them. The hours were brutal, and most women—the smart women—quickly tired of the life: Miles leaving work at five a.m., sleeping till noon, and even then not waking rested.

Jules left him for that reason, and lucky for her that she cut him loose when she did, otherwise his tax problem and debts would be hers as well.

Suddenly Miles is regretting his decision to return home. What if they did find Elena? And what if Trask's plan worked? He was, after all, trying to help her, no? A favor to the man who meant so much to him.

The man Miles never really knew.

A man worth—what was it?—tens of millions.

Difficult to believe your father didn't make some provision for you in his will.

Miles's doubt lingers, his thoughts drift from here to there, and soon enough he realizes that Angelina, dressed in yoga pants and a tight-fitting tank top, is standing in his doorway.

———

She says she wants to show him things.

The telescopic baton—six inches of hard steel surrounded with black foam rubber—is in her hand.

She hands it to Miles and first instructs him on how to open it: make a sharp, downward motion with the wrist, and out of the handle slides a thinner rod, and out of that slides yet another, this one fitted with a round metal tip.

There is a click as the extended pieces lock into place, and suddenly eighteen inches of hardened steel is in his hand.

They move to the middle of his small, dimly lit room, and there she demonstrates what she says are the four basic strikes. The first two are an angled downward pattern that draws an invisible X in the air, and the second two are a level horizontal forehand to backhand pattern. She shows him how to put his shoulder behind the first two strikes to give them power, and how turning sharply at the waist gives the second two power.

From there she covers basic footwork—based on a V-shape, it allows Miles to easily slip to either side of an imaginary opponent. And each slip not only moves him out of harm's way but also brings him within effective striking distance.

Finally, Angelina addresses what targets Miles should be aiming for. Nearest ones first—elbows and knees and hands. She calls strikes to the hands "de-fanging the snake" because a blow to the hand would render it instantly useless and likely cause any weapon being held in it to be dropped.

The next targets are the face and skull, which can be struck with either the downward X motion or the forehand to backhand motion.

To attack the lower targets, she instructs, one doesn't bend at the waist but rather drops into a crouch or down to one knee. From there, springing suddenly upward and taking a step forward—she calls this technique the "kangaroo hop"—allows one to both close the distance and add force-via-momentum to the subsequent blow to the head or face.

After thirty minutes with Angelina, Miles has an understanding of techniques he could actually see himself using. Techniques that could actually work, that he has already seen work.

An angry bear driven off by a persistent and fearless bee.

⌣

Later, stretched out on his bed but not yet under the blankets, Miles can only think of the woman in the other room.

He can smell her on him, that mix of jasmine and peppermint that makes him think for some reason of warm summer nights.

He can see her, too, in those yoga pants, baggy and yet clingy in places, and the tight-fitting tank top that hides little.

Despite the workout—or maybe because of it—he is nowhere near drowsy.

Inside his head is a single thought: *Is Angelina awake as well?*

This thought lingers, and then another arises: *Might she, too, be thinking of me?*

Not long after this Miles hears a sound coming from the hallway. It is followed almost immediately by a soft knock on his door.

He says, "Come in," and watches as Angelina, dressed now in a short silk robe, her dark curly hair pulled back into a ponytail, slips into his room.

Bare feet on the old floor planks, bare legs looking pale in the light coming in through the one window.

Reaching his bed, she looks down at him, then unties the sash and opens her robe.

Small breasts, dark nipples erect in the room's chill. Toned stomach and, between a pair of delicate hip bones as sharp as weapons, a narrow strip of jet-black pubic hair.

The robe slips from her athlete's shoulders and falls to the floor. As she gets under the covers with him, hurrying a little because of the room's chill, he feels her smooth legs brush against his own.

Lying on her left side, she places her right hand flat on his chest, covering the exact spot where the man disguised as a panhandler had driven his fist.

Two insomniacs, face-to-face in the dark. Neither says a word. All Miles can smell now is her. Skin, hair, breath.

A long silence, then, at the same instant, they come together and kiss.

Sunday

Seventeen

Elena is wakened by the first gray light of morning.

Standing at the window overlooking rue de la Commune, she switches on the tracking device. Immediately five of its ten lights are lit and holding steady, just as they were when she lay down a few hours before.

Looking at the clock through tired eyes, she sees that it is half past six. Doing the quick math, she concludes that thirty-six hours of battery life remain. But since the signal will steadily diminish during the last twenty-four hours, really only twelve hours remain before the precise location of the man who possesses the tracer bills can be known.

Not a lot of time.

She has a choice: pursue the new lead provided by the man her father called Don Quixote, or set that aside for the time being and, while she still can, go hunting for the man who killed Pavol.

This option all but paralyzes her, and the powerful current that has carried her this far—a current she willingly surrendered herself to, that she couldn't fight even if she wanted to—has suddenly stalled.

She must pick a direction and swim in it.

But how could she possibly make the choice?

One beloved man avenged or the other.

Could it really come to this?

She is beyond exhausted. The little sleep she manages to grab isn't restful—every time she closes her eyes, she sees dead men. They crowd her, call to her, speak to her. At times she even flinches.

Unconsciousness offers even less relief—she slips into dreams of these dead men, their deaths are replayed, and she cannot look away.

And through all this, Pavol's absence.

His absence, and terrible silence.

⁀

Alone, Miles wakes in his narrow bed.

Angelina is nowhere to be seen, so he listens for any sound that might tell him her location in the apartment.

He hears none, though. The door to the adjoining bathroom is open, and he can see through it to the door leading to the back bedroom, which is also open.

Stepping into the bathroom and through it to that second door, he glances into her room but sees no sign of her there.

Returning to his room, he dresses, then walks down the short hallway and out into the open living room.

Angelina is there, sitting in a chair, her cell phone in her hand. Her eyes are unfocused, and she has the trancelike look of someone lost deep in thought. She is already dressed—motorcycle jeans, bone-white turtleneck sweater, black leather boots. When she senses Miles's presence—it takes a few seconds—she is startled, but only slightly. Coming back from her thoughts, she looks at him and quickly smiles.

Before either can say more than "good morning," her cell phone rings. Miles immediately recognizes the tone as the one assigned to an incoming text.

She glances at the display, then looks at Miles again and says, "Trask wants to meet with you before you leave."

"What's going on?"

"He didn't say."

She stands and steps to the sofa, on which lies her field jacket and Belstaff bag.

Opening the bag, she reaches in and removes the telescopic baton, then tosses it to Miles.

"Carry it with you," she instructs.

"Don't you need it?"

"I can get another one. There's a military surplus store up in Chinatown that always has them in stock."

"You sure?"

"Yeah."

He extends the baton with a downward flick of the wrist. There is something very satisfying about this weapon, Miles thinks. Maybe that's because it is a weapon he actually knows something about. Slamming the rounded tip at the rod's end straight into the heel of his palm causes the baton to collapse back down to six inches.

Slipping it into his back pocket, he says, "What time is it?"

"A quarter to seven."

They had finished making love around three a.m. The longer it lasted, the longer it would be before either would have to face their respective sleeplessness. So no point in hurrying. As far as Miles knows, he fell asleep quickly—quickly for him, anyway. A little over three hours of sleep, then. Exactly what he is used to.

He asks Angelina if she slept at all.

"I think I maybe got an hour."

"You okay?"

Putting on her jacket, she nods and says, "Yes. We need to get going. He's meeting us at seven."

"Where?"

"It's just a short walk from here."

Her answer strikes him as slightly evasive, but it probably means nothing, so he says nothing.

"What time does the train for New York leave?"

"Nine. We'll get you there in time, don't worry." She pauses.

"Make sure you have everything. I'm not sure if we'll get to come back here again."

Miles touches his hip pocket, where his stack of a little over four grand is stashed. "That's everything."

Angelina's eyes go to his pocket for a quick second.

"You still want to go home," she says.

Miles can still smell and taste her, can still feel her hands on him—easily the strongest hands he has ever known. He can still see her above him—the look on her beautiful face, the frame of curly hair, the sweat clinging to the bridge of her nose. Her orgasms racked her entire body, causing her muscles to flex hard and a prolonged guttural sound to fly from her throat.

Of course things have changed, and he sees no reason to be dishonest. "I don't know."

She smiles slightly. "Because we could do a lot of damage to each other between now and Tuesday, don't you think?"

Elena unfolds the paper she pulled from Don Quixote's printer tray.

This list of locations and times represent yet more choices for her to make. Which location might give her an advantage? Which time would be best?

She doesn't even know if any of the corresponding codes, once sent as a text from one of her prepaid cell phones, would even draw out the man code-named Hamlet.

Getting out the tourist's map of Montreal, she goes through the list and searches for each location. Quai King-Edward is literally outside her window. Parc La Fontaine isn't far from the Latin Quarter. And Olympic Parc isn't far from La Fontaine, but the assigned time of ten a.m. probably isn't enough notice.

She is making her way down the list when the tracking device catches her eye.

Suddenly six lights are lit.

As she watches the device, a seventh light suddenly begins to glow.

Rolling the volume control up, she hears the sound of rapid beeping. Within a few seconds, its speed increases and the number of lights swells to eight.

Knowing she is best when she has no choice, Elena is more than willing to let this tell her which course of action take.

Without a second thought, she quickly gears up.

Angelina leads Miles down Saint-Sulpice to rue de la Commune.

Crossing the wide, curving boulevard to the river's edge, Miles notes that the street is utterly devoid of activity in both directions. Old Montreal in the early morning is, apparently, a ghost town.

On the left-hand side of the street are several blocks of gray stone buildings that look to Miles to be two hundred years old, at least. The block nearest to them is a mix of restaurants and shops, as well as a hotel called Auberge du Vieux-Port.

At the end of that first block is what appears to be an abandoned building. He recalls searching all over Manhattan with Jimmy for the right place for their jazz club, finally finding, when hope was nearly lost, the small, dilapidated space on Delancey.

Despite the emptiness of this street—and despite the skilled woman beside him, not to mention the weapon in his own back pocket and the knowledge that she passed to him last night—Miles feels suddenly wary and exposed.

Angelina turns right onto a long pier called quai Jacques-Cartier—the second of four piers jutting out into the river. As she leads him past a large pavilion, Miles sees two men standing at the pier's far end.

Trask and Cohn, shoulder to shoulder.

As he walks toward them, Miles wonders why in the world they are meeting out in the open like this.

For that matter, why are they meeting at all? Certainly whatever it is Trask has to say or wants to hear could have been conveyed via a text or phone call, no?

———

Exiting her hotel, Elena removes the tracking device from her jacket pocket and sees that eight lights are now lit.

Searching up and down rue de la Commune, she sees not a single person or vehicle.

She has another decision to make, but this one is not difficult. Turning right, she heads south, but it isn't long before there are only seven lights glowing.

Wrong direction.

She turns and heads north, and by the time she is in front of her hotel again, the eighth light blinks back on.

Still, the street ahead is empty. The fact that the lights increased while she was stationary in her room means that the person in possession of the tracer bills was in motion just moments ago. But since her movement is the only cause of any increase or decrease now means the bills are currently at rest.

The question, of course, is at rest where?

In one of the many buildings up ahead? Or maybe even the abandoned building at the end of the block?

Could the man who killed Pavol have somehow determined that she had been in that building and is there now looking for clues to her whereabouts?

None would be found, she knows that much—Jean-Claude was slovenly but not sloppy. The equipment left there could in no way be traced to her.

As she approaches that building, the number of lights increases from eight to nine. Crossing Jacques-Cartier, a wide street that rises steeply toward rue Notre-Dame, she continues north along Commune. It isn't long, though, before the number of lights drops back down to eight.

She quickly returns to Jacques-Cartier and crosses back to the southern corner where the abandoned building stands. The ninth light is once again glowing steadily. She looks up the inclining street—west—but sees not a soul. The shops and restaurants have yet to open. Above those businesses are what must be apartments. Could the person she seeks be in the window of one of them? Watching her?

Stepping back around the corner and out of sight, she looks east across Commune.

It is then that she at last sees something.

Two people are standing at the end of the pier, and two others are walking toward them.

They are all too far away to identify, but the corner she is standing on is too out in the open for her to bring out the binoculars.

A quick survey of the area tells Elena that the best place for her to observe these people unseen would be the next pier to the south—quai King-Edward, the pier directly across from her hotel.

Walking quickly at an angle across Commune, she sees by the time she reaches the river side of the street the tenth and final light flicker on and off.

There is no doubt in her mind now; at least one of these four people has the tracer bills.

Elena reaches quai King-Edward's entrance in less than a minute.

Stepping onto it, she hurries past the IMAX theater toward the bi-level parking area at the pier's end. Concealing herself behind one of the thick metal beams that supports the upper level, she places her backpack at her feet and removes the binoculars.

Three of the four people are standing together. Elena focuses in on that trio first. One of those three—a man—has his back to her, but the man he is facing, the man who is doing the talking, she of course recognizes immediately.

Harold Trask.

Uncle Harold, he always insisted she call him.

She isn't surprised to see him; the longer one stays put, the more likely it is that one will be found, and she has, after all, been in Montreal for a month now. Even if Trask hadn't managed to find her prior to Wednesday night, Pavol's murder—his name made the papers by Friday morning—would certainly have brought him here.

What she does find surprising—alarming, actually—is the possibility that he is in possession of the tracer bills taken from Mephistopheles.

Could it really be that simple? Could her father's closest friend— the first man her father hired when he put the pipeline into action— have turned on him? Could the man who found her in Amsterdam and pleaded with her to quit her search and live her life be the man she has been hunting for close to a year?

A woman with dark curly hair is standing beside the man whose face Elena cannot see. When this woman turns her head to look at the man beside her, Elena glimpses her face.

It is all she needs.

The woman is the little mutt who was with Trask in Amsterdam. The mutt with the French accent. What was her name? Angel-something.

Panning the binoculars over to the fourth person, Elena doesn't recognize him, but it is clear by the way this man is standing—away from the other three and looking around—that he is some kind of security. Trask's bodyguard—yet another of his mutts.

There is, however, something else Elena notices about that man.

He is the only one of those four whose build is even remotely similar to that of the man who killed Pavol.

But aren't all men in that line of work more or less built the same?

Since these people arrived in separate pairs, it is possible that they will leave in the same manner, so all Elena needs to do is wait for them to depart, at which point the tracking device should tell her which pair to follow.

From there all she needs to determine is which of that pair is in possession of the tracer bills.

And then what?

First things first.

Eighteen

Trask says, "We're running out of time."

Angelina, eager as always to please her boss, asks, "What's going on?"

Trask directs his answer to Miles. "There was another man here who worked for your father. The only thing I knew about him was that he lived somewhere in Montreal and owned some kind of underground gentlemen's club. The man who was killed last night was found in a building that may have been such a club. According to my police contact, a neighbor on the same street suspected something strange was going on there. Cars and cabs came and went on certain Saturday nights. Women only before eleven, and then nothing but men after that. The neighbor set up a surveillance camera to make a record of the activity, and last night being Saturday, he turned it on and left it running and happened to get footage of a woman stepping onto the property, then leaving it again a short while later in an SUV. As she's pulling out, fire can be seen in the upper windows."

"Were they able to make out her face?" Angelina asks.

"The camera is low-tech, so the footage is too grainy. But the police can see that it's a woman, and they've determined her height and build. Needless to say they're actively searching for their suspect now, and this . . . complicates things." He looks at Miles. "We need to find her before the police do. If she's picked up here, there's nothing I can do to help her."

"It's possible she could have taken off, right? If she knows the police are after her."

"Like I said, we're running out of time."

"So what do you plan on doing?"

"If she is here, we need to draw her out."

"How can you do that?"

"Frankly, we use you as bait."

Miles says nothing.

"She has already gotten two men killed," Trask says. "And she might have killed another herself last night. The man found in that house wasn't killed by the fire. He'd been shot. And if your sister did send someone to take you out, well, that means she's watching you somehow."

Miles suddenly understands why Trask wanted to meet out in the open. He glances at Angelina, then back at Trask. "You want me to stay."

"You won't be in any danger. I promise you that. We don't know exactly how your sister is monitoring you, but until we find out, the safest place for you to be is Angelina's apartment. If Elena is serious about killing you, she can easily put someone on the train with you, in which case you'd never reach New York alive. For that matter, she could just as easily wait till you get home and then send her man down there to kill you. If we could track you down, then he could. Do you really want that, Miles? Do you really want to have to keep looking over your shoulder everywhere you go, day and night? And what if you have your son with you when he finally strikes? The best-case scenario is that the poor kid sees his father get gunned down in front of him. I don't even want to think about the worst case."

Miles turns away and glances toward the river. It is, he notices, as wide and fast-moving as the Hudson. Till today, the Hudson and the East River were the only rivers he has ever seen.

Trask gives him a moment, then: "The sooner we get this over with, Miles, the better for all of us. Don't you agree?"

Looking back at Trask, Miles says, "What other choice do I have, right?" It isn't long, though, before a thought occurs to him. "What if the man who got killed last night was the man she's been after all this time? I mean, if she's done, wouldn't she just disappear? What then?"

"If that's the case, then I failed. With her skills and resources, it's fairly certain that no one will ever see her again. And you'll never see a penny of your father's money." Trask pauses. "We find her here, Miles, we find her in the next few days, or we never do. Do you understand?"

Miles nods.

"So will you help us? Will you stay?"

It takes a moment, but Miles nods again.

Trask says, "Thanks," then turns to Angelina. "Keep an eye on him. Don't let him out of your sight for a minute. Neither of you leaves your place till you hear back from me. Is that clear?"

"Yes," Angelina says. She then glances at Cohn standing on the periphery.

Miles notes that the man has stopped surveying the area and is staring at Angelina with what seems to be utter disapproval.

Realizing he is being watched, Cohn turns his attention away from Angelina, but only after pausing for a moment to stare at Miles.

It is nothing less than a hateful stare.

———

Elena watches through the binoculars as the man with his back to her turns his head and looks out over the river.

It is only her need to be thorough—as her father taught her to always be—that leads her to take this opportunity to glimpse the unknown man's face.

The sight of his profile, however, causes her heart to race.

She finds the presence of mind, though, to take a second, closer look at his face before he turns to face Trask again.

What she sees only causes deep confusion.

This man is not someone she has ever met. She has, in fact, only ever seen a single photograph of him—one that her father always carried in his wallet.

In that photo a young man in a blue sweater and jeans is walking alone on a New York street at night.

A sad young man, hands plunged deep into his pockets, eyes focused at his feet.

The fact that this photo had been taken from inside a vehicle—the edges of a car door window, as well as a side view mirror, were visible—told her it was taken during the course of surveillance.

Even if she hadn't ever been shown that photo, the resemblance this man, now in his midthirties, bears to her father would have been more than enough for her to instantly recognize him.

A younger version of her father—shorter and thinner, yes, but in all other ways identical.

Her brother, Miles.

It takes all she has to refocus her mind, and when she does, the first thought to come to her is a question.

What in the world is he doing here?

With Trask and his two mutts?

Elena watches till her brother is finally led away by the dark-haired woman. Trask is joined at the end of the pier by his bodyguard, and, after conferring for a moment, these two begin to walk away as well.

Exiting in two pairs, just as she hoped they would.

Returning the binoculars to her backpack, Elena leaves her position and hurries toward the end of her pier, reaching it just as the woman and Miles reach the end of theirs. Taking shelter beside the pavilion, Elena removes the tracking device from her jacket pocket and watches the lights.

Nine glowing bright.

And the tenth flickering on and off.

She is convinced that the device will tell her to follow Trask and his bodyguard, so she waits for those two to reach the end of the pier. If she is lucky, the woman and Miles will go in one direction and Trask and his mutt will go in another.

The first pair walks straight across Commune and starts up Jacques-Cartier, disappearing from sight. It takes almost a half minute for the second pair to reach the wide boulevard. Instead of crossing it like the first pair did, however, the second pair turns right and heads in the direction of Marché Bonsecours.

The very same direction in which the man disguised as a panhandler had fled after killing Pavol.

Elena follows, careful to remain as far back as possible. Up ahead is the fourth pier—quai de l'Horloge. She can see the old hangar standing at its entrance, its orange awning with the white lettering clear in the muted morning light.

Looking down at the tracking device, she is surprised to see the LED lights begin to drop.

Down to eight, then to seven, then six, then five.

By the time she is parallel with the fourth pier, only four lights are lit.

Stopping dead in her tracks, she stares at the device in her hand. Only three lights are lit, and then only two.

This can mean just one thing.

The tracer bills are not with either of these men.

They are, in fact, with her brother and the dark-haired woman.

By the time she looks up from the device again, Trask and his bodyguard are nowhere to be seen on the long, empty street.

Turning around, she quickly backtracks. The lights hold steady at three, then rise to four. Reaching Jacques-Cartier, she turns right and hurries up the steep incline.

Five lights.

Crossing rue Saint-Paul, the lights hold at five for a moment, then drop down to four.

Backtracking yet again, she turns right onto Saint-Paul, heading south.

Saint-Vincent, Saint-Gabriel, Saint-Jean-Baptiste, Saint-Laurent—with every street she passes, the LED lights increase by one, so by the time she reaches rue Saint-Sulpice, nine lights are once again lit.

Heading up toward the Basilique Notre-Dame, the tenth and final light begins to flicker.

It is when she is standing outside a building directly across from rue le Royer—a building that is mere feet from the back of the massive, ancient church—that the tenth light at last glows solid.

A brass plate beside the door shows the address.

418 Saint-Sulpice.

Walking calmly away, Elena watches as the tenth light begins to flicker, then go dark.

There is no doubt now where the tracer bills are located.

But who is in possession of them?

Her brother or Trask's little mutt?

Or maybe both?

And if it is her brother, then what does that mean?

Slipping the device into her jacket pocket, she turns right onto rue Notre-Dame, stopping the instant she rounds the corner and doubling back to peek around it and take another look at the building down the sloping cobblestone street.

What she needs to determine next is which floor her brother and the dark-haired woman are on.

Once she knows that, she'll need to figure out exactly how to get to him.

And what it is she will do when she does.

───────

In a coffee shop on rue Notre-Dame, the tracking device on the chair beside her, its lights holding at nine, Elena is forced to acknowledge that everything has changed.

The money wasn't the only thing her father—their father—had sent prior to his murder.

Instructions he had mailed—postmarked the day of his murder—were waiting for Elena when she and Pavol returned to Haifa after the funeral.

Continue to protect your brother as I have, a part of it read.

There was more to that handwritten letter, of course, but this was the main point, the last wishes of the man she'd loved so much.

The last thing Elena needs is a third thing from which to choose. But there is nothing she can do about that.

Checking her watch, she sees that it is half past eight.

Ten hours remain before the batteries in the tracer bills begin to weaken, and with them the accuracy of the transmitted signal.

So, really, she thinks, *little choice here at all.*

Exiting the coffee shop to a significantly busier street, she finds a cab and gives the driver the address of the apartment in the Latin Quarter.

Passing from Vieux-Montreal and into Chinatown, she realizes there is something her father might not have considered when he composed that final letter.

Could his son—by all appearances abandoned when he was a boy and denied his inheritance as an adult—be looking for his own kind of vengeance?

From a distant corner she studies her old apartment.

Its entrance, its windows, the surrounding buildings and street.

Fifteen minutes pass before she has the nerve to approach it.

Entering through the street door, she draws the CZ-75 from its shoulder holster and quietly climbs the stairs. When she reaches the top step, she pauses to check for the matchstick she'd wedged between the door and frame.

It is exactly as she left it.

Still, she enters the apartment cautiously, completing a thorough room-to-room search before finally returning the weapon to its holster.

There is a stillness to this place that is disturbing to her, a silence that is, though now familiar, utterly unbearable. She is not surprised by this, but she also has no time for it, so she quickly goes about gathering the specific gear she has risked returning for: the laser-sighted listening device in its carrying case on the oak table, a small digital voice recorder, and the keys to the vehicle Jean-Claude had provided, which are hanging on a hook screwed into the bottom of the tabletop.

Stepping into the kitchen, she removes two paper shopping bags from the cupboard beneath the sink and begins to fill them with all the goods she can. She'll need something to eat, yes, but she has more than that on her mind.

Once the bags are full—food, cleaning products, anything and everything—she places both bags in one arm and returns to the oak table in the living room. Pocketing the digital recorder and keys and grabbing the carrying case, she exits, doing so this time without pausing to even look around at the place she had for a time called home.

The vehicle—a black Nissan Xterra with dark-tinted windows—is parked three blocks away, in a narrow private lot belonging to a friend of Jean-Claude's.

Placing the two grocery bags and the carrying case on the passenger seat, she hurries in behind the wheel.

By ten a.m. she has parked a few car lengths down from the corner of Notre-Dame and Saint-Sulpice.

With the five-story building visible straight ahead, she unpacks the listening device and switches it on, then connects the digital recorder to the output jack with a patch cord. Since the first floor is a business, and not yet open, she begins by aiming the invisible laser through the windshield at a window on the second floor.

Any words spoken in proximity to that window will cause vibrations on the glass that will be sent back to the listening device via the invisible beam and instantly reconverted into speech by a microprocessor.

Switching the digital recorder on, Elena moves the beam from window to window. At first she hears nothing at all. She gets the same silence from the windows on the third floor.

When she reaches the fourth floor, however, she hears a conversation between two men. This leaves the fifth and final floor. Aiming the laser onto the first in its row of windows, she again gets nothing.

It is when she aims it on the very last window in that row that she picks up a conversation between a man and a woman.

A woman with a French accent.

With eight and a half hours of full battery life remaining, Elena settles in and listens.

Nineteen

At noon they finally break for food.

Toast with butter and raspberry jam, which they bring back to her bedroom on large plates and eat while sitting face-to-face on the unmade bed.

Upon their return at half past seven, they immediately began making love, doing so in a way that was as much the striving for exhaustion as the pursuit of intimate pleasure.

The way two insomniacs would, Miles thinks.

He has never before been with anyone who shares his affliction, never looked into eyes that hold something even remotely close to the same ghostly gaze he sees whenever he looks at his own reflection.

There is, to his surprise, real comfort in that.

As they eat their toast, they talk about what it is like to go through the day feeling always just a little drunk—the most prevalent side effect of getting little to no sleep over a long stretch of time.

Study after study has proven that sleeplessness leads to insanity, Angelina points out. It is a repeat, more or less, of what she had said during the long car ride up from New York, but Miles knows that forgetfulness is par for the course. Elena tells him that she read once the most a soldier is allowed by his officers to go without "sacking out" is thirty-six hours because any longer than that renders a person utterly useless.

Miles knows this state of mental decay well—has gotten there, or at least dangerously close to it, a number of times, particularly when his sleeplessness first began. Angelina asks what he thinks is the cause of his insomnia, and he tells her, spelling it all out. There is for him somehow no shame in admitting to her his failure—*failures*, actually.

Maybe his being hundreds of miles away from the place where he had failed has something to do with that. There is, after all, a guarded border between here and there, between his cheap place in a city of crumbling brick and Angelina's apartment above this storybook city. Miles sees himself suddenly as a man who has escaped some war-torn country for its neutral neighbor to the north.

Or maybe his candor is a result of the fact that Angelina already knows so much—Trask had come to New York well researched, after all, and certainly Angelina knows everything her boss knew.

Knows everything and still came knocking on Miles's door last night.

Still undressed herself in her living room upon their return to her place this morning while he watched.

Whatever the reason, Miles hears himself speak as a man who has nothing to hide would. A rare thing, though now that he thinks of it, he wonders if it is less the talk of a man who has nothing to hide than that of a man who has nothing left to lose.

Well, that's not true, now, is it? There is the boy waiting for his father to return. The son he cannot abandon, and will not, no matter what.

Whether or not he has nothing to hide or simply nothing left to lose, whatever questions Angelina asks him, Miles answers them all without hesitation. It almost becomes a game—how much will he reveal?

She asks him about his own father, but Miles has little to say about the man because he knows so little about him.

After that Angelina is quiet for a moment. It seems she is trying to decide how best to phrase what she wants to say next.

He waits, watching her.

Finally, she asks about his mother.

"You must have been scared when she died. On your own like that."

"I was terrified."

"Tell me about her."

She'd sung in jazz clubs, starting back when she was sixteen—that was how she'd made her living for many years, and that was how she eventually met his father. She was in her late thirties when she had Miles—she was older than his father by over ten years. By the time he had left her—left to begin his second family, with a much younger wife—all the jazz clubs were long gone, that whole way of life had disappeared, and the only work his mother could find was as a cleaning lady.

Angelina listens quietly, watching him closely. She asks if that is why Miles started his own jazz club, as some kind of tribute to his mother.

He nods. "Something like that."

"How did she die?"

"She was mugged coming home from work one night. Killed for the contents of her purse."

"I didn't know that."

"How could you?"

She shrugs, then smiles tenderly, ignoring his question. "My father left my mother and me when I was young, too," she says. "Life was never the same. A parent leaves, for whatever reason, it's never good." She touches his hand. "Don't worry, we'll get you back to your son. You'll watch him grow up, and then he'll watch you grow old."

"Promise?"

"*Oui.*"

Neither speaks for a long time. Finally, Angelina asks, "Do you think the man who attacked you last night was sent by your sister?"

It is clear to Miles that this is the very heart of the matter, the one question to which he must find the answer. At all costs.

He shrugs. "Maybe. Who else would have a reason to send someone after me?"

Another long pause, and then Angelina says, "Trask is right. The sooner we get this over with, the better. Your son is beautiful, and I'd hate to think of anything happening to him."

In her vehicle, Elena listens.

There is for her no mistaking what is going on there.

The questions asked, their leading nature.

More than two lovers simply getting to know each other.

It is when she hears around three o'clock another round of love-making begin that she switches off the listening device and disconnects and rewinds the digital voice recorder.

She listens to the conversation all over again, and when she reaches the moment when her name comes up, she pays close attention.

Do you think the man who attacked you last night was sent by your sister?

Maybe. Who else would have a reason to send someone after me?

Elena rewinds that exchange for another listen, then lets the playback continue.

Trask is right. The sooner we get this over with, the better.

She presses the "Pause" button.

Get what over with?

She needs to hear that several times more, and once she has, she knows there is only one thing to conclude.

Trask is up to something, yes.

But more than that—worse than that—her big brother is clearly in danger.

She thinks again the words she read in her father's final letter.

Continue to protect your brother as I have.

How could she possibly disobey?

But what exactly might the act of obeying cost her?

What opportunities might she miss?

At four o'clock she switches on the listening device and aims its invisible beam again at that last window.

For a long time she hears nothing, and then through the headphones comes whispered voices and words she cannot fully make out.

———

"I'm going to take a shower," Angelina says. "Want to join me?"

"I'm actually kind of liking the way I smell right now."

She smiles. "Suit yourself."

Crossing to the bathroom, Angelina closes the door behind her. A few seconds later, Miles hears the door leading to his room shut.

He lingers for a moment, then gets up and puts on his jeans and shoes. The heavy telescopic baton is still in his back pocket. He removes the weapon and leaves the bedroom with it.

In the living room he sees a darkening sky beyond the two front windows. On a chair by the door is Angelina's Belstaff bag—her gear bag, ready go. Hanging from one side of the chair's back is her shoulder holster and gun. On the other side is Miles's Belstaff jacket, brand-new and shiny save for a few scuff marks on the left elbow and shoulder.

And the bloodstains.

Hearing the sound of the shower starting, Miles steps to the chair and slips the baton into the bag. Suddenly tired of the bulky bills jammed into his front pocket, not to mention what they represent—the entirety of his fortune—Miles removes the stack and slips it into the cargo pocket of his jacket, then moves to the window and looks out.

Night falls earlier here, and faster. Something to do with being almost five hundred miles farther north, he assumes. Looking down at the street below, he sees a handful of people strolling about: some window shopping, others heading down toward rue de la Commune, couples all.

Nightlife. His domain—how he made his lavish living back when he had his own club, and these days how he barely scratches one out at his friend's restaurant.

Stepping into the kitchen, Miles opens the refrigerator, looking for something to eat but seeing instead the bottle of Bailey's Irish Cream.

He fills a coffee mug with crushed ice, then carries the mug and the bottle to his small room, which is lit now by the soft, bluish glow of the streetlamps standing in a row several stories below his single window.

Standing shirtless in front of his window, he takes a sip of the sweet slush and focuses on his reflection in the glass.

He sees the bruise, like some horrible birthmark dead center in his chest, and thinks of the man who gave it to him.

Studying the scene, Miles sees nothing unusual. More couples walking, a car moving slowly down the cobblestone street, its tires making that now familiar thumping sound.

Not far up the street a black SUV is parked at the curb.

Its driver's side door opens, and a lone, dark-haired woman carrying two brown paper grocery bags exits and starts down Saint-Sulpice.

⁓

At the first sound of running water, Elena quickly switches off the listening device and lays it on the backseat, then takes the lock-pick gun from its carrying case and a roll of duct tape from her backpack.

Placing those items into the pockets of her coat, she gathers together the two grocery bags from the passenger seat and, one bag in each arm, exits the Xterra and heads down the sidewalk toward the building.

A woman coming back from a trip to the market—nothing more than this.

At the street door she shifts the bag in her right arm over to left, balancing both on a raised knee as she reaches into her pocket for the lock-pick gun.

Using the bags to block her actions from passersby, she expertly unlocks the door and enters. At the top of the third flight of stairs she pauses to place the bags on the floor and draw the CZ-75, then makes her way up the final flight as slowly and as quietly as she can.

Standing to the left of the only door in that short, dimly lit hallway, she holds her breath and listens carefully.

When she is certain she hears nothing from the other side of the door, she silently inserts the pick's serrated blade into the lock.

The knob turns freely, and she withdraws and pockets the tool. With the CZ-75 held ready in her right hand, she slowly eases the door open with her left.

A quick visual search tells Elena that this room is unoccupied.

Closing the door, she pauses to locate the source of the running water, which is coming from somewhere down the hallway straight ahead.

To her left is a kitchen, which she checks first. Seeing that it is empty, she returns to the living room and looks down the hallway, spotting two doors on the right. The door nearest to her is open, but the one beyond it is not.

From the open door comes the sound of movement.

Entering the hallway, Elena takes three careful steps, then pauses just before reaching the door to listen.

She takes a breath, then pivots into the doorway and scans the unlit room till she spots a man standing by the only window.

His back is to her, and he is dressed only in jeans. His right hand is raised to his face. It takes Elena a quick second to ascertain that he is sipping something.

On the wall inside the door is a light switch. She flips it.

The man by the window turns to face her. The smile on his face—he was clearly expecting someone else—quickly disappears and is replaced by a look of sudden realization.

And that look quickly shifts into fear.

Twenty

Miles's first instinct is to raise and extend both hands to show that he is holding nothing more than a coffee mug.

The woman—dressed in black, the gun in her steady hands aimed at his forehead—takes two steps into the room and closes the door, then backs up and presses the heel of her heavy boot against the door's bottom edge.

"Get down," she orders.

Dumbfounded, his heart is pounding harder than it ever has before.

It takes all he has to find the air with which to speak.

"Elena, right?" he says.

"Get down on your knees."

Miles does.

"Put the cup on the floor."

He does this, too. "It's me," he says. He hesitates, then: "It's your brother. It's Miles."

"Put the back of your hands over your heels."

He obeys her and then starts to speak, but she cuts him off.

"Sit back on your hands."

The instant Miles does this he realizes the reason she has ordered him to do this.

His hands are now pinned by his own weight between his butt and his heels. Removing them would first require that he sit up.

"It's me," he says again.

"I know who you are. I need you to tell me what you're doing here."

"Trask brought me here."

"Why?"

"He thinks you're in trouble."

"Did he contact you?"

"Yes."

"When?"

Miles has to think. He has never looked down the barrel of a gun before.

More than that, he has never stood face-to-face with someone who might have tried to have him killed.

"Friday," he says.

She thinks about that, then says, "Get dressed."

"Where are we going?"

"I'm getting you out of here."

"Trask wants to help you."

"Get dressed." Elena quickly glances toward the bathroom door. The sound of running water continues. Looking back at Miles, she says, "Now."

He rises off his heels and brings his hands out and up to indicate his compliance.

It is when he is standing that Elena's eyes go to his bare chest.

A look of concern immediately crosses her face.

"What happened?" she says.

At first he doesn't understand, but then he remembers the bruise. "You don't know?"

"How would I know?"

"They said he might have been sent by you."

"Who?"

"The guy."

"What guy?"

"The one who beat me up. It was just on the other side of that courtyard down there."

She pauses to think about that, seems genuinely thrown by this. But her confusion doesn't last.

"Where's the money?" she demands.

"What do you mean?"

"The fifty grand. Where is it? Do you have it or does she?"

"I don't have fifty grand."

"It's here. It's in this apartment. I know it is."

"All I have is a few thousand dollars."

"Where did you get it?"

"Trask's man gave it to me."

"What man?"

"Cohn."

"The man who was with him at the pier just now? That man?"

"How did you know—?"

"That man?"

"Yes."

"Is the money he gave you all in fifties?"

"Yeah."

"American fifties?"

"Yes."

"Where is it now?"

"In my coat pocket. Out in the living room."

She again thinks for a few seconds, looks to Miles like someone piecing a puzzle together. All the while, the gun in her hand remains expertly trained on him.

"Get dressed," she orders.

"What's going on?"

"Get dressed."

The sound of the running water abruptly stops. Elena waves the gun in a way that tells Miles she wants him to hurry.

His shirt, he realizes, is in the back bedroom. He remembers, though, that his hooded sweatshirt is in the bag on the floor not far from his bed. He steps to it, and as he is quietly pulling the sweatshirt on, Angelina suddenly calls from behind the bathroom door. "Miles?"

Elena raises her left hand and holds her extended index finger in front of her lips.

Miles freezes.

"Miles?" Angelina says. "You there?"

Elena takes two steps forward and opens the bedroom door, then backs out into the hallway, the gun still trained on Miles. He follows her down the short hallway and into the living room, where she directs him to stand by the front door while she steps to the side so she won't be immediately seen when Trask's mutt emerges from the bathroom.

Miles reaches for his jacket hanging on the back of the nearby chair, but Elena shakes her head. He drops his hands to his side.

Angelina calls for him again. "Miles? Where'd you go?" He can tell by her voice that she has exited the bathroom and is in his room.

He looks down the hallway just as she enters it. She is dressed in her short silk robe, her curly hair hanging wet.

Seeing him and heading toward him, she smiles, though a bit uncertainly. He says nothing, isn't sure whether he should smile back.

"What are you doing out here?" Angelina asks.

The instant she steps into the living room, she spots Elena out of the corner of her eye and turns her head with a snap.

The gun is now aimed at her, and she stops.

Elena removes a roll of duct tape in her coat pocket and tosses it to Miles.

He catches it. "What this for?"

Elena gestures to the chair by the door. "Tape her to it."

"I can't do that—"

"She's not your friend," Elena barks. "You have to trust me right now. Just do it."

Miles senses that his half sister is on the verge of losing her cool. Though he has never met her before, he knows what a person who has been pushed past exhaustion looks like.

Elena tells Angelina to step toward the chair. At first Angelina doesn't move. Finally, she crosses the room and faces Miles, the chair between them.

He takes the jacket off the chair back and picks up the bag, dropping them both to the floor.

The bag, containing the telescopic baton, lands with a thud.

Miles says nothing—what is there to say? What choice does he have but to do what he is ordered to do? Angelina sits down, the silk robe, held closed only by the sash around her waist, hanging loosely around her torso.

Elena instructs Miles, telling him to tape Angelina's hands behind her back. As he does, the lapels of the robe separate, exposing her breasts. As Miles tapes her ankles to the chair legs, the bottom of the robe opens as well.

When he is done with the tape, he quickly fixes the garment as best he can, arranging it to better cover her—or at least he starts to do this but stops when Elena gives him a final order.

"Tape her mouth."

Miles does, reluctantly, then looks at his half sister.

"You and I are leaving," she says.

"Where are we going?"

"Just get moving."

Miles reaches for the jacket on the floor, but Elena tells him to leave it. Before he can explain that his money is in there, she crosses the room to him and places her left hand on his shoulder. With a strength that surprises him, she pushes him toward the door.

They quickly exit the apartment. With her left hand on him and the gun in her right, she guides Miles down the three flights of stairs.

Opening the street door, she leans out, looking up and then down Saint-Sulpice. After a quick glance toward rue le Royer, she grabs Miles's sweatshirt and moves through the door, pulling him with her.

She immediately takes position beside him, placing her left hand on the back of his neck and bending him forward at the waist like a bodyguard would. As if they are about to come under fire at any moment, she half pushes, half pulls Miles forward, leading him up the street and toward an SUV parked at the curb.

The SUV he had seen from his window just moments ago.

As they reach the vehicle and she grabs the handle of the passenger door, however, a car suddenly turns onto Saint-Sulpice from Notre-Dame. By the speed with which it moves around the corner and heads down the cobbled street toward them, there is for Miles no mistaking the intention of its driver.

Intercept course.

There is, too, no mistaking who is inside.

Trask and Cohn.

Angelina manages to shove her brother into the passenger seat as the sedan passes the driver's side of the Xterra.

At first she hopes they have gone unseen by the sedan's driver, but when its brakes suddenly lock up and the vehicle skids to a stop, she realizes they have been spotted.

Hurrying around the back of the Xterra, she opens the driver's side door and climbs in behind the wheel. Through the heavily tinted windshield she sees both the sedan's driver and passenger doors open and two men emerge.

Trask and his other mutt.

The man from the pier.

The man her brother had said gave him the fifty-dollar bills.

The tracer bills.

The man already has his weapon drawn and is aiming it at the driver's side of the darkened windshield. A command from Trask forces him to lower the weapon and return it to the inside of his jacket. He does not holster it, however, keeping it instead in his hand so it can be quickly drawn again if necessary.

They approach the vehicle slowly but steadily, Trask on the sidewalk and his mutt, Cohn, on the street.

Elena feels her brother looking at her as she reaches across the steering wheel with her left hand and turns the ignition, the CZ-75 still in her right. Once the engine catches, she places her left hand on the wheel and grabs for the stick shift with her right while still holding the firearm.

Moving forward would mean she'd have to run down Cohn, and as much as she wants to do this, she knows she can't, not yet.

She has to be sure first.

Sure that this is the man who killed Pavol.

Trask is speaking, and as he and Cohn get nearer, his words can be heard through the glass. Muffled, but clear enough.

"Let's all remain calm," Trask says, as much to Cohn as to the occupants of the vehicle. "We're here to help you, Elena. Let's talk, okay? All we want is to talk. I know the police are looking for you. I know what happened last night. If you come with us, we can get you out of the country. We can get you to safety. But we don't have a lot of time. Do you hear me? Elena? I know you can hear me."

Elena lays her gun on her lap to get a better grip on the gear shift. She doesn't want to hear any more. Her eyes focus on Cohn.

Maybe she's sure enough.

Or as sure as she'll ever be, anyway.

And will she ever have this chance again?

"Your father wouldn't want you to throw your life away like this, Elena," Trask says. "I know he wouldn't. Pavol's dead. He didn't deserve that. Do you want any more innocent people to die?"

All she can see is Cohn.

She pushes in the clutch, throws the gear lever into first, and as she reaches up with her right hand and grips the steering wheel, her brother suddenly moves, lunging across the seat and grabbing the CZ-75 right off her lap.

He doesn't aim it at her; he is holding it, in fact, in a way that tells her he has never before in his life held a handgun.

Her brother's right hand is grasping the door handle; he is about to pull on it. They look at each other. She says the only thing she can.

"Don't trust them, Miles. Don't, please."

Cohn reaches the nose of the Xterra and places one hand on the hood, then steps around to the driver's side and approaches the door.

Elena knows there is nothing she can do to stop her brother, so she says, "How did they get here so quickly just now? How did they know I was here?"

A look of confusion crosses her brother's face, yet he is still clearly seconds from bolting.

She repeats, "Just don't trust them, Miles."

He jerks the handle, opening the door, and scrambles out, her CZ-75 in his hand.

The instant he is clear, she lets out the clutch and presses down on the accelerator.

The Xterra lunges forward, and Cohn quick-steps into the middle of the street.

She sees his face clearly as it passes by her window, sees the anger in his eyes. She hears him slam the door and then the rear fender as the vehicle speeds past him.

⁓

Before Miles even realizes it, Cohn is next to him and yanking the gun from his hand.

As Elena did, the man takes hold of Miles's sweatshirt and pulls him, this time toward the sedan. Trask, just ahead of them, is watching the Xterra. It reaches the bottom of Saint-Sulpice and turns left onto Commune.

Miles thinks of Angelina upstairs, barely covered by her short silk robe and bound to a chair. He doesn't want to leave her there like that.

"Angelina's upstairs," he tells Trask. "She's tied up."

He snaps, "I know. It doesn't matter. Get in."

Cohn shoves Miles into the backseat, then climbs in behind the wheel. As Trask is closing the passenger door, Cohn steers the sedan away from the curb.

They turn left on Commune and race across several blocks, but there is no sign of the Xterra anywhere ahead.

Frustrated, Cohn slams the dashboard with his heavy palm, then looks back at Miles.

His look is nothing less than hostile, and Miles is reminded of the disapproving look the man gave him back on the pier.

Trask spots a police car up ahead and tells Cohn to slow down. After a few more blocks, Trask concludes that they've lost her, then asks Cohn, "The item is in place, right?"

Cohn nods. "It is."

"I think we're going to need a backup."

"I'll take care of it."

"All right, let's get him back to the apartment."

Miles, sitting quietly in the back, takes note of how many times Cohn looks at him in the rearview mirror.

Looks at him with those hostile eyes.

Twenty-One

Standing outside the Marriott hotel on rue Saint-Jean-Baptiste, Elena looks across the courtyard of rue le Royer to 418 Saint-Sulpice, only just visible through the distant wrought iron gate.

The Marriott is a foreboding brick building, the closest to modern-looking as any building in Old Montreal. Its entranceway, hidden deep within a low overhang, is a rare dark corner in this otherwise brightly lit city.

Two hours have passed since her escape from Trask and Cohn, and during that time she made a circuit around the edge of Montreal, parked the Xterra in an attended lot in Chinatown, and then made her way on foot down to the Marriott.

Her tracking device is on, but just as Jean-Claude warned, the signal transmitted by the tracer bills is beginning to weaken. Three lights were lit—the third just barely—when she first arrived, and now only one is glowing.

The fact that there are lights in all the windows of that top-floor apartment tells Elena that it is still occupied. And obviously the bills are still there; otherwise, she wouldn't be getting any signal at all.

For a while all she sees are empty windows, but then someone passes one of them, and does so again a few seconds later. This is repeated several times—someone, no doubt, in that living room, pacing.

But whoever that someone is, he or she is too far away to be identified with the naked eye, and despite the shadow of the brick building beside which Elena now stands with her hands in the pockets of her coat, pulling the binoculars from her backpack is not an option.

When that last illuminated LED light begins to blink, Elena retreats into the hotel. She requests a room facing rue le Royer and is told by the young man at the front desk that she is lucky: one such room is available.

Five minutes later she is standing at a third-floor window of a dark room and looking at the top floor of 418 through her binoculars.

It takes a moment, but finally someone passes the window again.

Trask.

Having known the man her entire life, she is capable of reading his mood, even with only this glimpse of him.

Agitated.

She is faced again with a choice. Make another attempt to get her brother away from them, or continue with her search for the men who betrayed her father.

Only maybe it isn't a search for them anymore. Maybe it's now a search for confirmation that she has found them.

Trask didn't come here from Amsterdam—stopping to pick up her brother along the way—just to offer his help.

There is nothing that she can do right now. Even if she had her gun and launched some kind of rescue mission, chances were it would fail in one way or another—she'd get killed, or her brother would, or both would. What good would that do?

And if she is right about Trask's intentions, the man will not harm Miles.

Not yet, anyway.

If only for the reason that it eliminates her having to make the choice, Elena embraces this line of thinking—and the course of action it makes inevitable.

She must draw out the man called Hamlet while she still has the chance.

Taking one of the prepaid cell phones from her backpack, she removes it from its clear plastic packaging, attaches the precharged battery, and powers it up.

Checking the list she got from Don Quixote, she finds the appropriate time and location.

Parc La Fontaine, 9:00 p.m.

One hour from now, and, according to her map, just above Chinatown, so a straight line to the northwest from where she is now.

Entering Hamlet's number into the phone, she selects "Send Text" and types the six-letter word that corresponds with her desired time and place.

She holds her breath, remembering all too well waking beside Pavol, unable to breathe because of the nightmare gripping her heart like a claw. Exhaling at last, she presses "Send."

The reply comes through fast—faster than she could have hoped for. Its quickness feels a little like mercy.

And maybe too good to be true.

It reads: *Received. Will be there.*

Too good to be true or not, she must see this through.

From the backpack she removes one more item: a Spyderco Police model folding knife. A four-inch blade of serrated high-carbon, cobalt-enhanced stainless steel, razor sharp, and an ergonomic grip made of ultra-light, textured black G-10 steel.

No better knife on the planet, Pavol once told her.

She clips the closed knife inside her hip pocket.

It is when she is at the door, ready to leave, that a thought crosses her mind that causes her to pause.

Better safe than sorry, no?

Taking out the small Gerber multi-tool she carries with her always, she steps to the wall socket nearest to the door and goes to work on the single screw holding its cover plate in place.

Reaching into her turtleneck, she pulls the chain over her head, then looks at the titanium flash drive dangling from it.

Should Trask turn out to be the man she has been after all this time, then what else could he be after but this?

Releasing the clasp, she winds the chain around the plate bracket several times, then reconnects the clasp and lowers the flash drive down behind the wall till the chain is taut.

After screwing the plate back into place, she pockets the tool and leaves.

Out in the hallway, she finds the ice machine in an alcove not far from her room and tosses her key card on top of it.

Better not to have anything on her that could lead someone back here.

———

Trask, having spent the last hour making everyone aware of how unhappy he is, finally leaves.

Cohn remains behind to stand watch in the living room, a large black canvas gear bag he removed from the trunk of the sedan at his feet.

He occupies himself by examining Elena's gun, doing so, Miles notes, in the way one would a newly won prize.

Angelina, of course, had taken the brunt of Trask's considerable rage. She stood there the whole time, stoically, dressed in nothing but her short silk robe. Excusing herself now, and deeply embarrassed, she heads down the hallway and into the back room to dress.

Miles watches Cohn for a moment, who begins to disassemble Elena's gun. For some reason Miles thinks of a kid pulling wings off a fly. Grabbing his jacket, Miles returns to his bedroom, where he finds his bottle of Bailey's and coffee mug waiting for him.

The ice in the mug has melted, so he dumps the diluted contents down the bathroom sink and pours himself a fresh drink. He has no ice, and the bottle has reached room temperature, but he doesn't care. After the dressing down he had just witnessed—not to mention his half sister holding a gun on him—he needs a drink.

Stretching out on his bed, he thinks about everything that has happened. It doesn't take long at all before he comes around to what Elena had said to him.

How did they get here so quickly just now? How did they know I was here?

From there Miles wonders about Trask's reaction when he told the man that Angelina was tied to a chair.

I know.

How could he have?

There is only one answer to this second question—an answer that also addresses the question raised by Elena.

Years ago, while he worked as an electrician, Miles frequently did business with a wholesaler who also sold surveillance equipment. He remembers well the large variety of listening devices that hung in clear plastic bags behind the counter of the man's shop on the Lower East Side.

It takes Miles less than a minute to find such a device in the ceiling-mounted light fixture—there are, he realized quickly, only so many places in a room that a bug could be hidden. This device is significantly smaller than any of the ones he'd seen all those years ago, but despite its size—or rather lack of size—it is a listening device nonetheless, powered by nothing more than a small 9-volt battery.

Don't trust them, Elena had warned.

Miles leaves the device where he found it and steps to his only window.

What was once a safe perch above Montreal is now suddenly nothing less than a cell from which he must escape.

But how to escape?

And once free, what to do then?

———

The park is, of course, well lit.

In its southern corner, which Elena approaches first, is a lake around which a tree-lined path winds. Since she has no idea where exactly the man called Hamlet will be waiting, or even what he looks like, she decides to begin here, then work her way deeper into the park and, if necessary, walk its every path.

It is, however, when she is about halfway around the lake that she spots on a bench up ahead a solitary man.

As she gets nearer to him she sees that he is dressed in a long overcoat and expensive shoes. Covering his head is a tall sable hat.

A man as well dressed as her father had always been.

And, too, older than her father. A stout man with a barrel chest and large hands inside black leather gloves.

She continues to approach the bench, and when she is ten feet away, the old man looks straight at her and offers a smile.

A quick and warm smile, full of both recognition and fondness.

Despite the confusion this causes her, Elena doesn't waver. When she is only a few feet from the bench—and suddenly completely uncertain what exactly she is going to say—the old man, still looking at her and still smiling, speaks.

"I've been expecting you, Elena," he says.

She stops beside the bench and makes a quick survey of the cluster of trees behind it—the only available cover in the immediate area.

"I'm alone," the old man says. "Please, sit down. We have a lot to talk about."

He pats the open space beside him.

—⁓—

Miles hears a knock on his door.

Gentle, familiar.

"Come in."

The door opens. Angelina, dressed now in her jeans and boots and a heavy sweater, stands in the doorway.

She can barely look Miles in the eye. Shame, no doubt—Trask had been hard on her, and in front of both Miles and Cohn. She'd had no choice but to stand there, barely dressed, and take it all.

Like a good little soldier.

If she had come to his door just moments before, Miles would have felt for her, would have told her to come to him so he could comfort her, say supportive things, hold her, tend to her.

But not now.

There is, he knows, the possibility that she had no idea his room was bugged. And there is, too, the possibility that their encounter could have been real.

Two lonely insomniacs thrown together, no reason at all for them not to fill a few of the long, sleepless hours with pleasure.

But these are slim possibilities at best. And he can think now of nothing that has happened between them since the moment they met that could turn those odds in her favor.

After all, she came to his room last night only after he announced that he would be heading back to New York.

A reason for him to stay—what better reason to risk more violence than a beautiful French woman with dark curly hair and the slightest of overbites . . .

It had worked. Of course it did.

"I'm going to make us some dinner," Angelina says.

Miles nods but says nothing. After a few seconds, though, he begins to regret his silence—despite what he now believes, it feels a little too much like cruelty—so he says, "I'm not hungry."

"You have to eat something."

"Maybe later."

Now she nods silently. A pause during which she studies him, then: "Sorry about before."

"He's got a temper, doesn't he?"

"He's under a lot of pressure."

"He'd have to be to lose it like that. It's none of my business, but maybe you should find a new boss."

"There aren't really any want ads I can go through for the kind of work I do."

"Then maybe you should think about a change of career."

It is obvious that she has sensed the shift in his demeanor.

Sensed it, and not at all interested in fighting it.

"I'll be in the kitchen if you need me," she says.

"Okay."

She leaves without closing the door. Miles, still at the window, looks down on Saint-Sulpice. He focuses at the exact spot where the Xterra had been parked.

He keeps waiting to see it again, hoping that every vehicle making the turn onto Saint-Sulpice from Notre-Dame will turn out to be Elena's, or at least another car driven by her.

What, though, if she were to appear? How to get past Cohn standing guard—no, standing watch—in the living room?

But the point is moot; Elena never shows.

Eventually Miles starts to think about the money in his jacket pocket and Elena's numerous questions about it.

Who gave it to him? Where is it?

And how did she know it was all in fifties?

He thinks, too, about her wanting him to leave it behind.

That's what that was, right? Her insistence that he leave his jacket. She knew the money was in it. He had told her that, right?

Grabbing the jacket, he unbuttons the pocket's flap and removes the stack, then begins looking through the bills.

He finds nothing unusual about them at first. All brand-new fifties, fresh from the bank. But when he comes to one of the last bills in the stack, he notices there is something very different about it.

Heavier than the other bills—not by much, but by enough. And thicker, too.

He holds it by its two edges with his thumbs and forefingers, studying it.

Finally, he holds it up to the streetlight coming in through the window.

He both sees and remembers something.

What he remembers is the old tailor holding the bills Miles had given him in this exact same way, just as Miles was leaving his shop.

What Miles sees is a small square the size of a large postage stamp embedded inside the bill and connected by a hair-thin wire to a long ribbon that runs from the top of the bill to the bottom.

What the hell?

Miles knows one thing: this device, whatever it is, is not his friend.

Another bug? Not likely. The postage stamp–sized square looks more like the kind of card slipped into store merchandise—inside the pages of books and into the pockets of clothing—that, if not deactivated at the time of purchase, will trigger an alarm when passing sensors positioned at a store's exit.

So, what? A tracking device?

If so, then the ribbon connected by the hair-thin wire to the card has to be some kind of power source. Without one the card wouldn't transmit a signal.

But Miles has never before seen a battery like this. Nor has he heard of one in theory. Granted, it has been a long time since he made his living as an electrician. And the surprising smallness of the listening device is itself a testament to the march of progress he has missed.

Out of all this confusion and uncertainty, however, Miles is still able to conclude what his next action should be.

Tearing the bill in half, he removes the circuit card and severs the wire connecting it to the ribbon.

Then he stares at the pieces for a bit.

Okay, what now?

Twenty-Two

Elena sits beside the man she now knows is Hamlet.

They face the lake, two strangers making small talk on this chilly November night.

She starts with the question that is foremost on her mind.

"How did you know who I was?"

Hamlet nods once, as if agreeing to a comment she has just made about the weather or the view. "Your father carried photos of you. He had a new one every time I saw him. He was quite proud of you, of the woman you'd become." He pauses, then adds, "I was the first person he came to when he launched his pipeline. This was right before you were born. He and I were friends for a very long time."

"Why weren't you surprised to see me just now?"

"When I heard what happened to Don Quixote, I knew it was only a matter of time before you contacted me. I'm assuming, of course, that you didn't murder him in cold blood. Knowing him as I do, I can easily imagine him leaving you no choice." He pauses, then: "And that's the thing, isn't it? Everything comes down to choice. I myself have struggled over what do about your father's murder. It is obvious he didn't kill himself. And maybe, as you have done, I should have searched for his killers at any and all costs. But I'm an old man, and vengeance, I think, is a young person's game, no?"

Elena looks at him then. She no longer cares about keeping up the charade of them being two strangers.

She has come too far—and paid too much—to get here.

"I'm hoping you'll be able to answer some questions," she says.

"What would you like to know?"

"My father's files indicated that things weren't running so smoothly during the last few months of his life. You were late for drop-offs a few times, and a man my father called Faust was a no-show. Something was going on. Do you have any idea what?"

"One of your father's biggest clients was a high-ranking official in the United States government. No one but your father knew who this official was—or at least no one was supposed to know. He could have been a senator or congressman. He could have been a general. Whoever this official was, he was taking large cash bribes from a military contractor. The money needed to be laundered, so it was transported out of the States and into Montreal, then to Europe, where it was used to purchase diamonds. The diamonds were then smuggled into another European city and converted to euros that were deposited into a numbered Swiss account belonging to the government official. A simple service—routine, really. Just one of the many services your father provided for his select clients."

"So what went wrong?"

"Faust went wrong. He somehow found out who this official was and decided to blackmail the man."

"Why?"

"Faust, it turns out, had his own side business—moving and protecting assets belonging to known terrorist organizations. In 2004 a certain Swiss bank was caught funneling cash into Iran, Cuba, and Libya, in violation of international trade sanctions. It paid a one-hundred-million-dollar fine—chump change, as they say—but that didn't stop the transfer of money. Those involved—Faust among them—just got better at it. His particular sideline involved funneling money into Iran—money that was then distributed to Hamas and Hezbollah, which the United States considers terrorist groups." He looks at Elena. "And you being Israeli, there's a pretty good chance that you agree with that."

Elena nods once but says nothing.

Hamlet continues. "In 2008 a lawsuit was filed in New York City on behalf of fifty victims of several terrorist attacks in Israel—Americans who were in Israel and were either wounded or killed in bombings linked to Hamas and Hezbollah. That same Swiss bank was on the line again, and for closer to a billion dollars this time. This was around the time that the United States was leaning on Swiss banks to reveal the identities of US citizens holding numbered accounts. The bank decided to cooperate with authorities and froze certain accounts deemed suspicious. Funds were eventually seized, and certain men—scary men—whose money Faust had promised to keep safe were very unhappy. They made it clear that if he didn't compensate them for their losses, he was going to die in a most unpleasant way. He scrambled for a plan—any plan—that would net him a big payday, and there was this government official sitting on a large amount of untraceable cash. When your father found out what Faust was up to, he knew right away that his life—as well as the lives of his children—were in danger, so he laid a trap for Faust. But somehow Faust got the upper hand. I was in Antwerp when I got the news that your father was dead. I wanted to come to Geneva and pay my respects, but it would have been too much of a risk. With your father dead, none of us were safe. We all went into hiding, and as you can imagine, it is very difficult to make a living while in hiding."

"So why was Faust missing scheduled drop-offs?"

"I can only assume he knew your father was onto him. A scheduled drop-off can easily become an assassination attempt. That was the power your father held over all of us. He knew who we were and where we lived. He knew where we were going to be at any given time."

"Mephistopheles worked for the Department of Defense. Could he have helped Faust determine the identity of the government official?"

"It's possible." He pauses. "I'm assuming, since he was killed here a few nights ago, that he was in some way helping you."

"He sold me my father's files."

"And the man the newspapers identified as Pavol Jelinek. He was your lover? Your father had mentioned that you had found someone he approved of. He was very happy for you, by the way."

Elena nods. "Yes, that was my Pavol."

Hamlet says solemnly, "The price we pay." Then: "I'm curious. Did Mephistopheles by any chance tell you how he'd come into possession of those files?"

"No. Why?"

Hamlet scans the lake thoughtfully, then shrugs. "The problem with wanting something for so long, and paying such a high price for it, is that when you finally get your hands on it, you tend not to question its authenticity. You tend to only look so close. It's possible those files weren't your father's. Or were at one point but had been altered in some way."

"By whom?"

"That's certainly one question, yes. The other is why? Why would someone alter them? What exactly would providing you with altered files accomplish?"

Elena's conclusion comes quickly. "To send me in a particular direction."

"The files led you straight to Don Quixote, and Don Quixote led you to me."

"Why would someone want that?"

"I can only think of one reason: to draw out the men who worked for your father so they could be killed."

Elena remembers Don Quixote's sudden attack. He was a man fighting for his life, that much was clear to her. Had he come to this conclusion as well?

"Why, though?" she asks.

"Faust knew you were looking for your father's killers. He needed to eliminate any and all possible leads to himself. It was just you he was afraid of. There were others more dangerous and better funded than even you after him."

"But you said no one in the pipeline knew who anyone else was. How could they be used to find him?"

"The handoffs were face-to-face, which means some of us knew what Faust looked like. With Don Quixote dead, there'd be one less person who could identify him as Faust. And with me dead, there'd be no one. Faust had to have known that if you found Don Quixote, only one of you would walk out of that meeting alive. If Don Quixote killed you, then Faust had nothing to worry about. If you killed Don Quixote but he still somehow led you to me, then no doubt I'd kill you the minute you showed up."

Elena pauses, then: "So why didn't you?"

"Because I have information you want. And people with information aren't killed by those who want it—at least not right away." Hamlet shrugs. "Mainly, though, it's because I know you're not a killer. You could no sooner kill in cold blood than your father could have." Hamlet surveys the lake with the manner of a man who is pleased by what he sees. "I want what you want, Elena," he says finally. "I want the men who killed your father to pay for what they did. Maybe between the two of us we can accomplish that."

Elena can't help but remember what this man said just moments ago.

The problem with wanting something for so long, and paying such a high price for it, is that when you finally get your hands on it, you tend not to question its authenticity.

These words are still fresh in her mind.

But she has come this far.

Whether she has been led here or not, here is where she is.

How could she possibly choose inaction now?

"What do you have in mind?" she says.

Miles can think of only one way out of this apartment.

Taking the bottle of Bailey's into the bathroom, he raises it above his head and then drops it to the tile floor, where it smashes into several pieces.

The sound echoes sharply, and he hears footsteps in the hallway almost immediately.

Cohn reaches the bathroom door first, then Angelina.

"It just slipped out of my hands," Miles says.

He and Angelina clean up the mess while Cohn watches. With the exception of an occasional warning to be careful with the broken glass, no one speaks.

When they are done, Miles states that he needs a drink, and badly. He has been through a lot, isn't used to this shit, needs something to calm down. He even insists on making the run to the SAQ himself. He'll be back in ten minutes, and the night air will do him good.

Cohn says that isn't possible, which is exactly what Miles was hoping for. Angelina suggests that Cohn goes.

"I'm not an errand boy," he says. His eyes, as before, are hostile.

"Look, the guy's a fucking alcoholic, can't you see?" she says. "Why do you think he owned his own bar? Go get him something to drink."

"You don't have anything here?"

"I don't drink, you know that."

It's clear that she is eager to get rid of the man for a while. Why, Miles doesn't know or care.

Cohn hesitates, then relents.

After he has left, Angelina looks at Miles for a moment, as if waiting for him to say something. He just looks at her, stone-faced, and thanks her for her help. She is hurt by this, he can tell, and it takes all he has to keep up his front.

She returns to the kitchen to continue making dinner, and it is then that Miles makes his move.

The first thing he does is slip into the living room, careful not to make a sound, and grab Cohn's gear bag.

Bringing it back to his bedroom, he places it on his narrow bed and zips it open. Before going through it, however, he puts on his jacket and shoes so he is ready to bolt.

The first thing he finds in the bag is Elena's gun, which just fits inside one of his jacket's large cargo pockets.

He considers leaving the search at that and making his break for it while he can. Cohn won't be gone for long. But something makes him curious about what else this bag contains, so he digs through it.

What he finds at first puzzles him, then sends a cold shiver spiraling down his back.

A wig of long, scraggly hair, and, rolled up inside it, a fake beard that is a perfect match.

He also finds tattered clothing—the very same clothing worn by the man who had attacked him.

He digs deeper and finds something else.

Knee pads—foam rubber with hard plastic plates for extra protection. Next to them are elbow pads with forearm guards.

He remembers all the blows Angelina had thrown at the panhandler.

Strikes to the knees and forearms. Every blow aimed at the man's head had been blocked by his forearm.

And the one that hit his shin caused him to cry out.

Jesus.

Cohn is the panhandler.

Miles then remembers what was taken from him and quickly searches deeper still. He finds a folded handkerchief and pulls it out. The weight feels right. He unfolds the thing, and there it is.

His Rolex.

Jesus.

Slipping the watch into one of his jacket's breast pockets, then snapping the storm flap closed, Miles moves as quietly as he can to his bedroom door. Only after he hears the sound of running water coming from the kitchen does he move into the hallway.

Once in the living room, he makes his way to Angelina's Belstaff bag, carefully lifting the flap and reaching inside till he finds the keys to her Audi.

Cohn left the door unlocked, making opening and slipping through it, both quietly and quickly, that much easier.

It crosses Miles's mind that his leaving will no doubt cause trouble for Angelina. Again, maybe she knew about the bug, maybe she didn't. And she did help him just now by getting rid of Cohn. She even told the man a blatant lie.

But Miles doesn't dwell on that. He can't.

Once he reaches the bottom of the final flight of stairs, Miles opens the street door and looks around—up Saint-Sulpice, then down, then across to the courtyard.

No sign of Cohn.

Stepping out into the night, he hurries to Angelina's Audi, unlocks the door, and gets in behind the wheel. He knows not to take the vehicle; if the device inside the fifty is what he thinks it is, then the Audi could be equipped with a similar device as well.

No, what he wants is in the glove compartment.

The Mylar pouch in which he placed the E-ZPass when he and Angelina first left New York.

Finding it, he removes the transponder it contains and drops it onto the seat, then stuffs his stack of fifties inside and seals the pouch shut.

It is overkill, he knows; the battery is disconnected. But if there is some kind of residual signal being transmitted—a small amount of energy could be stored within the device itself—the Mylar will easily block that signal.

Leaving the keys on the driver's seat, he climbs out and closes the door. He has no idea from which direction Cohn will be returning, so he chooses the nearest corner—at the top of Saint-Sulpice.

As he reaches Notre-Dame, he crosses to the other side, then pauses to look for Cohn.

He spots the man immediately, watches as he rounds the corner and, his back to Miles, starts down Saint-Sulpice.

Turning and moving quickly in the opposite direction, Miles doesn't know where he is going, only cares that it is away from here.

———

Hamlet leans to one side and reaches into the pocket of his overcoat.

Elena instinctively thrusts her cupped hand forward, pressing and trapping his forearm against his side and making it impossible for him to remove his hand from his pocket.

"I'm just getting my cell phone," he explains.

It nonetheless takes Elena a moment to withdraw her hand.

Hamlet removes a phone and presses several buttons on the keypad till an image appears on the screen.

It is a photograph of a man.

"I was able to get this the last time I met with the man your father called Faust. Tell me if you recognize him."

The photo is a surveillance shot, so it hadn't been taken by this phone originally.

A night shot showing a close-up of a man with what looks like dark buildings behind.

It is a man Elena recognizes immediately.

"That's Harold Trask," she says.

"You know him."

"Yes."

"When was the last time you saw him?"

"This morning. Down by the waterfront."

Hamlet nods. "This is the man who killed your father, Elena."

He presses another button, and a second photograph is displayed.

It shows Cohn, Trask's mutt.

The man she could have run down but didn't because of her brother.

She feels a wave of nausea in the pit of her stomach.

"This is Faust's thug. He goes by a number of names. The one I know him by is Cohn. He's a vicious bastard. Was this man with Faust—Trask—this morning?"

"Yes."

Elena immediately relives the man disguised as a panhandler showing up on the pier and opening fire.

She sees, too, the very thing she'd rather not see.

Pavol dropping into a lifeless heap.

She is pulled from these terrible memories by the sound of Hamlet's voice.

"Was there anyone else with them this morning?"

"A woman," she says. "I've seen her before."

"Where?"

"In Amsterdam." She stops short.

Hamlet pockets the phone and looks directly at Elena. "What's wrong?"

"There was someone else with them, too."

"In Amsterdam?"

"No. This morning. Here."

"Who?"

"My brother."

Hamlet seems genuinely concerned, almost alarmed. "Miles?"

"Yes."

"What the hell is he doing here?"

It takes only a few seconds for Elena to put it together. "He's being used as bait."

"How?"

"After Cohn killed Pavol, he took the money Pavol gave Mephistopheles in exchange for the files. That money contained tracer bills, and those tracer bills ended up in Miles's pocket. He said Cohn gave him that money. They had to have known what the bills were and planted them on Miles, then brought him up here to bait me."

Hamlet looks out over the water again, thinks for a moment, then nods decisively and says, "This changes things."

"Trask took my father's files the night he was killed, doctored them, and gave them to Mephistopheles to sell to me."

"That sounds about right."

"But Cohn killed Mephistopheles during the handoff. Why do that?"

Hamlet shrugs. "Dead men can't betray."

Elena looks out over the water. "Miles is in danger, isn't he?"

"Yes. The guy's in over his head. His father wasn't around to prepare him for this the way he prepared you. Cohn is as dangerous as they come. And Trask is desperate, which makes him just as dangerous."

She thinks of the letter she received from her father.

Continue to protect your brother as I have.

"So what do I do?"

"The last thing you want to do," Hamlet answers. "Contact Trask and give him what he wants. What he's been after for nearly a year."

"My father's money."

Hamlet nods. "He'll call it an exchange. The money for your brother. He probably brought the poor guy up here with some story. Convinced him he had an inheritance coming and you were holding out on him. Which isn't a complete lie, is it?"

Elena says nothing to this.

Hamlet waits a moment, then asks Elena if she has access to her father's money.

"Yes."

"You're using the same security protocols that he used? The encoded flash drive, correct?"

"Yes."

"I have a six-digit code that I can text to Trask. If he still has his contact phone, that is. I can try to contact him and negotiate a deal for you. This way you wouldn't have to deal with him yourself."

"I'd need to see my brother first," Elena says. "I'd need to know that he's alive and unharmed. So it would have to be face-to-face."

"I'll see what I can do."

"I want it somewhere out in the open, where there are plenty of people. And it would have to be during the daylight."

"Okay," Hamlet says. "Where are you staying?"

She almost tells him that she is at the Marriott, then catches herself.

"I'm at the Auberge du Vieux-Port. Do you know it?"

"On rue de la Commune."

"Yes."

"Have you been there all this time?"

"I have," she lies.

Hamlet nods, then says, "I'll be in touch."

Later, in her room overlooking Commune, Elena watches the surveillance video captured from Pavol's button camera.

She waits till she has a clear view of the man disguised as a panhandler, then freezes the frame and stares at the image.

Blurred, black-and-white, grainy, but she can see his eyes.

The same eyes that had looked at her through the windshield of the Xterra not hours before.

She is staring at this image when her prepaid cell phone rings.

"We're all set," Hamlet says.

"Miles is okay?"

"They said he's fine."

"What time is the meeting?"

"Tomorrow at ten."

"Why ten?"

"You wanted a crowded place. You might have noticed that Old Montreal is pretty much a ghost town before nine."

"Okay. Meet me here an hour before."

"I'll be there—"

She ends the call.

Monday

Twenty-Three

A hotel room in a neighborhood called, according to the tourist's map in Miles's hand, "Quartier Chinois."

By the look of the neighborhood, that has to mean Chinatown.

Just a dozen blocks northwest of Vieux-Montreal, but another world entirely. More modern, busier and dirtier, full of shops, none of which could be mistaken for a boutique.

As he made his way through this neighborhood yesterday, looking frantically for a place to hide and think, Miles happened to pass an electronics supply shop. According to the hours posted on its door, the shop, closed on Sundays, would open at nine Monday morning.

In his small room now, checking his watch, Miles sees that it is just past seven.

A little less than two hours to kill.

A long time to sit and wait.

He begins to wonder if he should run while he can. Certainly there must be a train to New York City that he could catch. But would the fake passport still work? Since Trask had provided it, couldn't he also have it canceled? Or at least flagged as false?

Or would Trask only do that as a last resort? At the last possible moment? Once canceled, could a passport even be made valid again? If for any reason Trask needs Miles back in the States, why would he make it more difficult for him to get there?

Miles remembers the border guard running the passport under a scanner. He remembers, too, what Cohn had said about the questions asked going into Canada being nothing compared to the questions asked when one is coming back into the States.

Is he up to even trying that?

But there is, Miles knows, another thing to consider. Even if he makes it across the border—makes it all the way to his cheap apartment in SoNo—what then? Spend the rest of his life looking twice at every bum he crosses paths with?

For that matter, would Cohn even bother with his disguise? Might Miles leave work one night and find the man waiting for him around a corner? Or inside his apartment, eager to act on the hostility in his eyes?

Relocating and living in hiding, Miles knows, won't make a difference. First, it would be akin to abandoning his son, so that isn't an option. Second, Trask certainly has what it would take to find him eventually. And if he couldn't find Miles, Trask could find Jack and Julie—easily.

Call Julie right now, tell her to hire bodyguards for herself and their son. She could afford it. That might keep them safe—might—but not Miles.

That leaves for him only the option of running and hiding.

No, running isn't the answer.

So, then, what is?

Maybe, he thinks, it's time to trust the very person he'd been told not to trust.

Angelina driving him up to Montreal, the attack in the courtyard by Cohn in disguise, Angelina coming into his room that night—these were things that were done, no doubt, simply to manipulate Miles, engender a mix of both trust and fear.

He remembers what Trask had said to him back in New York.

You really should pick your friends more carefully.

Since Elena had been right about not trusting Trask, she could be right about everything else, too, no?

Had their father been murdered?

And if so, Miles wonders, *could I have just spent two days in the company of the very people who had killed him?*

Folding the map, he places it on the bed, then takes the Mylar pouch out of his jacket pocket and looks at it. He can't be sure for how long he stared at it, but finally, he picks it up and opens it, removing all but the fake bill.

After sealing the pouch again, he quickly goes through the remaining bills, making certain that none of them contain a similar circuit card.

None do.

He thinks of the money he gave Julie before leaving New York.

Three stacks of five grand in fifties.

Could each stack have contained a similar fake fifty?

Opening the bag again, he takes out the circuit card and the thin, silvery ribbon it had been connected to. If this were in fact a battery, how much power could it store? How long could it last?

Sliding the circuit card back into the Mylar bag, Miles refolds the seal, then puts the real bills back in his jacket pocket and heads out the door and down the dark hallway to the stairs.

Elena had been able to find him in Angelina's apartment, and she knew about the money in his possession, so that means she had been tracking him by the signal being transmitted by the circuit card.

How she got the tracking device into the money Cohn gave him, Miles doesn't know. But he doesn't need to.

All that matters is finding Elena.

And maybe, with a few alterations easily within his skills as a one-time electrician, Miles can use this very same device to draw his sister to him.

⁓

He eats something at a coffee shop, watching through its storefront window the electronics supply shop, next to which is a military surplus store.

At nine precisely he sees the owner of the electronics supply shop arrive.

A minute later Mile is inside that shop and pulling from its shelves everything he'll need. After he pays for his items—the man behind the counter has no problem taking American fifties—Miles decides to show the silvery ribbon to him and ask if he knows what it is.

"I've read about those but have never actually seen one," the man says. "Where did you get this?"

"It doesn't matter. So it's a battery, right?"

"Yeah. But these aren't available to the private sector yet, won't be for a while. They're only for the military and government agencies." The man pauses and regards Miles with sudden suspicion. "Do you know how many companies would pay to get their hands on this tech?"

Miles thanks the man and exits the shop, seeing as he does something in the window of the store right next door.

A telescopic baton, identical to the one Angelina carried.

And showed him how to use.

Despite his encounter with the neighboring store owner, and the suspicion it aroused, Miles enters the military supply store and purchases the weapon, then quickly makes his way with his head down to his tiny hotel room two blocks away.

———————

Hamlet, standing at the window of Elena's room in Auberge du Vieux-Port, looks down on rue de la Commune.

Then the angle of his head shifts, and Elena knows he is now looking toward the pier on which the old hangar stands.

"According to the papers, that's where Mephistopheles was killed," he says. "And Pavol. Were you here when it happened?"

She tells him that she was, then looks for any indication that he knows she is lying.

She sees none.

"Good thing," he says. "Otherwise you might be dead, too." He turns and faces Elena, then looks down at the tracking device in her hand. "Any luck with that?"

"No. The battery in the tracer bill only lasts for five days."

"Then we don't have any other choice, do we?"

Elena, in her overcoat, ready to go, pockets the device but leaves it switched on. Predicting battery life, she thinks, can't be an exact science. There still may be some juice left in the bill's battery, and a signal, no matter how weak, may still be out there somewhere, waiting to be picked up if she gets close enough.

Hamlet removes his cell phone and places the call.

Elena watches.

Hamlet talks briefly, then ends the call.

"Place Jacques-Cartier, in fifteen minutes," he says. "Do you know where it is?"

The inclining street rising up from Commune, outside the very building at the end of the block from which she had watched Pavol get shot down.

An open area, no doubt filling at this moment with tourists and locals.

"I know it," she says. "And he's bringing Miles?"

"That's what he said."

Elena waits a moment, watching the man. "Are you coming with me?"

"If you don't mind, I think I should lay low."

She isn't surprised by this.

"You're welcome to wait here."

"Thanks."

"Make yourself at home," she says.

A battery tester indicates that the ribbon battery is in fact dead, so Miles uses a foot of red-white wire to connect a toggle switch equipped with a small indicator light to a snap-on connector affixed to a 9-volt battery.

With the switch in the off position, Miles then connects the other end of the toggle switch to the circuit card's hair-thin wire.

After pausing to recheck his work, he flips the switch to the on position.

The small indicator light glows red. Flipping the switch to the off position, the light goes dark.

Miles carefully places his fragile invention into a small plastic shopping bag, then turns his attention to the bag containing his newly purchased weapon.

Removing it from its box, he sees that it comes with a nylon holster. He clips that to his belt, then slips the weapon inside.

He wonders whether he should bring Elena's gun as well. But he knows nothing about firearms—not how to handle them safely, let alone how to use them properly—so he places it under his mattress.

With his jacket on, no one can see the baton. And leaving the jacket unzipped and the belt hanging free means he can access the weapon quickly.

Grabbing the plastic bag, he leaves his tiny room.

Out in the cold, bright morning, he heads down the hill toward the very place he fled last night.

Elena once again feels a deep, almost crippling nausea.

It hits her like a fist as she exits the hotel.

Similar to the nausea she felt last night in the presence of the man called Hamlet, and yet different.

She can't help but take note of the fact that it is now morning.

She was pregnant once before, a careless mistake when she was young that ended with a miscarriage.

She remembers feeling this same morning sickness just days after conception.

Pushing this from her mind, she follows Commune, connecting the earbud to the tracking device as she does. She then wedges the earbud itself deep into her ear.

The device is dead silent and remains so as she makes her way to meet the man she had been raised to call Uncle Harold.

Twenty-Four

A wide, cobbled street, rising up on a sharp incline from rue de la Commune, place Jacques-Cartier is a popular square with locals and tourists even at ten o'clock on a weekday morning in November.

Upon turning onto the street and passing the abandoned building on its corner, Elena takes a quick note of the many ways out of the area, then heads straight toward the man standing alone in the dead center of the open square.

The man who, according to Hamlet, killed her father.

And who employed the man who killed Pavol.

More than that right now, the man who was supposed to bring her brother with him but clearly didn't.

It is when she is standing face-to-face with Trask that she feels the urge to reach for her knife, flip it open, and thrust its four-inch blade deep into his gut.

The urge almost overwhelms her, but she tells herself, again, *first things first.*

"Where's Miles?"

"He's safe, Elena. It's good to see you."

She ignores that. "Why isn't he here? That was the deal."

"He has become a bit . . . difficult to control."

"What does that mean?"

"Bringing him to a public place in his current condition would have been problematic."

"Why is that?"

"Frankly, he's a bit on the hysterical side. Scared to death and begging for us to just let him go home. He's not at all like his father—or you, for that matter. As I said, though, he's safe. You'll see him soon enough."

This is a possibility, she thinks. Yes, her brother hasn't had any of the training she has, she knows this much about him. A pampered American male, no military service, untested.

Not in any way ready for this the way you are, her father's letter to her said.

Wanting to get this over with, she says without hesitation, "How much do you want?"

Trask is caught off guard by the question. "What?"

"How much do you want for my brother? That's why we're here, right? To bargain for his life."

He studies Elena closely for a moment, then says, "It's obvious that Hamlet has taken it upon himself to tell you some things about me. Let me guess: I'm the one who betrayed your father."

"He made a very compelling case, yes."

Trask nods, thinks about that, then says, "I'm wondering, did he by any chance show you any kind of proof?"

Elena says nothing.

He nods again, this time confidently. "Of course he didn't. And of course you believed him. Why wouldn't you? He's a kindly old man, well dressed. He showed up just when you needed him, told you everything you wanted to hear. But what if I told you that it was Hamlet who betrayed your father? Would you believe me? Would you just take my word for it the way you took his?"

Again, Elena says nothing.

"Would it help if I had proof? Would you believe me then?"

Maybe this is a stall, maybe it isn't. Elena is aware of this but still can't help herself. "What kind of proof?"

"Your father's files weren't all that Mephistopheles had to sell. The fact that he had them in his possession was in itself a pretty good indication that he was involved somehow, don't you think? After all, the files had to have been removed from your father's apartment at the time of his murder."

"You're saying Mephistopheles killed him?"

"No. He was one of three men there, though. He grabbed the files, along with something else."

As to what the something else was, there is only one conclusion to make. "The surveillance gear that Don Quixote installed," Elena says.

Trask nods, even shows a degree of pride in her. "Video captured by that equipment shows your father's murder. You can see the three men who betrayed him as clear as day. Mephistopheles, Hamlet, and a thug who works for him. A thug who is an expert at disguises, though I'm told he favors a certain disguise. A panhandler."

"It wasn't your man Cohn I saw on the pier?"

"No."

"I saw what I saw."

"You saw what they wanted you to see. You saw a man dressed as a panhandler."

"So you had nothing to do with Pavol's murder. Or my father's."

"I've been trying to help you, Elena. I told you that in Amsterdam."

"Why would Mephistopheles sell you a video that shows him present at my father's murder?"

"Insurance." He pauses, then elaborates. "Because it also shows who actually killed your father. Who pulled the trigger. And who gave the order."

"I don't believe you," she says flatly.

Trask opens his coat, first to show that he has no weapon and then to reach inside. He removes an envelope from its inner pocket, opens it, and takes out several five-by-seven photographs, then offers the stack to Elena.

"Maybe you'll believe your own eyes," he says.

Miles crosses rue Saint-Antoine and enters Vieux-Montreal.

His knowledge of the area is limited, but what he does know, along with the map he has with him, tells him that if his best hope is to find some place that is busy so he can blend in with the crowd, the Basilique Notre-Dame should be his destination.

Though this location is right around the corner from Angelina's apartment, it nonetheless feels right to him—tourists are gathered outside the cathedral's front door, and dozens of pedestrians pass in clusters along a street congested with morning traffic.

Add to that the fact that the small square directly across from the cathedral is a construction site full of workers and loud equipment and is surrounded with orange netting on two sides and tall plywood walls on the other two, and Miles knows he has found exactly what he needs.

Chaotic—or at least the closest thing to it that he has encountered in this otherwise tranquil place.

He chooses a small café on rue Notre-Dame, not far from Saint-Sulpice, to leave the contraption.

Entering, he heads straight for the restroom with his backpack. Removing the pack and reaching inside to flip the toggle switch, he then stashes the pack into the garbage can and exits calmly.

No one in the café even notices him as he crosses to the door and steps outside.

Crossing the busy street, he stands on the far side of the construction site and looks for a sign to tell him where he is.

Rue Saint-Jacques.

Looking over the construction site, he watches the café and waits for someone to show up.

Either his sister will, or the people who lured him up here.

For that matter, it could be all of them.

Elena is surprised by the sudden beeping present in her ear.

Strong and steady—stronger and steadier than any signal she has heard in a long time.

Uncertain what this could mean, she keeps any hint of the confusion from crossing her face, then takes the stack of photographs Trask is offering her.

The first photo is a type that by now is very familiar to her: a still-capture from a video source.

It shows her father and a man with a beard and long hair—the same getup as the man she saw murder Pavol—standing inside the doorway of her father's Geneva apartment. It is obvious that they have just entered. She sees that the man is behind her father and has a gun pressed to his lower back.

The next photo shows the man known only as Hamlet and her father standing face-to-face while the disguised man holds a gun against her father's right temple.

A nine millimeter Sig Sauer, she notes.

She remembers the dreams that have haunted her since the coroner's report labeled his death a suicide.

Her father facing her, blood pouring from the bullet holes in both temples.

The man asking her, *What will you do?*

She can tell by the thickness of the stack in her hands that there are many more photographs still to be viewed. Maybe they show Mephistopheles, but she doesn't care.

She knows now what she has come this far—and paid so dearly—to know.

"I have the entire video," Trask says. "It is, of course, disturbing to watch, but, as I said, it's proof of not only who murdered your father but why."

"How is it proof of why?"

"The equipment also recorded audio."

She almost doesn't dare go any further. Finally, though, she says, "And?"

"Simple robbery, Elena. That's all it was. Hamlet wanted your father's money. He needed it. Whatever he told you about me last night was probably a lie, to frame me and drive you to me. Hamlet knew your father wore his flash drive on a chain around his neck. He wanted it and the ten-digit code that activated the account. He came to Geneva to get them both, brought Mephistopheles to deal with the surveillance equipment and that thug, whoever he is, to do the 'heavy lifting.' But what Hamlet didn't know was that your father was onto him and wired all the money from his Swiss account to another one he didn't have access to. An account he set up for you. His last act was to show Hamlet proof of the transfer."

He pauses again, then: "Do you understand why he did that, Elena?"

She says nothing.

"He did it to protect your brother. It would prove to Hamlet that your brother got nothing. And if your brother got nothing, then Hamlet would have no reason at all to go after him. The last thing your father said—the last words he uttered—was to warn Hamlet not to go after you, that he was no match for you. Your father had so much confidence in you, Elena. He groomed you for this—your whole life was to prepare you for this. And maybe the one thing he wanted, the thing he died for—to keep both his children safe—wouldn't be at risk right now if you had just done what I told you to do in Amsterdam: take his money and go into hiding and stay there. If you'd done that, your brother wouldn't be in the middle of this. Pavol would still be alive, and I wouldn't have wasted so much of my own money chasing after you."

"You're the one who brought my brother all the way up here. You're the one who put him in the middle of this."

"I brought him up here to protect him. If he was with me and my people, he'd be safe from Hamlet and his. And, yes, I thought maybe if you saw him you'd be reminded of what it was your father died for. What he sacrificed himself for. I thought maybe the sight of your brother would bring you back to your senses and bring an end to this nonsense."

Elena knows that a deceiver—a skilled real deceiver—balances many lies with just enough truth. And she knows, too, a stall when she hears one.

She can only imagine what Hamlet is doing now back in her hotel room.

Searching, high and low.

Would he know the hiding places she knew? Could he have learned them from her father, just as she did? Could he have been the one to teach them to her father?

Certainly she has given the man long enough to find what he is looking for.

Of course, in truth, it only resembles what he is looking for.

The actual item is in another hotel room several blocks away.

She needs to get there, retrieve the true flash drive, and get out.

But she can't do that without Miles.

The signal in her ear is now her only hope of doing that.

It is holding steady, never getting faster or slower, and this means its source isn't currently in motion. She decides the thing to do now is use this to her advantage.

"Can you get us somewhere safe?" she asks Trask.

"Yes. We should all of us get out of the country as soon as possible."

"Bring me to my brother. We leave right now. And once we're safe, I'll reimburse you for all your troubles. A reward for your loyalty to my father. It's the least I can do."

To her surprise, Trask takes the bait. He nods toward the northeast. "We're this way."

Elena doesn't move. The apartment—where she found Miles, and the last place she saw him—is in the opposite direction.

She points this out.

"We've had to move him to a new location as a precaution," Trask tells her.

Elena nods and tells him to lead the way.

By the time they are at the top of the incline and about to follow rue Notre-Dame northeastward, the rapid clicking in her ear diminishes slightly.

It is enough of a decrease, however, to tell her that they are moving away from the tracer bill, not toward it.

"Miles is this way?" she confirms.

"Yes. He's just a few blocks away. Another apartment. We really should hurry. Hamlet's thug could be watching us right now. He could be anywhere."

Elena doesn't move.

Trask looks at her and smiles. "Elena, what's wrong?"

She doesn't answer.

His eyes go suddenly to the earbud in her ear, and his smile instantly disappears.

Elena reaches for the knife clipped to her pocket.

Her move is smooth but fast.

Before she can withdraw it, however, Trask takes several long, panicked steps back, putting as much distance as he can between them and saying quietly but urgently, "Get out here. Get out here now."

He is wired with a listening device—of course he is. A quick look in the direction Trask was trying to lead her confirms this.

Cohn enters the wide square from his hiding place between two buildings.

Moving toward her with determined strides, a man on an intercept course, he reaches into his jacket.

There is, at this moment, no choice for Elena but to run in the opposite direction.

As she does, the rapid beeping increases in one ear while from the other she hears Trask say in the same quiet but urgent voice, "Rabbit is running. Rabbit is running."

A message, Elena can only assume, meant for everyone listening in—Cohn, Angelina, and perhaps even Hamlet.

Elena heads southwest, in the direction not only of the signal but of the apartment on Saint-Sulpice as well.

Maybe not the direction in which she should be moving.

One block below is Commune—and Auberge du Vieux-Port, where Hamlet is waiting.

Or having heard Trask's announcement that she was running, he, too, could be on the move.

Elena could be running straight toward any of them, or all of them. She could be leading them to her brother—if the reactivated signal is in fact coming from his tracer bills.

But what else could it mean?

What really matters to Elena, though, isn't what is ahead of her but what is behind her.

Pursuing her.

Closing in.

Cohn, moving at an all-out sprint and ready to draw his firearm.

It is now or never.

What will you do?

Twenty-Five

Like a rabbit, Elena makes a quick last-minute course change and heads down through the square toward the waterfront.

Commune being a wide boulevard means there would be many more directions in which to run than up in those narrow, mazelike streets of Vieux-Port.

As she reaches the bottom of Jacques-Cartier, her instincts tell her to turn left since turning right would bring her toward her hotel nine doors down—and Hamlet.

Straight ahead is the palatial Marché Bonsecours, but directly across from that is quai de l'Horloge.

And the hangar that stands upon it, with the automated city-run parking lot inside.

She remembers seeing glimpses of it via the buttonhole camera in Pavol's jacket. All but empty of vehicles that night—and utterly devoid of people—might it be the same this morning?

She heads straight for it. Trask and Hamlet will want her alive—there would be no extracting from her the ten-digit code otherwise, nor any hope of finding where she has hidden the flash drive—the real flash drive—that will allow online access to her account.

Knowing they want her alive means she has the advantage over the man behind her. He cannot kill her, yet she is under no such restrictions, and this more or less negates his clear advantage in weaponry.

Glancing back, she sees that Cohn is moving with the determined, powerful strides of a sprinter. A fit man, yes—his profession, no doubt, requires that he be. She will have to let him grab her, needs to let him in that close, and once he does, once he has hold of her, she will likely only have one chance.

The privacy that the interior of the hangar may offer will be exactly what she needs, so yanking the earbud from her ear, and ignoring her nausea and exhaustion and fear, she bolts toward it, pushing herself to the limit.

———

She reaches the end of the pier, passes the orange awning that reads "Labyrinthe," and slips through the first of the seven open doors that run the length of the hangar.

It is dim inside, like a cave, the light coming in through the open doors more harsh glare than illumination.

The large parking space isn't even a quarter filled, and as she makes her way deeper inside it, she takes a quick look around and determines that she is the only being present.

Not for long, though.

Cohn, breathing hard, his handgun drawn, reaches the oversized door and takes cover along its edge. She cannot see him, but his shadow on the pavement is clearly visible.

It looks a little like a downed man.

Like Pavol when she last saw him.

Elena has moved between two cars; it's the only cover there is.

But it'll do, because it means Cohn can only approach her from one of two directions.

"It's over," he calls, still breathing hard. "There's nowhere left to run. Just come out, okay. Come out and you won't get hurt."

The sound of his voice—maybe the very last voice her father ever heard—brings her quickly from fear to anger.

Her exhaustion and nausea are suddenly gone.

"Fuck you," is all she says.

"What about that wimpy brother of yours? He's useless to us now, which means he's as good as dead. Another Aureli man dies by his own hand. Like father like son, right? Is that what you want? Is that what your father would want?"

"I don't care about anyone else," Elena bluffs. "You should know that by now. You killed Pavol, and it didn't stop me. Why would killing a brother I never knew be any different?"

"There's an easier way to do this, Elena. Be smart for once."

He does not bother, she notes, to deny killing Pavol.

"Fuck easy," she says. "Fuck smart."

"You're at the end of the line. There's nowhere else to go. We've got you."

"Not yet you don't. You'll have to come and get me."

Cohn steps out from the cover of the hangar wall and appears in the doorway.

To her eyes he is at first nothing more than a black and faceless silhouette holding a gun affixed with a suppressor.

But as he steps inside the hangar and clears the glare, she can see him clearly.

Again, she sees that his eyes are those of the man in the video captured by Pavol's buttonhole camera.

More than that, she sees that the gun he is holding is a Sig Sauer.

Identical to the gun held to her father's head in the photo Trask showed her.

Not the same gun, of course; that one had been placed in her father's hand to help sell the suicide cover.

Cohn's weapon of choice, then.

And chances are, the gun he used to kill Pavol.

Cohn knows roughly where she is, had plenty of time to determine her general whereabouts inside the hangar as they spoke, so finding her precise location doesn't take long at all.

She stands still, facing him, does so boldly.

Aiming his gun at her, he takes several more steps forward, then stops.

She knows what's coming next but does not move.

His aim is dead center, her chest in his sights.

"There's an easier way to do this," he says again.

She thinks suddenly of what Pavol had told her. *Killing a man isn't easy.*

"Is that what you told him?" Elena says. "Is that what you told my father when you held a gun to his head?"

"We all have our jobs to do."

"And I'm doing mine."

"Oh, you're such a badass, aren't you? Tough little soldier girl. Pride of the Jews. Do you want me to tell you how many mistakes you've made? In the past three days alone?"

"My only mistake was not running you down when I had the chance."

"If only you knew then, right?"

"I know now. That's what matters."

"Too little, too late."

"We'll see."

"I'm going to give you just one more chance. It doesn't pay to be stubborn, trust me. He was stubborn, and look what it got him."

"Fuck you."

Cohn almost smiles. Delight shows in his eyes. "It's going to hurt."

"I don't care."

"But it won't compare to what Hamlet will do to you later. I'm going to enjoy watching that. You act all tough, but I bet you're a screamer. Frankly, I hope you hold out for a long time. I hope you don't crack too soon. I want to hear your screams. I want to see you cry and beg. And when he's done with you, after you've told them what they want to know, I get to have you all to myself. I get to make you scream in a whole different way. Eventually I'll have to kill you, but not for a while. Not till I've grown bored of you."

The fear has returned; she can't help it, but she refuses to let it show.

Hiding herself is all she has.

"I wouldn't count on that," she says.

Cohn smiles again, even shakes his head in amusement. Then his smile quickly disappears, and after making the slightest adjustment in his aim, he fires off a single shot.

The shot echoes, but she barely hears it because before the sound can reach her, the bullet does. As if it were a razor, it instantly slices through the outer edge of her right deltoid.

Though only a grazing shot, as intended, the bullet's impact— along with the shock that immediately courses through her like an ice-cold wave—is enough to cause her to drop.

Suddenly flat on her back, she is overcome by a sensation of utter cold. And then, just as suddenly, a burning pain radiates through her shoulder.

She can do nothing more for a moment than cup her left hand over the open wound and let out a scream.

She cringes at having given Cohn just what he wanted—a scream.

But she can't dwell on that. She knows she has to push through the pain—all of the pain, the physical as well as the psychological.

She forces herself to concentrate and reaches across to her right pocket with her already bloodied left hand.

The clipped knife comes free, and as she opens it, locking the blade into place with a click, she rolls onto her left side and curls into a fetal position, then tucks the knife into the archway created by her ribcage and hip and the cement floor.

A perfect little hiding place.

Keeping still as if passed out, she watches as Cohn—only his feet are visible beneath the car beside her, and the echoes of each step he takes are all she can hear—makes his way toward her.

As he reaches her, she closes her eyes, even though her back is to him. She hears nothing for a moment, assumes that he is standing over her with his handgun aimed down at her. Then she feels the toe of his boot nudge her shin.

He is close now, but not close enough.

She makes no move, ignoring the pain and the blood flowing from her shoulder, some of it spreading into her clothing and going quickly, sickly cold, the rest of it spreading like a spill around her.

Stepping so he can see her face, Cohn places his toe on Elena's chest and pushes her roughly, rolling her onto her back.

The knife is beneath the small of her back now, and both her hands are empty and visible to Cohn. He nudges her again, and she opens her eyes and looks up at him.

"Nice try," he says scornfully. "I'm not carrying you out of here, so you'd better fucking walk. Do you hear me?"

Removing his jacket, he tosses it onto the hood of the nearby car, then holsters his weapon and reaches down, impatiently grabbing Elena by the lapels of her overcoat with both hands.

He pulls her up, making no effort to do so with any amount of care, but the instant she feels herself leaving the floor, she reaches beneath her with her left hand and grabs for the handle of the knife.

She almost misses it completely but then manages at the last second to grasp it and hold it firm.

As he yanks her up to her feet abruptly, Elena brings her left hand around so it is between them.

Cohn sees this—he sees something—but it is too late.

The force of him yanking her toward him—his own brutal, careless force—is in itself enough for the tip of the knife to enter just an inch below his sternum.

Elena takes over then and thrusts the knife even deeper with all her strength.

A gutted man, no matter how strong he may be, cannot stand. Cohn's grip on her lapels, however, tightens, and as he drops to the cement floor—dropping just as Pavol had—he pulls Elena down with him.

As she lands on top of him, the blade is driven even deeper still.

The last two inches of the ergonomic handle are all that can be seen of the thing.

Elena locks eyes with Cohn, watches as the look of surprise that filled them when he first glimpsed the weapon gives way to shocked realization.

It takes Cohn a good minute to die, but Elena stays with him—astride him, his fading exhalations touching her face—the entire time.

———————

After, she grabs his overcoat—she'll need it to hide her own bloodied clothes.

She can only get her left arm through the sleeve, has to drape the other side of the coat over her injured right shoulder. But this will do. Picking up and pocketing Cohn's Sig, she steps to the open doorway and looks out.

A part of her expects to see Hamlet or Trask or the mutt Angelina approaching, or standing guard at the pier's end so she could not possibly escape.

But she sees none of them.

What she does see is the long walk through broad daylight that awaits her.

Her strength is draining along with her blood, and she knows she doesn't have much time. Too little sleep, too little to eat for too many days.

Returning the earbud to her ear, she hears a weak signal. Stepping out of the hangar, moving toward the end of the pier, the signal picks up slightly.

Turning left onto Commune, heading southeast toward place Jacques-Cartier, she hears the signal grow louder and more rapid.

Remaining on the river side of the wide street, she is soon enough opposite the inclining square. Looking up it, she cannot see Trask among the dozen or so people.

Nine doors down, and she is across from Auberge du Vieux-Port. She looks up at her windows; they are empty. She looks toward the lobby door. It, too, is vacant.

She almost wishes that Hamlet would appear, either in that doorway or somewhere on this open street. Even in her weakened condition, she could still find what it would take to pull out Cohn's weapon and shoot Hamlet down.

With that done, all this would at last be over, and whatever happened to her from then on wouldn't matter.

But then she realizes that isn't true. Her brother is still in harm's way. She has to get to him, make sure he gets back home safely. Even with Hamlet dead, there would still be more for her to do, more duties to be performed for the father she loved.

And then the nausea returns, and with it comes the realization that what happens to her from now on does matter.

If she is carrying Pavol's child, how could she not protect it?

As she continues along Commune, the beeping in her ear increases. She passes rue Saint-Sulpice and looks toward the building halfway up that incline, and the row of apartment windows running the length of its top floor.

No sign of anyone.

What the hell? Where have they all gone?

Where could they be waiting?

Or could they have scattered? But if so, for what purpose?

As she approaches the next street—place Royal—she hears the signal begin to diminish, so she crosses to the other side of Commune and climbs Royal to rue Saint-Paul, then follows that to rue Saint-Francois-Xavier and climbs it.

She has made a zigzag behind the rear of the Basilique Notre-Dame and is approaching the street that shares its name.

Her weakness increases, as does the sound of the beeping in her ear. She takes the tracking device out of her pocket and looks at the row of LED lights.

Her vision is blurred, but she can see that nine out of ten are lit.

As she reaches rue Notre-Dame, the tenth light is flickering on and off.

So, too, is her mind. The loss of blood and the walk here through dangerous ground have taken their toll. She feels as if she is about to faint, sees nothing but the chaos of spinning scenery around her. The beeping in her ear stops suddenly, but so do the sounds of the automobile traffic and the clamorous noise from the construction site across from the cathedral.

She forces herself to remain standing and puts all her will toward stopping the spinning, does this long enough to see someone approaching her from the edge of the construction site.

A man, moving quickly, but she can see nothing more than that.

Her will is suddenly spent, and she wavers for a moment and then feels herself collapsing.

She expects the sensation of landing on hard pavement to be the next thing she feels, but to her surprise a pair of arms catch her.

She wants to look for the face of whoever has her, fearing that it is Hamlet or Trask—who else could it be?—but she is quickly lost in darkness.

From this darkness, however, comes a voice that is vaguely familiar.

"I've got you," it says. "I've got you, Elena."

Miles.

She says to him the only thing that matters.

"No hospital. No hospital."

Twice is all she can manage.

"I need you to stand right now," he says. "Can you do that, Elena? Can you stand for me?"

Her eyelids open as if by a will of their own. She eventually finds his face, nods, and says, "Yes."

He pulls her to her feet. She senses from him a surprising strength. People have gathered around—pedestrians, a few construction workers—and she hears her brother telling them that she has fainted.

She is suddenly walking, her brother wedged beside her like a crutch. The next thing she knows she is being led into the back of a cab, and the next thing she knows after that the cab is in motion.

Her brother is seated beside her now, and she hears him say, "You're going to be okay. Everything is going to be okay now. I've got you, Elena. I've got you."

Twenty-Six

A brother and sister, strangers once but together now and hiding in a small hotel room in Montreal's Chinatown.

Elena had held on to consciousness long enough to instruct Miles in the best way to approach their destination—a cab ride to where they could easily catch another cab, and from there a ride not to his hotel directly but to a street several blocks away. The rest of the distance, once that second cab had pulled out of sight, was to be crossed on foot.

After making it to his room on the second floor and easing his sister down on the bed, Miles had hurried to a pharmacy for a first aid kit. As he walked to the store and back, he watched for the faces he did not want to see. To his relief, he saw none of them.

Upon her brother's return to the room, Elena talked him through the tending of her wound. It took six butterflies to close the gash, and several compression bandages held down by feet of surgical tape for the bleeding to slow to an uneven seeping before eventually stopping altogether.

Miles pointed out that Elena would probably need stitches at some point, but she assured him it could wait. It was almost noon when she allowed herself at last to rest. Every ounce of her strength was gone.

Unlike the bedroom window back in the apartment in the Latin Quarter, there were no heavy curtains the color of blood and gold hanging like guards against the daylight here. But that was not stopping the unconsciousness that beckoned her. She gave in to it the way the exhausted survivor of a shipwreck finally gives in to the deep ocean below.

Sitting silently in a chair by the window, his telescopic baton in his hand, Miles carefully watched the street below. Elena glimpsed him through fluttering eyes and was reminded of Pavol standing at the living room window and waiting for Jean-Claude to show.

How many nights ago was that now?

⁓

When Elena wakes again the room is dark, and for a moment she doesn't remember where she is or how she got here.

Then she sees her brother in the chair by the window, still looking out and with his back to her, and she remembers everything.

After a moment she tries to sit up, but her head feels as if it is full of some sickeningly dense, sloshing liquid, so she lies back down.

It takes another a minute for her to gather the strength necessary to speak. "Hey," she says.

Miles looks over his shoulder. "You're awake." He stands and steps to her bedside. The room is so small it only takes two steps to get him there. "How are you feeling?"

"Nauseated."

"What about your shoulder?"

"It throbs like hell. But the stomach is worse."

"You must be hungry. How long since you last ate?"

She shakes her head. "No, that's not it."

"What is it then?"

She ignores the question, tells him instead that she needs to ask a few questions of her own. He says, "Okay," and waits.

It takes her another moment, then: "Tell me, how did you reactivate the transmitter in the tracer bill?"

"I attached a new power source. A 9-volt battery."

"How did you know how to do that?"

"I used to be an electrician."

This jibes with the little she knows about him.

All in her father's letter.

"When did you figure it out? That there was a device in the bills?"

"After I saw you. The things you said made me curious, so when I was alone I looked closely at the money they paid me, and I found it."

"How did you know what it was?"

He shrugs. "I wasn't actually sure what it was, but what else could it be, right? I don't understand something, though. Why were you tracking the money they gave me?"

"The money was part of what I paid a man for our father's files. But he was killed by Cohn, who took the money before taking off. They must've given it to you so they could draw me out."

Miles thinks about all that, then says, "They tricked me, Elena. They told me you were crazy and that you needed help. They knew I was desperate for every penny I could get my hands on, so they threw twenty grand at me. And that woman, too. Angelina. And right after I got up here they had that Cohn guy beat me up and then blamed you for it, said you were the one who had sent him, maybe even to kill me. I fell for it. I fell for it all. I was a fool. I'm sorry I doubted you."

She shakes her head. "It's okay. They tricked me, too."

Another pause, then Miles says, "I resented you for a long time. I resented our father for leaving me and my mother the way he did. Off he goes to start his new and improved family, not a word from him for fifteen years. Not even when my mother died. Not even when *he* died. Trask played on that. He told me there was a shitload of money in a secret bank account somewhere and that you were holding out on me. He told me that if I helped them get you back to the States, he could arrange it so I would get control of that money. Just like that, all my troubles would be over."

She takes a breath and lets it out. "I probably would have done the same thing."

"Anyway, I just wanted to say I'm sorry. Sorry for all the trouble I caused you. Sorry for being so wrong about you."

"It's okay. You didn't know. Listen, there are some things I need to tell you. Some of them I didn't even know until recently. In fact, if it weren't for Trask, I wouldn't have ever known. And neither would you."

"Know what?"

"Sit with me."

Miles lowers himself onto the edge of the bed, carefully so he doesn't jostle her.

Elena takes his hand and begins by telling him of the letter that was waiting for her when she returned from Geneva.

Later, Miles is at the window again, this time standing.

A man who has been barely more than a vague memory for most of his life is suddenly something else entirely.

A shadow, or, in his own way, as close as one.

"He knew you were in trouble, and he wanted to help you out," Elena says. "He had your bank routing and account numbers, so he could have wired you money at any time, any amount you needed. But to do so would have put you in Trask's sights. As long as he ignored you—as long as everyone thought he didn't care about you— you'd be left alone. He died to save your life, Miles. He sacrificed himself so you'd be safe. If that isn't an act of fatherly love, I don't know what is."

Miles thinks about that, about what it means—or at least he wants to think about that; right now it is almost too much to comprehend.

He recalls realizing that Jack might soon be in danger. He knows that if his running would have in any way saved his boy, he would have done it and not thought twice.

Done it, and done it well.

"According to Father's will, half his money is yours," Elena says. "And if anything happened to me, all of it would of course go to you. I left instructions with my lawyer in Haifa. But in the letter Father sent me, he instructed me not to release your share until his killers were apprehended. I wasn't even supposed to contact you till they were locked away. But the Geneva police bought the suicide cover-up and closed the case, so I had no choice—I had to search for his murderers myself. Just so you know, I hired someone to watch you for a few days and report back to me. I had to be sure you were safe. I knew the fact that you were in such financial trouble would work to your advantage. Obviously, a man with as many debts as you, working the jobs you were working, didn't have twenty-five million euros sitting in a Swiss bank."

This is the first time Miles has heard in exact terms the nature of his father's wealth.

He can't even imagine that amount of money, or even what he would do with it once his debts were cleared and his son's future was set.

Elena continues. "As long as Trask knew you were struggling—and trust me, he kept tabs on you, too—you would be left out of this. Or at least that's what we were counting on."

Miles remembers the early morning meeting on the end of the pier. He now understands the real reason why Trask hadn't just relayed what he had to relay with a phone call.

If Elena was watching, Trask wanted her to see her hapless brother in harm's way.

He remembers, too, Cohn playing lookout—when he wasn't staring at Miles with open hostility.

"You said Cohn was the one who killed our father."

"Yeah."

"You know this for certain."

"Yes."

"Jesus," Miles says. He shakes his head.

"You couldn't have known it," Elena says. "He was a pro. And anyway, if you had known, what could you have done?"

Hard to argue with that, especially with the memory of Cohn beating him still so fresh in his mind.

"This Hamlet guy," Miles says, "whatever his real name is, he's the one who ordered Cohn to do it. To shoot our father."

"Yes. He stood by and watched Cohn pull the trigger."

"How do you know this for certain?"

"I saw still-captures from surveillance video."

Miles sees no reason to doubt her. Of all the people in his world right now, she is the only one he trusts implicitly.

"So Hamlet and Trask are partners."

Elena nods. "Yes. They've been after our father's money for a long time."

"Trask said our father helped terrorist groups move money into the United States."

"That's a lie. Our father did a lot of shady things for his clients, but there was a line he wouldn't cross. Helping people avoid taxes was one thing, getting people killed was something else. If anything, that's a side line that Trask and Hamlet were in. I suspect they both owe the wrong people a lot of money."

Miles considers that, then says, "So what do we do?"

"*We* do nothing. You need to get out of this city as soon as possible. You need to go somewhere and lie low. It doesn't matter where, and I probably shouldn't know where, just to be safe. You still have the money Cohn gave you, right? You can survive on that till I figure out what to do."

Miles shakes his head. "No, I'm not doing that. I'm not going into hiding."

"I've already lost someone, Miles. I can't lose anyone else. This is the way it has to be."

He looks over his shoulder at her. "Who did you lose?" he asks gently.

"His name was Pavol."

He remembers that name from the article in the paper. "He was your boyfriend."

"Yes."

"I'm sorry. But you can't expect me to just go somewhere and lie low while you go chasing after Hamlet and Trask by yourself."

"No offense, but I'm better at this than you are."

"Maybe, but I'm not the one with a sliced-up shoulder. You wouldn't even make it down the stairs on your own. And anyway, Trask can always go after my son, use him to get me to cooperate. The only way I see any of us ever being safe again is if Trask and his partner are dead."

Elena is reminded of the warning Pavol had given her during their last night together.

"It's not as easy as that," she says. "Killing, I mean. It isn't an easy thing to do."

"If it means saving the life of my son, I'll do what I have to. Jesus, for all we know, Trask could be on his way to New York right now."

"He's not."

Miles turns to face her. "How can you know for certain?"

"Because chances are he thinks he has the thing he's been after all this time."

"What thing?"

"A flash drive that allows online access to my numbered account in Switzerland."

"He can access your account?"

"No. The flash drive he has is useless. But he thinks it's the drive he wants. The drive can only be accessed with a ten-digit code. To get the code, he needs me. Not you, not your son in New York. Me."

"Why does he think he has the drive he wants?"

"Because I led Hamlet to where I hid the one I wanted him to find. It contains our father's files and some surveillance video, nothing more."

"If it was hidden, how can you be sure he found it?"

"If I knew where to hide it, he'd know where to look for it. They have the drive, I know it, and as long as I'm in this city, neither of them are going anywhere."

"What if they already checked out the drive and know it isn't the one they want?"

"The instant it's connected to a computer, any computer, a prompt window automatically opens and asks for the code. You have thirty seconds to enter it, and if you don't, online access is permanently blocked and can only be unblocked by the account holder going to the bank in person. It's a fail-safe. Trask and Hamlet know this, so they know not to connect the drive to any computer until they have the code."

"So where's the real drive?"

"Somewhere safe."

"We should get it while we can. I'll get it now and bring it back here."

"No. I'm not letting you out of my sight. And I'd appreciate you not letting me out of yours. Deal?"

Miles nods. "Deal."

"We'll go later. I need to rest a few more hours. Then we'll get the drive and get out of the city. Once I've had a few days to heal up a little more, we'll figure out our next step. Does that sound good to you?"

"Yeah."

"In the meantime, Miles, I need you to do something for me."

"What?"

"I need you to make another run to the pharmacy."

"Sure. What do you need?"

"I'm thinking I should take a pregnancy test."

Twenty-Seven

Ten minutes later, in the cramped bathroom, Elena is looking at an e.p.t test stick.

Nothing at first, but according to the instructions it takes two minutes.

A long time.

She is reminded of the countdown that ran in her head as she downloaded her father's files back in that abandoned building.

Finally, something begins to emerge within the round-shaped window at the end of the stick.

A plus sign, indicating a positive result.

She closes her eyes to cut off the tears suddenly building in them, then tosses the stick into the wastebasket.

When those tears have fallen and there are no more to replace them, she returns to the room and sits on the edge of the mattress.

"Well?" Miles asks.

She nods once.

"Maybe we should just get out of here now," he suggests after a moment. "Leave the flash drive where it is and come back for it later. I mean, this changes things, don't you think?"

"What's his name?" Elena says.

"Who?"

"Your son."

"Jack."

She says nothing for a while, then, "No, we stick to our plan."

"What about your child? If something happens to you . . ." He doesn't finish his thought, doesn't have to.

"This has to end, Miles. It has to end tonight."

He hesitates, then nods in agreement. "Okay. What do you have in mind?"

"Call Trask, tell him you know where I am and that you want to betray me for a cut of the money."

"Why would he believe me?"

"Because he has no choice. And because he knows he won't have to honor any deal he makes with you."

"He'll just kill me instead."

"Exactly."

Miles thinks of his son, and the potential—the real potential now, more so than ever before—of the boy being yet another child whose father simply disappeared, just as Miles's own father had.

Would Jack ever learn the truth someday? That his father died to protect him? Would he ever get the chance to forgive his father the way Miles has forgiven his?

"We won't give him that chance, though," Miles says. "Right?"

Elena nods. "Right." She says nothing for a moment, then: "Have you ever used a handgun before, Miles?"

"No."

"I'm going to teach you, okay? I'm going to show you what to do."

Miles glances at the nightstand. On it are two handguns—the one he took from Elena when she tried to rescue him, and the one Elena had with her when he got her back to his room.

"You got that other gun from Cohn?" he asks.

"Yeah."

"It's not the one he used to . . ." He can't finish the thought, but she knows what he's thinking.

"To kill our father? No. He had to leave that gun behind; otherwise, it wouldn't look like a suicide."

"Oh, yeah."

"But I think it's the gun he used to kill my Pavol."

Miles says nothing for a moment. All it takes is for him to think once more about his son.

"Yeah, okay," he says. "Show me exactly what to do."

———

Another crash course for Miles, given to him by yet another woman he has only recently met. A woman who clearly knows her stuff, just as Angelina did.

Afterward, he winds what remains on the roll of surgical tape tight around Elena's shoulder like a harness in an attempt to keep her wound from reopening as she moves. While she puts her sweater back on, its large bloodstain already caked, Miles holsters his telescopic baton and slides Cohn's handgun—a Sig Sauer, Elena called it, the suppressor still affixed to its muzzle—into the waist of his jeans.

His Belstaff jacket conceals both weapons nicely, and Cohn's coat, oversized and then some on Elena, keeps her weapon and bloodied clothes hidden as well.

It is almost midnight when they leave the hotel. As they step into the cold night air, Miles realizes that he doesn't know what their exact escape plan is, and that, considering Elena's condition, maybe he should. She tells him they can't head for the train station because chances are it is being watched. It would be the same with buses. Too risky, and they have come too far to blow it now.

Miles asks about the black Xterra she was driving earlier. She tells him that Cohn had placed a magnetic tracking device under its rear bumper when she drove past him yesterday. She'd heard him slap the vehicle and knew immediately what that meant. She found the device easily and could have removed and destroyed it, but she left it in place so that the vehicle, parked in an unmanned lot a dozen blocks away, would serve as a diversion—Trask, after all, didn't have an unlimited number of people working for him, and the more resources he was forced to squander, the better.

How she planned on them getting out of the city, once they got the flash drive from the hotel, was by a series of cabs. Drivers keep records, and while switching taxis wouldn't necessarily cover their tracks entirely, it would certainly make tracing their movements a laborious—and time-wasting—endeavor.

After they hopscotched their way out of Montreal in this manner, they would be free to catch a bus or a train to wherever they wanted to go. Once they were safe, Miles could then call his ex-wife and warn her about what might be coming her way—Cohn and Hamlet, after all, might eventually become desperate enough to play that hand. But this would give Miles's ex plenty of time to either flee or arrange private security to protect herself and their son.

This makes it even clearer to Miles that Elena knows her stuff. He envies her skills and knowledge—envies, too, the time she got to spend with their father, the man who obviously taught her much of what she knows. It isn't a hateful envy that he feels, or jealousy. If anything, he looks forward to hearing more about the man he barely knew, the man who sacrificed so much for his son.

Miles thinks to tell Elena this, but before he can say anything, she turns onto a side street.

As he follows her, he hears the sound of an engine suddenly gunning.

He spins to face the sound and sees a vehicle turning the same corner they just turned.

But not just any vehicle.

An Audi A4.

It races toward them, and though Miles and Elena are on a sidewalk, he at first fears that the vehicle is on a collision course.

But at the last possible moment its driver applies the brakes, and the Audi skids to an abrupt stop, its nose just inches from the curb—and mere feet from them.

Miles instinctively grabs Elena's arm and starts to run. He has all but forgotten that he is armed. Only as the driver and passenger doors of the Audi open and Angelina and Trask emerge—Angelina with her gun drawn—does Miles even remember the Sig in his possession.

By the time he begins reaching into his jacket— his movements are by no means expert—Miles sees that Trask has his handgun already drawn and aimed.

Angelina, too, has her weapon trained squarely on the same target.

Miles.

The threat is obvious: Elena makes a move, and her brother, not she, gets shot.

After all, they need to take her alive.

"No more running," Trask says to her. "End of the line." Then, to Miles: "Take your hand out of your jacket, slowly."

Miles has no choice but to comply. Helpless, he looks around for witnesses—any*one*, any*thing*. But there is no one but the four of them on this empty street.

He wants to ask how they found them. The need to know somehow competes with—and almost wins out against—the fear spreading deep in his gut.

A glance at Elena's face tells him that she shares his curiosity—more of a disbelief than curiosity—but if she also shares his fear, it does not show on her face.

She stares at Trask with cold and steady eyes.

Before Miles can speak, however, Trask says to Elena, "You're not the only one with access to the best equipment money can buy." He pauses, then looks at Miles. "I seem to remember warning you about picking your friends more carefully. I guess I should have warned you about accepting gifts from strangers as well."

It takes a second, but finally Miles understands. He glances at the jacket hanging open around his torso.

Not a gift, exactly, since he paid for it, but he gets Trask's point.

If a tracking device could be hidden in a fifty-dollar bill, then it could also be hidden inside a jacket.

Is the item in place? Trask had asked Cohn as they gave up on chasing Elena.

It is.

I think we'll need a backup, just in case.

I'll take care of it, Cohn assured him.

Miles and Elena at first refuse to move, but a simple nod by Trask sends Angelina to Miles's side. She aims her gun at his head.

Just as Cohn had aimed his at their father's.

Miles and Elena are quickly ushered into the back of the Audi. Trask is behind the wheel, Angelina in the passenger seat. Kneeling and turning around, she faces the back, her weapon again aimed at Miles.

No point, he realizes, in aiming it at Elena; one bump in the road could cause a misfire, and then the information Trask has been after for almost a year would be forever lost.

The Audi speeds for several blocks, then, on a secluded, poorly lit residential street, Trask pulls to the curb and kills the motor and lights.

Getting out, he moves to the back door and opens it, leans in, and binds Elena's wrists together with wire, and then leans across her and does the same with Miles. The wire, Miles notes, is thin but very sharp.

Angelina, still in the passenger seat, keeps her gun aimed at Miles's head. She refuses to look him in the eye, though, keeping hers instead fixed on Elena.

But Miles can see Angelina's eyes clearly.

Her left eye has a crescent of black beneath it, and one corner of her lower lip is split and swollen.

Trask's wrath, no doubt, at letting Miles escape.

To his surprise, Miles actually feels angered by this.

When Trask is done binding Miles's wrists, he leans back out and stands. Just as he does, a set of headlights fill the Audi's interior from behind. The headlights go out, and Miles glances back and sees the wide, shining grille of a vintage Mercedes-Benz sedan.

Its driver's door opens, and Hamlet emerges. He steps back to the sedan's rear door and opens it, then, looking around, waits.

Miles and Elena are moved quickly, and once in the backseat of the Mercedes, dark hoods are placed over their heads.

Nothing happens for a moment, and then Miles hears Angelina say, "I have my gun pressed against your sister's shoulder, Miles. You move and I shoot. Do you understand?"

Miles asks what's going on, but no one answers. It isn't long before he feels something—the sleeve of his jacket is being unbuttoned and pulled up his forearm.

Are they after my father's watch again?

Wait, it's in my jacket pocket.

But then he feels a pinch—the unmistakable sensation of the tip of a syringe needle piercing his skin and entering deep into the radial muscle—and he understands. He winces sharply through gritted teeth as the needle lingers there for a long moment before finally being pulled out.

Then he feels the muzzle of the gun pressing against his forehead. Angelina says, "I have my gun to your brother's head, Elena. You move and I shoot. Understand?"

There is for Miles very little after that, just the sense of the Mercedes carrying them along, first turning through city streets and then finally at steady highway speed.

Soon enough Miles feels Elena's shoulder touch his. Then he feels himself leaning against her, as if pulled toward her by gravity.

Then the powerful tranquilizer injected into him takes hold, and he collapses into nothingness.

———

Later, for Elena, nothing more than fragments of semiconsciousness.

The Mercedes coming to stop, the back door opening, then the sensation of her being dragged along, her shuffling feet barely able to keep up, the handlers on either side of her impatient and rough.

Around her, cold night and the steady hiss of wind moving through trees.

Then she's inside a house, and then she's being led down plank stairs.

Seated in a hard chair, her wrists are bound by sharp wire again, this time behind her. She can barely lift her head, and her eyelids feel as if they are glued shut. She wants to open them but simply cannot.

Will I ever be able to again? she wonders.

Her heart is pounding, and the throbbing in her right shoulder is like its echo delayed by distance.

There is nothing else for what feels like a long time, and then Elena hears the sound of scuffling feet and grunts of exertion. Miles is being brought in and placed nearby. At least she hopes that's what it is.

I'm not letting you out of my sight. And I'd appreciate you not letting me out of yours.

All they have now is, after all, each other.

Tuesday

Twenty-Eight

Murky light greets Elena when she is finally able to open her eyes.

Directly across from her, slumped forward in a chair, is her brother. Like her, his hands are bound behind him. It takes a moment for her to realize that he is speaking, and another for his words to actually make sense.

"You okay? Elena. Are you okay?"

Still groggy, she nods, then looks down at her right shoulder. She is dressed only in her camisole and jeans, her bloodied sweater gone. The cast of tape her brother had wound around her like a harness prior to leaving the hotel room has been removed, replaced by a single large bandage.

Crisp and white, the gauze shows no hint of seeping blood.

"Someone stitched you up," Miles explains.

Elena looks at him. She finds it difficult to keep her head up and senses it is the same for him.

"Who?" she says.

"I don't know. He had one of those black leather bags, though. Like doctors used to carry. So a doctor, I guess."

"When was this?"

"I'm not sure. A while ago, I guess. I'd wake up for a bit, and then the next thing I know I'm waking up all over again. Jesus, my head is killing me."

"Any idea where we are?"

"No."

Elena looks around. The room is obviously a basement. The floor is uneven concrete, an indication of years of frost heave, and the walls are fieldstone and crumbling mortar. In a far corner is a furnace the size of a ship's smokestack, and not far from that is a large, oval-shaped tank, most likely for heating oil.

So, the basement of an old house.

She finds only one window, directly above the tank, where the top edge of the stone wall meets the wood beam ceiling. It is boarded over. The source of the murky light, she realizes, is a small quartz heater standing several feet away.

There is a sense of responsibility that she feels for the man across from her. And it is a sense she cannot shake or ignore. She wants to tell him something—anything—but can think of nothing to say that would come close to offering comfort or even hope.

She is, after all, terrified, and if she, with her military training and all that her father and Pavol had taught her, is terrified, what must her brother, a man who has never been tested, be feeling?

She remembers what she read in the newspaper the other day— the Canadian journalist's time in a Tehran jail and how the lyrics of Leonard Cohen sustained him in his moments of despair. She tells Miles about this, then asks him if he knows any Leonard Cohen songs.

"I don't," he says. "Do you?"

She shakes her head. "No. So what songs do you know?"

"Old jazz standards, mainly. When I was a kid, my mother used to sing them to me."

Elena thinks about that for a moment. "Is that why you started your club? For her?"

Miles shrugs.

"When did she die?" Elena asks.

"I was sixteen."

"I'm sorry. I remember the day Father found out that she was killed. He immediately sent people to make sure it was really an accident. He wanted to pay his respects at her funeral but of course couldn't. You understand now why, right?"

Miles nods. "What about your mother?"

"She died when I was a girl."

"How?"

"Cancer."

"I'm sorry."

Elena thanks him, pauses for a long moment, and then says, "Up till now I've only been a child. Someone else's child. My mother's, and then after she was gone, our father's. It was how everyone saw me; it was how I saw myself, for the longest time. Even after he was gone, I was still his child. What I had to do, I had to because I was his child." She pauses again, then: "The idea of being a parent—of having a child of my own—scares the hell out of me."

Miles wonders why she is talking as if they are going to get out of this, as if she will live to give birth.

Does she know something I don't?

Finally, he says, "It scared me, too. When I first found out. Scared the hell out of me. It actually still does."

Neither say anything for a while, just look at each other.

Miles can no longer avoid the obvious.

"They're going to kill us, aren't they? When they get what they want, we're both dead, right?"

"Yes."

"And they'll make it look like suicide? Or a murder-suicide. I killed you, then myself. Two heirs fighting over their dead father's money?"

"That sounds about right."

Miles cringes, but less at the idea of dying than the idea of his son thinking his father had killed himself.

Growing up with that curse, living the rest of his life with it.

The father who had promised to come back no matter what.

It is a thought that is simply too much to bear.

And yet it is this thought that tells Miles what he has to do. Must do.

"I'm thinking there might be a way for you to get out of this," he says.

"What do you mean?"

"Offer to take them to where you hid the real flash drive. Maybe you'll get lucky on the way there and see a chance to make a break for it. They need you alive, so that gives you the advantage, right? Like you said, you're better at this than I am. Maybe you'll even see a chance to kill them all and end this once and for all."

"And what if they decide to kill you before they take me back to Montreal? Or if one of them stays behind with orders to kill you if the others don't come back? What then?"

It only takes Miles a second.

"Then you take care of my son, Elena. You provide for him and protect him. And you tell him that I didn't abandon him, that what I did was for him. Will you do that for me? When he's old enough to understand, will you tell him what happened? Will you promise to do that, Elena?"

She shakes her head. "I'm not leaving you, Miles."

"It's our only chance. So that makes it our only choice."

"I can't do that. I can't let them kill you. I won't." Tears—strangely hot tears—fill her eyes suddenly.

"If I die, Elena, my son lives. But if you die, then your child dies with you. Pavol's child."

"Miles, don't."

"It's the only way, Elena."

"I won't let them kill you."

"It doesn't matter what happens to me. Just say you'll take care of Jack. Take care of yourself and your baby and my son. That's all that matters now."

The tears spring from her eyes and stream down her face. "We'll think of another way."

"There is no other way."

"I can't lose you. You're all I have now."

"It's me or it's the both of us. You know I'm right."

Before Elena can respond to that, Miles raises his head and yells toward the ceiling, "Hello! Anybody up there? Hello!"

Elena whispers, "Miles, don't. Please."

He ignores her and keeps calling till the door at the top of the plank stairs finally opens.

A corridor of harsh light is cast downward. Though it doesn't reach them, it nevertheless causes both Miles and Elena to wince and turn their heads away.

Someone starts down the stairs. When Miles looks back, he sees that it's Angelina.

She stops a few steps from the bottom. Being backlit, her face is all but invisible. Miles remembers then the blackened eye and swollen lip but pushes the thought of them from his mind.

"Tell your boss I have a deal to make," he says. "Tell him I want to talk to him. Now."

Angelina hesitates, looks first at Miles, then Elena, and then back at Miles. Finally she turns and starts up the stairs. The door closes.

They are in near darkness again, and the long silence between them is eventually broken by Elena.

"Don't do this," she says.

"When you see a chance, you take it. Do you hear me? You take it and you kill them and you get out of there. And don't come back for me. Don't even think about it. Do you understand? Elena, do you understand?"

She does not respond.

"I'm your older brother, so you have to listen to me. That's the way it goes. Okay?"

Before Elena can protest, the door at the top of the stairs opens again.

Trask makes his way down, followed by Angelina and, finally, the man called Hamlet.

The three of them stand shoulder to shoulder like a wall, facing their captives.

Miles first looks at Hamlet, the man who ordered his father's murder.

He is an old man, yes, but he has a stout torso like a barrel and short legs and arms. His hands are large and powerful.

Dressed in a suit and wearing expensive shoes that shine even in this dim light.

"You have something you want to tell us, Miles?" Trask says.

Miles nods, then, looking finally at Trask, tells him to pull up a chair.

Twenty-Nine

Trask is seated facing Miles, his back to Elena.

Hamlet is standing not far from him. Angelina, several feet away, is positioned between the faint glow from the quartz heater and the patch of light at the bottom of the stairs.

"It's a bluff," Hamlet says.

Trask watches Miles's face for a moment, then says to Angelina, "Get me the computer."

"You connect that drive before we have the code and that's it, we're locked out," Hamlet warns.

"Just bring me a computer!" Trask snaps.

Angelina—ever-obedient Angelina—turns and quickly climbs the stairs.

Trask looks at Miles again. "You're not lying to me, are you, son? Because that wouldn't be very smart of you."

"The drive you have is useless. Elena said she hid the real one somewhere else."

"She told you that?"

"Yes."

"Where is it hidden?"

"I don't know."

"He's lying," Hamlet says.

Trask smiles—it is meant to be the reassuring smile of an old family friend. "I believe my partner here thinks you may be lying."

"Check it out and you'll see."

"And if it turns out to be the real drive, we're screwed," Hamlet says. "We only have thirty seconds to punch in the code. Let me get it out of her first, just in case."

Still looking at Miles, Trask says, "You hear that? He wants to get the code out of your sister first. Do you understand what that means?"

Miles says nothing.

"Have you seen my friend's hands?" Trask asks. He tells Hamlet to hold up his hands so Miles can see them.

The old man raises his hands. Eight thick fingers and two fat thumbs radiate from palms as wide as the pockets of catcher's mitts.

"His father was a butcher," Trask explains. "Which means back when he was a kid, before he made his way out of his miserable hometown, he worked in his father's butcher shop. So making your sister talk would involve cutting her. Cutting into her at first, and if that doesn't get immediate results, then cutting pieces off of her. The problem is, that might not work on someone as tough as our little Israeli soldier here. Or it might not work as quickly as we'd like it to. So do you know what *that* means? That means we'd have to cut pieces off of *you* instead. Generally speaking, forcing someone to watch horrible pain being inflicted upon another brings about much quicker results. And not that we're pressed for time; we've got hours to kill, even days, if necessary. Of course, my friend here knows all the right places to cut, places that will cause you the most agony possible but not put your life in danger."

Trask glances over his shoulder at Elena.

"You're paying attention to this, right?" he says.

Elena nods reluctantly.

There are, however, no tears in her eyes this time, just raw hate.

"Give us the code this very minute like a good little girl, Elena, or my friend here goes to work on your brother. I'm not going to ask you twice."

She looks at Miles.

"Just tell them," he says.

"Listen to your brother, Elena. Look, I'll even make you a promise. You tell us the code, and we'll not only let you live, we'll leave you enough to live off of for the rest of your life."

"Fuck that," Hamlet scoffs.

Trask ignores him. "I didn't want your father to get killed, Elena. I really didn't. I just needed his money. But he left us no choice. Don't make the same mistake he made. Be smarter than he was."

Hamlet says, "She'll come after us."

"No, she won't. You won't, right, Elena? You'll take the money that's left—let's say five hundred thousand—and you'll return to the homeland and stay there and live a long and happy life. I'm giving you the chance to make the right choice. All you have to do is give us the code. You and your brother can both walk away from here without a scratch." He glances at her shoulder. "Well, too late for that."

"Why should I believe you?"

"What's the alternative? Just so you know, the longer you take to decide, the less money will be left in your account. The amount is down to four hundred thousand now."

She looks at Trask for a long moment.

"Three hundred thousand," he says.

She nods. "Okay."

"Really?"

"Yes."

"So let's hear it."

She recites the ten-digit code. As she says it, though, she looks at Miles, as if telling him the code, not Trask, as if there is a chance that Miles might be the one to somehow get out of this alive.

Hamlet, caught a little off guard by her compliance, rushes to pull a notebook and pen from his pocket and write the number down.

"Got it," he says.

"Was that so terrible?" Trask asks Elena.

She says, "Yes."

Trask smiles. "Stubborn to the end, just like he was."

Angelina makes her way down the stairs. She crosses the room and hands the computer to Trask, who places it on his lap.

"It's online," she tells him.

Before stepping away, she looks once at Miles.

Their eyes briefly lock.

Trask removes the flash drive from his trouser pocket and pulls off its cap.

"If the code is a fake, Elena, you and your brother are both in for a long night."

"A very long night," Hamlet corrects.

"It's not fake," she says. "You've got what you wanted. You won."

"I'm guessing your brother was trying to bluff us. Or maybe you told him this wasn't the real drive so he wouldn't be tempted to run off with it himself." He looks at Miles. "Is it possible that after all this she'd still lie to you? I think it is. In fact, I think it's likely. I warned you about her, didn't I?"

Then he looks back at Elena. "But, my little rabbit, if somewhere along the way you did pull the old bait and switch, if this does turn out to be a decoy, we're going to need to know where the real drive is. And you understand what that means, right? For your poor, trusting brother here."

Elena says nothing. Miles looks at her, but she avoids meeting his eyes.

"Moment of truth, then, I guess, right?" Trask says.

He locates a USB port and inserts the drive. Hamlet leans down, and he and Trask watch the screen Miles cannot see.

What he can see is their faces. It takes a few seconds for the flash drive to open, and Miles knows by the reaction of these two men that drive does in fact contain only files.

"Fucking bitch," Hamlet says.

Trask shakes his head in disbelief. And yet there is also a hint of respect at Elena's ability to once again elude him.

It is, though, only a hint.

He stands and hands the computer to Angelina, then turns and faces Elena squarely. "So where is it?" he says.

"You let Miles go and I'll tell you."

"No deal."

"Just do what he says," Miles tells her.

Trask steps closer to her. "Where's the real drive?" Standing over her, his shadow all but swallows her. "Another hotel? In your vehicle? In a locker somewhere? Under a fucking rock? Where is it, Elena? We know you transferred funds to your scout's offshore account a few days ago, so you had it then. It's here in Montreal with you. It has to be. Just tell me where is it, Elena. Tell me now. Please."

Elena simply shakes her head.

Trask wastes no time. He turns to Angelina and barks orders. "Untie him and take him into the cold cellar. There's a drain in there we can hose the blood down. Strip him of his clothes and hang him by his wrists from the crossbeam." Trask nods toward Elena. "And we'll need to bring her, too. Don't want her to miss any of it."

Angelina is motionless. She looks quickly at Miles.

"Do it!" Trask shouts.

Angelina places the computer on the floor and heads toward Miles.

"Okay," Elena says. "Okay."

Angelina stops in her tracks.

All eyes in the room are on Elena.

"The Marriott on Saint-John-Baptiste. Right across the courtyard from her apartment."

"What room?" Trask says.

"Three-ten."

"In the same hiding place as the other drive?"

She nods.

"It's a bluff," Hamlet says. "To get us to waste more time."

"We've got nothing but time," Trask assures him. "It's only an hour away. Angelina will drive you. Call me after you've searched the room."

Hamlet points out that they would have found a room key when they went through her pockets.

"Not necessarily," Trask says.

"I'm not going on some wild-goose chase."

"Then what do you suggest? We have to find out one way or another whether she's telling the truth."

"I suggest that we make sure before we go." Hamlet nods toward Miles. "String him up. Give me ten minutes. If she didn't tell us the truth just now, she will when I toss the first piece of him onto her lap."

Trask looks at Miles, then at Elena. Finally, he nods once. "Yeah, all right. Just make it quick."

"I'm telling the truth," Elena protests.

As if to console her, Trask says assuredly, "We'll see."

Hamlet announces that he'll need to change his clothes first and turns toward the stairs. Trask orders Angelina to give him a hand with Miles.

But she does not move.

Hamlet stops halfway to the stairs.

Trask stares at Angelina. He seems stunned—almost hurt—that she hasn't jumped as usual at his command. "Now's not the time to get squeamish," he warns her firmly.

"I'll go," she says.

"What?"

"I'll drive to Montreal. I'll check out her hotel room. The minute I find it, I'll call. You don't have to do this."

"Where the fuck did you get *her*?" Hamlet scoffs.

Trask quickly closes the distance between himself and Angelina. Standing face-to-face with her, he says quietly but urgently, "You're going to help me, do you understand? You're going to do what I tell you, when I tell you. You got that?"

All she can do is repeat, "You don't have to do this."

Hamlet is shaking his head. "She can fuck Cohn nonstop for days and not think twice, it's all part of the job. But she fucks this loser twice and ends up caring for him."

Trask tells him to shut up, then focuses again on Angelina. Her eyes are closed. She looks to Miles like someone whose shameful secret has just been revealed.

Though it's the last thing that matters right now, Miles at last understands the hostile looks Cohn had given him, starting from the moment they met in New York City.

"We can end this right now," Trask says to her. His tone now is that of a coach talking to a tired player. "We get the money, you can take your share and go wherever you want. Frankly, I'm not sure you're cut out for this business anyway. But we're going to see this through to the end, okay? You know what you signed on for. You knew it might come to this. So let's string him up and end this. Right now. Okay?"

Angelina, her eyes open but down, nods.

"First," Trask says, "I want you to give me your gun."

She looks at him, then reaches into her jacket, removes her weapon from its holster, and hands it to him.

"Good girl."

Hamlet, still shaking his head, turns and heads again for the stairs.

Angelina crosses the room and steps behind Miles. She begins to undo the wire wound tight around his wrists as Trask, holding her gun, watches Miles closely.

When his hands are free, Angelina quickly applies a joint lock to Miles's right wrist and walks in a half circle till she is standing in front of him—and between him and Trask.

"Give me your other wrist," she says.

Miles has no choice but to comply. He brings his other hand around, and she puts his wrists together so she can rebind them.

He looks up at her and sees that her eyes are locked on his.

To his surprise he sees no shame in them this time.

He sees, instead, a determined look.

Her eyes dart downward, and he follows her line of vision as she discreetly opens her field jacket.

He suddenly sees something familiar.

A telescopic baton in a nylon holster hanging from her belt. As she lets go of her jacket and it hangs naturally, the weapon is well concealed and yet within easy reach.

She winds the wire around wrists again, but not at all tightly. In fact, the gap she leaves is more than enough for Miles to slip a hand through.

As she finishes with the wire, Trask, thinking that Miles is secure, places her gun inside his belt, then steps to the back of Elena's chair. He bends and begins to undo the wire binding her.

Miles glances toward the stairs. Hamlet is nowhere to be seen, and heavy footsteps can be heard on the ceiling above.

Angelina stands and, still facing Miles, pulls him by his wrists till he is standing. Walking backward, she leads him toward a door he hadn't before seen.

But she doesn't make a straight line toward that door. Rather, she makes a slightly curving one that brings her and her prisoner right past Elena's chair.

Trask is still working on the wires, yet he notices Angelina's strange course across the room.

The nature of this course, along with the fact that she is walking backward, quickly positions Angelina between Miles and her boss.

An obstruction.

Trask notices this, too, and begins to straighten up.

Curious, but not yet wary.

It is then that Miles slides his right hand free, and as stealthily as he can reaches for the weapon in Angelina's belt.

Grabbing it, he pulls it free of its holster.

Either Trask saw this motion or finally realized that Angelina's actions meant something was amiss, because he is already reaching for the gun tucked into his belt.

But he is too late.

As Trask grips the handle, Angelina pivots around and throws her body into his, wrapping her left arm around his right in an attempt to control the gun.

She is no match for Trask, of course—he is bigger and more powerful—but that isn't the idea, and Miles knows this.

Her tackle is merely to delay the man, tie up the gun so Miles can go to work.

And Miles does that without wasting any time at all.

Thirty

A flick of the wrist, and the steel baton extends to its full length.

Miles immediately drops down into a crouch, just as Angelina had shown him.

He swings at the back of Trask's knee, hitting the tendons there with a forehand blow, and then strikes the kneecap itself with the return backhand swing.

Trask's knee folds, but he remains standing.

Leaping up to a standing position and simultaneously taking a step closer, Miles goes for Trask's head. Though his first swing only grazes Trask's skull, his second is a more solid blow.

Trask is stunned but still standing, which allows Elena to grab for his gun hand and begin to apply a wristlock. But before she can attain it, Trask regains enough of his senses to resist and slip free of the hold.

His gun hand no longer trapped, Trask is in the process of bringing it to bear on Angelina when Miles lands another blow to his head, and then another.

Trask lumbers like a drunk, then crumbles.

Angelina lunges for his gun hand again, this time grabbing the weapon itself and ripping it free of his grip as he falls.

The instant he hits the floor, she is standing over him and holding the gun expertly with both hands.

Flat on his back, Trask opens his mouth to speak, but before he can say anything, before he can even take in the air with which to speak, Angelina fires twice.

Two shots to his head.

Miles, his ears ringing, looks at Angelina.

Before he can speak, she says quickly, "Hamlet has to have heard that. We need to move, now."

Through the ringing, and though only barely, Miles can hear footsteps above.

Heavy, running, not toward the door at the top of stairs but somewhere else.

Getting away?

"Untie your sister," Angelina orders.

Miles closes and pockets the baton, then hurries behind Elena and finishes the task Trask had begun.

Still weak from the blood loss, Elena needs help standing. As he did before, Miles wedges himself beside her like a crutch and holds her tight against him.

Every motion seems to cause her pain.

Angelina leads them to the bottom of the stairs, then gestures for them to stop and wait. Aiming the gun toward the open door above, she waits a moment, then carefully climbs the stairs, taking the steps two at a time. Only after she reaches the top and pauses to survey what she can see from the doorway does she signal for them to follow.

Up the stairs, Miles helps Elena along as Angelina guides them through the kitchen of what is clearly a farmhouse. The lights are off, and Miles glances toward the first window they pass and sees that it's dark outside.

More than that, there are no houses to be seen anywhere, just the shapes of trees lining the property's edge and, beyond them, the expanse of an empty field.

"Your gear's in here," Angelina whispers.

They enter a living room. On a sofa is Cohn's overcoat, Miles's jacket, and Angelina's Belstaff messenger bag. Miles drapes the overcoat around his sister's shoulders like a cape, then grabs his own jacket. He feels the pockets—his money is still there, as is his father's watch.

The last thing he checks for is his passport and driver's license—fake passport and fake license. *John Joseph Johnson.* These items are there as well.

Angelina grabs the jacket from his hands, and before Miles can do anything, she is feeling along its bottom seam. Finding what she is looking for, she tears at the cotton lining.

At first Miles doesn't understand why the heavy material gives so easily, and then he sees loose stitching and knows she has simply reopened a two-inch slice that had been hastily sewn closed.

Angelina reaches into the opening, quickly removes something, and hands it to Miles.

It is nearly identical to the tracking device he had removed from the fifty-dollar bill. The only difference is that it is attached to something resembling a watch battery.

He looks at her, then drops the thing and crushes it with his heel.

Angelina picks up her Belstaff bag and hangs it off her shoulder. The only things remaining on the sofa are Elena's prepaid cell phone and Cohn's Sig Sauer.

Elena wants to know where her gun is.

Angelina says that her guess is Hamlet has it. Then, with everyone gathered together and geared up, she says, "We're going out the back door. Understand?"

Miles nods, and as he starts to move, Elena reaches down and grabs the Sig.

Cohn's Sig.

The weapon he used to kill Pavol.

He and Elena follow Angelina through the dark kitchen and into a narrow pantry, which funnels them to a doorway. Though she still needs his help to stand, Elena is moving better now. Miles senses that she sees now the chance to kill the man who ordered their father's death, and that this is causing her, despite her injuries and exhaustion, to rally.

Reaching the door, Angelina pauses and looks through its paned window, shifting a bit to angle her line of sight so she can survey as much of the area outside as possible.

Then she looks back at Miles and Elena and whispers, "The Mercedes is still here, so Hamlet is around somewhere. My Audi is parked right behind it. That's what we're heading for. I'll go first. Once I'm there, I'll give you the signal. Don't move till I give you the signal. Do you understand?"

Miles nods, but Elena just looks at the woman she has only known so far as Trask's mutt.

Elena says to her, earnestly, softly, "Thank you."

Angelina nods, then reminds them to wait for her signal.

Opening the door, she moves out into the night. Miles watches as she makes her way across an open patch of ground toward where the vehicles are parked fifty feet away.

He looks at his sister. "You okay?"

"Yeah."

"Do you have your passports?"

"They're at the hotel. With the flash drive."

Miles nods. "Good. We're almost out of here," he assures her.

Before he can turn back to check on Angelina's progress, however, he hears a raised voice.

A male voice, calling Angelina's name.

Hamlet's voice.

It is followed quickly by a series of gunshots.

Several shots from two different guns, by the sound of it.

Chaotic fire, just a few seconds of it, and then silence.

Miles looks through the open door. Though it is dark, and she is just on the perimeter of the light that spills from the farmhouse, he sees that Angelina is facedown.

Whether she has been shot or simply hit the dirt after hearing shots fired, he does not know.

Her arm is raised, though, the handgun in it aimed at something beyond Miles's sight. This gives him hope that she has only hit the ground for cover. She fires once, fires again, and then her arm suddenly drops.

After that, nothing.

Miles pries the Sig from his sister's hand and, crouching, steps into the open doorway.

"Wait," Elena says, but it's too late, he has stepped outside.

Holding the gun the way she had taught him, he doesn't make a run in a straight path to Angelina but instead moves along the edge of the house, inching his way toward the direction in which she fired before finally collapsing.

As he reaches the end of the farmhouse—and his cover—he pauses, prepares himself, and then leans forward and peers around the corner.

He sees only darkness, the bordering trees, and the open land beyond them. Above it all, a clear night sky.

And then he sees something else.

A form, on the ground.

A heap.

A *man* in a heap.

Stepping around the corner, Miles aims the gun at the downed man and closes the distance between them carefully but steadily.

He hears nothing but the sound of the wind, his footsteps on the hard ground, and his own breathing.

He reaches Hamlet and remains in a crouch.

The man is on his back, conscious but gasping, Elena's CZ-75 just beyond the reach of his outstretched arm.

Miles looks around, then rises to his feet and stands over him.

Blood is pouring from the wound in the man's throat. He looks up at Miles, his eyes blinking slowly.

Bewildered—in shock, probably.

Miles sees something else in the man's eyes, though.

Terror.

Hamlet tries to speak, but nothing comes out.

And anyway, Miles doesn't want to hear it.

He says the only thing he can.

"This is for my father."

And just as he would an injured animal, Miles puts this dying man out of his misery.

Two shots to the head, exactly what Angelina had done in the basement moments before.

With the suppressor affixed and the trees hissing in the wind, the shots can barely be heard.

A moment later Miles is crouching beside Angelina. He places the gun on the ground and, touching her face gently, rolls her head toward him.

And is met with staring, lifeless eyes.

He looks at them and isn't sure what to feel. He isn't even sure how long he stays there, looking at her. The next thing he does know is that his sister is behind him.

"We need to go," she says softly. "Shots can carry a long way. Someone might have heard them."

Miles sees that she has reclaimed her CZ-75.

He nods, takes one last look at Angelina, and then picks up the Sig and stands. He hands the weapon to his sister, then takes the baton from his back pocket and hands it to her as well.

Bending down, he removes the Belstaff bag from Angelina's body.

Opening the flap, he turns the bag upside down, emptying its contents onto the ground.

He surveys the many items—her cell phone, extra clips for her gun, a folding knife, a roll of wire, what looks to Miles to be some kind of tracking device.

Among those things he sees only two that he wants: a first aid kit and a small silver cylinder.

Angelina's Migrastick.

All he cares about now are things that heal.

Picking them up and stuffing them into the bag, he empties the pockets of his jacket—the money, the passport and license, his father's Rolex—and tosses them in as well.

Then he removes his jacket and lays it over Angelina's torso and face like a shroud.

It is the least he could do for her, considering.

"But we need to take care of a few things first," Elena says.

Miles looks at her. "What things?"

Elena leads him back inside the house.

She is running on her last scraps of strength; he senses this as he follows her down into the basement, where she quickly searches a workbench till she finds what she is looking for.

Tools of some kind—Miles can't see which ones exactly, doesn't quite understand yet what she is doing.

She heads straight for the oval heating-oil tank under the boarded-over window, has to weave around Trask's body and spreading blood to get to it. She is as much stumbling as she is moving, and Miles remains close behind her, ready to catch her if need be.

Reaching the tank, she says, "I won't be able to do this with my shoulder the way it is."

She shows him the tools.

A large, study screwdriver and mallet.

"We have to make sure no one can ever prove we were here." She gestures toward Trask's body. "And we need to make it difficult for anyone to identify him. You were seen in Montreal with him. And the others, too."

Miles understands.

He takes the tools, tells her to step back, and crouches down, placing the tip of the screwdriver against the bottom of the steel tank and slamming the end of the screwdriver's handle with the rubber mallet.

It takes three hits before he punctures the steel and a red-colored liquid begins to flow out.

He makes several more holes, gets better at it to the point where only one strike is necessary to punch through, then drops the tools into the liquid spreading fast across the uneven cement floor.

Upstairs, Elena goes straight for the gas stove, lifts up the covering plate, and blows out the pilot light, and then she lowers the plate and opens up all the burners.

The sulfurous smell is immediate.

It takes the two of them to carry Angelina's shrouded body inside. They can only drag Hamlet's in. Both are left on the kitchen floor.

Hurrying into the living room, Elena grabs her prepaid cell phone from the sofa, returns to the kitchen, and begins rubbing the phone along the sleeve of Cohn's overcoat.

Cohn's *wool* overcoat.

Building up a static charge.

Miles quickly remembers Angelina telling him to discharge static before pumping gasoline.

Laying the phone on the kitchen table, Elena leads Miles outside and straight to the pile of Angelina's things. She bends down and grabs Angelina's cell phone, almost falling in the process. Miles knows she is on her last legs now, pushing through pain and exhaustion. He thinks of what Trask had said.

I wouldn't want to be the one she was after.

His arm around her waist, holding his sister up, Miles guides her toward the Audi but sees almost immediately that its right front and right rear tires have been slashed.

Hamlet the butcher's work, no doubt—his reason for running outside when the first shots were fired.

The act of a man determined to prevent their escape.

"Looks like it's the Mercedes," Miles says.

He eases Elena into the passenger seat, and by the time he has walked around the nose of the vehicle and is climbing in behind the wheel, she has already searched through the glove compartment.

In her hand is a map, the vehicle's registration, and a package of moist towelettes.

"What are you doing?" Miles asks.

"I'm finding out where we are." She reads off the name of the town listed on the registration, and though Miles is impressed by this—he wouldn't have thought to check the registration like that— the name of the town is meaningless to him.

Then Elena asks if he wants to know what Hamlet's real name is.

"No," he tells her. "Not really."

The key is in the ignition, so Miles starts the motor and shifts into drive. Making a U-turn, he follows the long dirt driveway toward the faraway road.

Elena lays the registration on her lap, then unfolds the map and, by the glow of the dashboard lights, quickly finds where they are.

"We're an hour north of Montreal," she announces. "The way back looks easy."

Miles nods. He realizes that they must be heading east right now because the horizon directly ahead is a long band of silver.

Dawn isn't far off.

Behind them, just darkness.

"The train to New York is at nine, right?" he asks.

"Yeah."

"Do you know where the station is?"

"I do."

Elena has taken out a towelette and is wiping down both guns, as well as the baton. After disassembling both firearms, she lowers the passenger window and tosses out the pieces one by one, waiting between throws so each piece lands a good distance from the one that went out before it.

Miles notes that there is nothing but wilderness out there.

Then she tosses out the baton, registration, and map—everything she had touched with her bare hands.

All that's left in her hand is Angelina's cell phone.

Opening it, she punches in the number of the prepaid cell phone she left in the kitchen.

As Miles continues driving, she turns and looks through the rear window.

He can hear the faint but steady sound of ringing coming from the cell phone in Elena's hand

One ring, two rings.

Nothing.

They look at each other. Miles applies the brakes, slowing the Mercedes to a stop.

"The gas needs to build up," Elena explains.

Still nothing but the dull ringing coming from the phone's earpiece. Three rings, four rings.

"Should we go back, set it off somehow?" Miles asks.

Elena says patiently, "Wait."

Miles has no choice but to trust her.

It's during the fifth ring that the dark horizon behind them suddenly lights up.

They see the flash of the explosion first, and then, a quick second later, they hear the deep, dense boom.

A second after that the concussion wave hits and rocks the Mercedes like a sudden gust of wind.

Elena lets out a sigh and, facing forward, simply collapses into her seat.

She closes her eyes for a moment, then opens them again and, after a quick wipe-down of the phone, tosses it out and raises the window.

Miles eases down on the accelerator, and the Mercedes is once again heading toward the silver horizon to the east.

The warm air flowing from the heater vents collects around them, and they ride on in silence.

Thirty-One

It is nearly first light when they reach Vieux-Montreal.

Wiping the interior of the Mercedes down and abandoning it several blocks from the Marriott, they then travel the remainder of the distance on foot.

A man and a woman, one clearly holding the other up, crossing early morning streets that are all but desolate.

In her hotel room, Elena grabs a Baggie containing her many passports from a backpack, then retrieves the flash drive from its hiding place behind the wall socket.

She hands it to Miles, and he looks at it.

It appears to be a simple thumb drive, the only noticeable differences between it and the other drive being that this one is encased in a much heavier metal and is connected to a long, sturdy neck chain.

How many are dead because of this?

"Do you remember the code?" Elena asks.

Miles nods.

"Good," she says.

He looks at the drive, then closes his fist around it.

She changes into clean clothes, stuffing all her belongings into a backpack. After she quickly wipes down everything that she and Miles have touched, they exit the room.

As a cab takes them into downtown, Elena removes the Baggie containing her passports from the backpack and places it into a pocket of her overcoat. After getting out of that cab, Elena tosses the backpack and all it contains into an overflowing Dumpster at a construction site.

"You'll need to get rid of your clothes and shoes the minute we get back," she says.

He nods. "It's the first thing I'll do."

Sitting together in the back of a second cab as it takes them toward Gare Centrale, they silently watch from their respective windows as the city, just coming to life now, passes by.

It isn't till the train is finally pulling out of the underground station that Miles allows himself to relax, though only slightly.

He has after all just killed a man.

A defenseless man.

But we've made it this far, right? he thinks. *All we need is to make it to the border, then across it, and then to New York. A step at a time. First things first.*

Miles hangs the chain around his neck, tucking the flash drive under his sweatshirt. To his surprise, and despite all that has just occurred and all that still needs to occur, his hands do not shake.

As the train clears the station, Elena rests her head on his shoulder and closes her eyes, but he realizes quickly that his sister isn't asleep.

She is, in fact, crying.

He does the only thing he can think to do.

He takes her hand and holds it.

⌣

A little over an hour later they are at the border crossing.

Miles hands the fake passport to the uniformed guard. It is a man this time, young and no-nonsense. He asks many more questions than the guard had asked when Miles was going into Canada, but he is prepared for this; Cohn, after all, had warned him to expect it.

The man runs the passport under the infrared scanner and watches the display screen.

Long second pass, and then he hands the passport back to Miles.

Elena's turn now. The guard looks her over once and asks what happened.

She answers him in a language Miles assumes is Hebrew. He notices the passport she handed to the guard is Israeli.

Immediately the guard looks to Miles to translate.

Thinking quickly, Miles tells him that she was in a car accident.

The guard nods. "Neither of you have luggage?"

"No."

The guard takes one last look at Elena, then hands back her passport.

"Welcome to the States," he says.

Later, as they are crossing south through Upstate New York, Elena once again rests her head on Miles's shoulder.

The rocking of the train, gentle but insistent, makes Miles think of a mother determined to lull her restless children to sleep.

Miles begins to drift, and with each mile crossed, he drifts further and further and a little further still . . .

When he opens his eyes again it is dark, and looking out the window he sees what can only be the Hudson River.

It isn't long before he begins to recognize other landmarks and knows that they have reached the upper Bronx.

Taking out his father's watch, he looks at the time. Almost eight p.m. He does the math.

He has slept for nine hours.

With Elena beside him, breathing the long, steady breaths of someone deeply asleep, Miles puts the watch on, doing so with care so as not to disturb his resting sister.

Then he looks out the window, and what he sees reminds him of the predawn train ride he made with Jack on Saturday.

So long ago. So far away.

And yet, just as he promised his son he would, he is heading home.

Almost there, in fact.

Only miles now—familiar miles—left to go.

About the Author

Photograph by Tracy Deer-Mirek, 2010

Daniel Judson is a Shamus Award winner and the author of nine novels, including *The Poisoned Rose*, *The Bone Orchard*, *The Darkest Place*, and *Voyeur*, taut, character-driven thrillers informed by the author's practice of taking on his creations' habits and milieus. Daniel's immersive research technique lends his work a distinctive authenticity and has fostered an ever-expanding, eclectic skill set that includes Vipassana meditation, Filipino knife-fighting, and playing jazz trumpet. A Son of the American Revolution, former gravedigger, and self-described one-time drifter, Daniel currently lives in Connecticut with his fiancée and four rescued cats.

Kindle Serials

This book was originally released in Episodes as a Kindle Serial. Kindle Serials launched in 2012 as a new way to experience serialized books. Kindle Serials allow readers to enjoy the story as the author creates it, purchasing once and receiving all existing Episodes immediately, followed by future Episodes as they are published. To find out more about Kindle Serials and to see the current selection of Serials titles, visit www.amazon.com/kindleserials.